Call To Battle

A SCRAPYARD SHIP NOVEL

Written By
Mark Wayne McGinnis

Cover design by:
Eren Arik

Edited by:
Lura Lee Genz
Mia Manns

Published by:
Avenstar Productions

ISBN: 978-0-9861098-3-6

www.markwaynemcginnis.com

PROLOGUE

It had been sixty-four days since Chrimguard, the ancient, highly-fortified, Grand Sacellum situated on Itimus-four, was attacked and destroyed by a relatively small Allied vessel. Any of the remaining high priest overlords still present within Craing space—those that weren't crushed beneath Chrimguard's tons of stone rubble—were now in hiding ... somewhere. *Good riddance*, Ot-Mul thought. They were the least of his concerns right now. He looked out through the observation window to the planet below, and shook his head.

Terplin, the Craing empire's predominant seat of power for thousands of years, was now in the throes of total bedlam. The last of the seven Craing worlds was on the verge of falling. What started with a dissident uprising ... a handful of university students ... had somehow turned into a full-blown revolution that had swept through the Craing worlds like wildfire. The Emperor's army had put up little resistance; in fact, most had joined the opposing side within days. Any day now, total victory lay within reach of the young revolutionaries.

Ot-Mul had been in the process of the *Transformation of Eternity*—the final step necessary to his becoming the Craing

Emperor. A position he'd come to realize he didn't want. Perhaps the attack was a godsend, after all. In any event, he'd barely escaped. If it hadn't been for his four Caldurian battle droids he, too, would be lying beneath the walls of Chrimguard. But he had survived—the droids had blasted through the massive stone walls and, eventually, they had fled to a waiting light cruiser he always had on standby. If he'd learned anything over the course of his distinguished military career, it was to never leave anything to chance when it comes to self-preservation. He and his four battle droids were well into space as the last of the towering obelisks fell onto the ancient Craing compound.

Ot-Mul had inherited his predecessor's ambitious Great Space initiative. In reality, perhaps it was too ambitious of Lom, the past acting-Emperor, to undertake such a monumental task: the destruction of thousands of worlds, all in the hopes of building a buffer zone against any possible insurgency by the growing list of enemies of the Craing Empire. Now, exiled from the Craing worlds, Ot-Mul had to put further dreams of continuing the Great Space initiative on hold … at least until sanity returned to the populace. For now, he would have to be content leading the combined Craing military forces from outer space.

The sheer number of vessels at his disposal was staggering. They had previously been recalled from hundreds of light-years away to support the Great Space initiative. The same assemblage of Craing military strength, thousands of warships, had taken place at other key locations within the sector. Here was the greatest combined military force ever assembled. Ever. In Craing space alone, there were nearly one hundred thousand warships of various sizes—all standing at the ready. The problem was that not all were fully manned. Even out in space there were many deserters … crewmen who had heard from family or friends of the great revolution taking place back on Terplin, or Halimar, or any of the five other Craing worlds.

Keeping control of crews that were still intact had become a full-time endeavor. Sure, at first putting a plasma bolt into a deserter's head had done the trick ... but that had eventually lost effectiveness as a deterrent. Within the last few weeks entire vessels, or even groups of vessels, were making a run for it. How many ships had deserted Craing space ... one thousand ... five thousand?

His eyes rose to the twinkling lights outside the porthole on the vessels moored around his command meganaught. Yesterday, Ot-Mul had a revelation ... *why hadn't I thought of it before?* He had at his disposal the ultimate deterrent. Actually, he had four of them.

"Increased heat signatures are prevalent within a cluster of Craing light and heavy warships at the outer reaches of the assemblage, my Lord. They're getting ready to run."

Ot-Mul turned a furrowed brow in the direction of his second-in-command. How many times had he corrected him that he now wanted to be called Admiral? Any reference to his former emperorship title was counter-productive.

"How many vessels, Captain Gee?"

"No less than ten, my Lor ... Um, Admiral."

"Send all four ... do it now!"

Both Ot-Mul and Captain Gee moved to the admiral's ready room where Gee used a wall-mounted intercom panel to convey his orders to the bridge. Irritably, Ot-Mul gestured toward the wall display with a raised brow. The captain sighted the cluster of warships on the viewer within seconds. Ot-Mul, looking at a split screen, saw his meganaught command vessel on the left and a group of ten ships, lying at a different section of Craing space, on the right. Movement. One by one, his magnificent battle droids appeared from one of the command ship's many flight decks. It was strange, even after all this time, how these four technological wonders could have such a physical effect on him. Stirred, he felt blood rushing to his loins. His heart rate increased and his small mouth opened, taking in bigger gulps of air. The display changed to a full-screen view. Ot-Mul wasn't aware that he'd begun to rapidly tap his left foot. And then, there they were: Each one was twice the size of an average Craing male, but much wider, with four squatty-looking legs, a barrel-like torso, four arms, and a circular turret that comprised its head. Every surface was reflective—covered with thin, razor-sharp plates that constantly spun. They were beautiful.

Ot-Mul adjusted his uniform to compensate for his now-hard member.

"Put them to work, Captain Gee, and ensure this feed is transmitted to all our vessels," Ot-Mul ordered, not taking his eyes from the display.

Again, Gee was on the intercom to the bridge. The four battle droids moved into position around the cluster of ten Craing ships. Ot-Mul forced his eyes to stay open, not wanting to blink—he knew the speed of their attack would be lighting fast.

They attacked in unison. As expected, they moved with incredible speed. Each droid was firing continuous plasma bolts from their head-like turrets, strategically firing on the multiple targets around them. Now, each battle droid zeroed-in on a single ship, and quickly annihilated that ship's defensive shields, then blasted through its thick outer hulls and bulkheads. As they disappeared into the bowels of the four ships, for the moment all was still. A smile appeared on Ot-Mul's thin lips. He waited. He knew the seeming silence was anything but still. He knew if he could look into any of these four vessels, he'd see the workings of a blender … first the shredding of metal … then, soon, the crew too would be … macerated. They'd see it coming … their own demise.

The first of the four warships, a heavy cruiser, had begun to implode. The battle droid reappeared at the stern of the vessel and took up position at the same outer perimeter location it had started from just minutes earlier. The other three battle droids soon followed suit, returning to their overtaken ships' entry position. All four cruisers were in various stages of implosion. Ot-Mul was left with a sense that it was all a bit anticlimactic. He'd far prefer to see these ships explode in bright balls of fire.

"Shall I order the destruction of the remaining six vessels, Admiral?"

Ot-Mul continued to stare at the display. "How many deserters were just … subdued?"

Captain Gee took a moment to answer, first double-checking the numbers in his head. "Close to a thousand … give or take a hundred."

"No. I think we have made an effective point here, don't you think, Captain?"

"Most effective, Admiral."

"Leave me now, Captain. Return to your duties on the bridge."

Ot-Mul watched as his second quickly bowed, turned, and left the ready room. He let out a long breath and sat down at his desk. He needed to deal with other, perhaps even more important, matters. He had little doubt the desertions would soon stop. Perhaps there would still be a few errant ships attempting to make a run for open space … and again, he'd send for his battle droids. Ot-Mul looked to the display again. Next time, he'd transmit live feeds directly from the droids themselves. Show the carnage. That should quell any further desertions.

His mind turned to other issues he'd been forced to shelve for far too long—to Earth and what remained of the Allied forces. Their influence over the Craing populace was the crux of the problem. Yes, he'd need to remove those outer influences first, before dealing any further with this Craing populace situation.

CHAPTER 1

Captain Jason Reynolds stood in the mid-morning sun, shirtless and wearing board shorts. He stood barefoot on the deck with his hands on his hips. In the distance he could see one of the droids, but couldn't make out whether it was Dewdrop or Teardrop. A bright, white-hot point of light danced, ten feet up in the air, a half-mile away—it was one of Old Gus's welding guns. He watched as a continuous fountain of amber sparks showered down to the ground, then he scanned the far outer perimeter of the scrapyard where the new thirty-foot-high fence had been erected. He'd insisted the ultra-high fence be installed in order to keep them out. From what Mollie said, they could climb virtually any surface, like a spider. It was her idea to cover the steel bars with a thick layer of grease—something they'd come up with to keep the molt weevils from climbing up the sides of the big dump truck. The molt weevils were no longer a problem … but the zombie-like creatures which had ripped themselves free from millions of molt weevil cocoons around the world most definitely were.

Mollie and Boomer were in the pool, arguing over whose turn it was to use the one inner tube. One of the droids emerged from the house and hovered at the edge of the pool. Jason recognized it—Teardrop. It lingered there, keeping a silent vigil over the two girls.

"Teardrop … why don't you make yourself useful? Find another inner tube for us to play with somewhere in the scrapyard."

It was Mollie, bossy as usual, who'd barked off the command. The droid hesitated for a second and then scurried off toward the mass of rusted-out old cars, trucks, and buses.

"What are you looking at, Dad?" Boomer asked, dripping wet and now standing at his side.

"Hey, kiddo … the fence."

"Looks like it's almost done, huh?"

"I think so. There's not much more we can add now for security."

"That mean we can stay in the house tonight?" she asked hopefully.

"I'll think about it." Jason and his daughters had been staying far below ground, at the base, within its newly constructed quarters there. The novelty of the ultra-modern facility had occupied the girls' attention over the last few days, but their initial enthusiasm was quickly waning. He, too, would like to spend more time outside, free of the confined spaceship compartments and living in subterranean quarters. Life was not back to normal, not even close. There were still countless *peovils*, the name Mollie had come up with for the molt-weevil-people, those zombie-like creatures still roaming the earth. And the alien fleet of five thousand Craing warships was still relatively close by in space. Two months previously, Jason had little doubt they would attack Earth within days, but it later became apparent they were in no hurry to do so. He wasn't entirely sure why, but his suspicions centered around the revolution taking place on the Craing worlds.

Jason's attention turned upward. The sudden appearance of *The Lilly*, quickly descending from above, brought his focus back to the present. The ship's black, matte, nanite-coated hull, her sweeping, streamlined curves still induced the same reaction it had the very first time he'd seen this advanced Caldurian ship, right here, below ground, at what had become her secret home base the past few years. The ship disappeared in a flash, phase-shifting below ground. And then Jason was reminded of something he didn't want to think about. Something heart-wrenching. Dira ... beautiful ... amazing ... Dira. She was gone! Oh, god ... how many times over the last few weeks had he pushed the very thought of her leaving from his mind?

Boomer was now back in the pool and several more inner tubes were bobbing on the choppy surface. Teardrop was already patrolling the outer fence perimeter.

Two months had now passed since they'd returned from their mission to Terplin—the destruction of the Chrimguard compound and what had become the acting-emperor's seat of power. Feeling victorious, Jason's team had returned to the small transport vessel, the *Streamline*, and then flew her back to the Orange Corridor, where *The Lilly* was awaiting them in orbit around Allaria.

News from Earth was not nearly as fortuitous. Nan and Mollie had, somehow, miraculously survived. But the infestation of molt weevils around the globe had dramatically changed Earth's milieu forever. Millions if not billions of people had been cocooned ... placed in a kind of suspended animation. Nan and Mollie had made their way to the joint NORAD and USNORTHCOM Alternate Command Center, sited deep within Cheyenne Mountain in Colorado. There, they'd been told Washington, D.C. had been overrun. The government, even the first family and the president, had been taken. As the lone remaining cabinet member, the Secretary of Inter-Stellar Relations, Nan had become acting president of the United States.

Jason recalled seeing Nan's face on the display screen within his ready-room quarters. She was barely recognizable, her pretty face pale and drawn. Her left cheek scratched— her eyes revealing the magnitude of her new situation—the weight of the world resting on her shoulders. He'd wanted to reach through space and hold her, tell her everything was going to be all right.

"No, Jason, I'm not going to be okay. Things will never be

okay ... never okay again," Nan told him, pushing her long hair back behind her ears.

"What can I do? How can I help you right now?"

Nan took in a breath and slowly let it out. She attempted a smile and seemed to relax some. She looked to her right and then turned back, facing him. "Keep Mollie for a while longer?"

"Of course."

"Where does that leave you? Are you still needed there, in Washington?" Jason asked.

She was nodding before he'd finished. "Are you serious? There's barely a working government here, Jason. Until the president is fully functional ... if that ever happens, I'm still calling our nation's shots. And there are other concerns, too, other than the cocoons and the damn zombies roaming the streets ... there's possible agression heading from outside the U.S."

"What does that mean?"

"Think about it ... The U.S. and Europe were hit hardest by the molt weevils. But some countries, namely parts of Russia and North Korea, are relatively free of the infestation. Both countries were already vying for more international power. Now, with the world's super powers in disarray, it's a perfect opportunity for them to strike. Your father is already en route back to Earth to meet with me and help us derive a workable plan for our own national security. But with the Craing fleet still a threat, he's hesitant to return our warships home from space. You asked what you can do to help ... we may need *The Lilly* to make an impromptu visit to the Far East, to remind the North Koreans that we are anything but an easy prey for aggression on their part. I know you needed a break ... but we need you—"

"No, it's time I returned to reality. When do you need me there?"

"Plan on returning to Washington tomorrow," she replied,

looking somewhat more hopeful. "It will be good to see you again … we need to talk."

Jason saw movement out of the corner of his eye. Someone had just entered his ready room.

"I look forward to it," he said, ready to sign off.

Nan continued to stare at Jason for several beats. "I'm starting to show now. I think I felt it kick last night." Nan looked down at herself and then up, with the beginnings of a smile. "Can you believe it? We're going to have another kid …" Nan's smile disappeared when she saw the figure standing behind Jason.

Jason turned to see Dira standing at the entrance to the ready room. She was staring at the display, her expression a mixture of confusion, then shock. Her eyes shifted to Jason. Tears welled up in her eyes and overflowed. Without saying a word, she spun and fled from the ready room. Jason turned back to the display.

"She didn't know? You hadn't told her?"

Jason felt his cheeks flush hot. He hadn't told Dira yet—there hadn't been the right moment. How do you tell the person you're in love with that you're having a baby with your ex-wife? How does one even approach such a subject?

"No. Was going to tonight," he said, finding it hard to talk.

"I'm sorry. I really am, Jason. Things are complicated … I need to go. I'll see you tomorrow." The connection was cut before he'd had the chance to respond.

Now, standing on the back deck of his San Bernardino house that overlooked his family's scrapyard and the hazy-blue San Bernardino Mountains beyond, he felt the familiar tug on his heartstrings. He'd tried numerous times to get Dira to just talk to him—let him explain the situation. But she hadn't wanted anything to do with him. She hadn't spoken to him since. She'd immediately contacted the admiral, his father, and arranged for transport back to Jhardon. She needed to be with her family, she'd told him, whose world, and hers, was still reeling from the recent attacks by the Craing Vanguard fleet. At least half of Jhardon had been destroyed. Her mother, the queen, was ill and it was time for Dira to assume the role she'd been avoiding for too long. She was a princess, heir to the throne, and it was time she returned home and assumed her rightful duties there.

CHAPTER 2

The next morning, Jason was up early. He and his daughters had enjoyed several weeks home, at the scrapyard, hanging out in the customized house Nan had builders create for them; languishing around the pool, they were basically free to do nothing much at all. With only a few minor emergencies to attend to, he was able to decompress to some extent, and, more importantly, reconnect with Mollie and Boomer. The truth was, it wasn't his idea to take this leave of absence. His father had insisted. The toll on his son of a year battling the Craing made it look like he was on his way to total burnout. Added to the fact he was still mourning the departure of Dira, Jason hadn't put up much of a fight. He'd spent the last several hours getting the house pre-locked-up, tightly secured, for another indeterminate span of time when he'd be away, returning once again to outer space.

He decided to take one more patrol around the property before leaving. When he stepped out onto the deck, he saw Boomer was already there, dressed and waiting for him.

"Where's your sister?"

"She's not my sister."

"Where's Mollie?" Jason asked, correcting himself.

"Sleeping still." She looked up at her father and scowled. "How is it she and I share the same DNA? We're not even a little bit similar."

Jason chuckled as he headed down the steps leading into the scrapyard. He opened the metal gate and let Boomer walk through first; then he followed, latching the gate behind him. This wasn't the first time he'd had the same conversation with either one, or both, girls. Several months earlier, after combating a Craing-induced, multiple-time realms situation here on Earth, there had been several significant time alterations, subsequently, in their own time-frame reality. One of its by-products was the merging of two, parallel, time frames, which resulted in two identical Mollies, and two identical Teardrops, co-existing at the same time. As Jason watched Boomer walk ahead in front of him, he had to agree with her earlier statement. The two girls couldn't be more different. Mollie, equally bright and rambunctious, was a normal nine-year-old in most every respect, while Boomer, who had been fine with changing her name, on the other hand, was a little warrior. She'd already been trained in close-quarters combat—had learned to kill an opponent—was an expert at knife throwing. Yes … her interests seemed to be well suited for space, and life aboard a warship.

Mollie, though, seemed better suited to live on Earth, with her mother. Smart and tenacious, she had a personality that worked its way into anyone's heart—not unlike her mother. Jason was happy to have them both with him. They may not consider themselves true sisters, but they were. In some ways, their bond was even stronger than what most siblings had. They often finished each other's sentences—seemed to know what the other one was thinking.

Boomer had picked up a long piece of metal and was using it as a walking stick.

"Be careful with that, it's sharp and full of rust."

Boomer pointed the end of the long spike in the direction of the fence. "I see two *peovils* moving around out there, Dad."

Jason stopped and looked where Boomer was pointing.

"Ignore them. They can't get in here. Even if they could, the drones would take care of them," he added, gesturing to the two droids that were approaching them from opposite sides of the yard. Dewdrop came within several feet of Boomer and hovered there, close by. Teardrop rose into the air and drifted above the high fence, then, lowering back down, placed itself between the two peovils and the fence.

"They creep me out. I don't like the way they slink around."

Jason watched as the two figures kept coming. They looked like middle-aged men. One was tall and wore a scruffy beard, while the other one was chubby and mostly bald. Both were wearing ragged, stained pants and were shirtless. The taller of the two was drooling—long strings of saliva dripped down from the corners of his gaping mouth.

"Stop your progress!" Teardrop commanded.

The two kept coming, moving in the direction of Jason and Boomer. Teardrop deployed its primary weapon from its torso. "Stop now, or be destroyed."

"Come on, let's keep moving," Jason said, turning Boomer away from what was about to happen. Several times in the night he'd heard the droids fire their plasma weapons. He wasn't sure what they'd done with the bodies afterwards—he'd have to ask them later.

Jason heard one pulse engaging and then a loud clang, startling him, and he instinctively pulled Boomer in close. The chubby peovil lay motionless on the ground. He looked up and saw that the taller peovil had jumped and was now high up, close to the top of the fence. Its arms and legs flailed to get purchase on the greasy metal—but, immediately, it began to slip back down. Dewdrop fired twice and the zombie creature's body was catapulted out onto the desert sagebrush. The two droids retrieved the dead bodies and then transported them further out into the desert. A moment later Jason heard more, extended, plasma fire. *Well … that answers my question:*

The droids are cremating the remains.

"Didn't Mom get bit by one of those things?" Boomer asked.

"Yep … on the neck."

"Is she going to turn into a peovil?" Boomer questioned, looking concerned.

"Your mom, and the rest of us, are immune. The nanites in our bloodstream protect us."

"Oh yeah, forgot about that." Boomer smiled and looked relieved. "Is there no way to … I don't know, help them? Cure them?"

"Not sure. Scientists are working steadily on that but so far haven't had any luck. Ricket, and the technology on the *Minian*, or even on *The Lilly*, may provide an answer. As soon as Ricket returns from his mission, he'll look into it." They continued their trek around the outside of the scrapyard, just inside the fence's perimeter. More peovils were approaching in the distance. These were former men and women. All were naked.

"Let's head back to the house, Boomer." He steered her away from the fence and pointed toward a concrete pathway that intersected several other paths—the one leading back toward the house.

★ ★ ★

Mollie was up and busy in the kitchen when they reentered through the sliding glass door at the back of the house.

"Something smells good!" Boomer said, quickly taking a seat on a barstool under the expansive granite countertop.

Jason took a seat next to her and watched Mollie at work. She had an apron wrapped around her waist. A dusting of flour covered the tip of her nose, and she was using just about every pot and pan in the kitchen. He really wanted them to get going, clear out of the house right away, but with a smile, instead, he watched his daughter as she flipped the flapjacks on the grill. Each was perfectly golden brown. "How does a nine-year-old learn to cook so well?" he asked her.

Mollie looked up for a brief second before returning her attention to the job at hand. "You've eaten Mom's cooking … right?"

Jason and Boomer nodded at the same time. Nan was a terrible cook. It made sense now: Mollie, who was spending most of her time living with her mother, would either have starved, or learned how to cook. Obviously, the latter case had prevailed.

Mollie used a spatula to place pancakes onto three awaiting plates. "Boomer, can you get off your rear end and pour us some OJ?" Mollie ordered.

Boomer made a face at her and headed off toward the fridge.

"You excited to see your mother again?" Jason asked, as Mollie put a plate down in front of him.

"I am," Boomer replied, returning with a carton of orange juice.

Mollie said, "I guess … she works a lot. I don't see her all that much. Mostly, I'm asleep when she gets home at night. And when she is around, she's crabby … I guess she has a hard job. Lots of people always bugging her."

"She has a very important job—" Jason started to say.

"She's the frigging president, Mollie!" Boomer butted in, coming back from the cupboard with three glasses.

"I know she's the president, dip-wad … guess who's been living with her all this time?"

"Hey, I don't like that kind of talk from either of you," Jason said, giving them each a stern look. He put a heaping forkful of hot, syrupy pancakes into his mouth and gave Mollie two thumbs up. "Really, really good, Mollie."

Boomer stuck her tongue out at Mollie, displaying a mouthful of half-chewed food. About to reprimand her, Jason stopped when he heard repeated, distant, plasma fire. He stood and looked out the back window. The fence was moving—teetering back and forth.

"What the hell …" He moved to the sliding door and stepped out onto the deck. The fence was covered with climbing bodies. One after another, peovils were jumping onto the fence before sliding back down. The two droids were firing toward those making it anywhere near the top of the fence. In truth, he felt they were using a surprising level of restraint. He signaled to Teardrop with a waving hand.

Within seconds the droid was hovering in front of him. Jason gestured toward the scrapyard and what remained of a plasma turret gun—a gun destroyed months earlier by the pirate Captain Stalls. "We're leaving soon. What can be done to repair that turret gun?"

The droid turned in the direction of the black-charred dome, with its drooping plasma weapon. "New parts would need to be manufactured. I would need access to *The Lilly*'s phase-synthesizer."

"How long?"

"Two hours and eleven minutes, Captain Reynolds."

"Get started now. I want this location secured against all future attacks, even if no one's living here."

Jason watched as the drone moved away, heading towards the old yellow school bus at the far side of the scrapyard. The surrounding fence was again being rocked back and forth. To his left, another peovil was attempting to climb over it. Jason recognized him. It was Larry Gipson—he owned the filling station just down the road.

CHAPTER 3

Both Mollie and Boomer had overstuffed backpacks slung over their shoulders, while Jason carried a Navy-issued duffle bag. All three were not only tan, but had sunburnt shoulders, foreheads, and noses. Jason felt a tinge of guilt as they came up the rear gangway and entered into the back airlock chamber of *The Lilly*. The hatchways were open—letting fresh air replace weeks of stagnant, recycled air. He heard the ship's AI make the announcement, "Captain Reynolds has boarded *The Lilly*."

"Good morning, Captain Reynolds."

Jason stopped in his tracks, seeing Petty Officer Miller waiting just outside the airlock. The girls ran forward and wrapped their arms around her waist. This alone would have been a miracle two months earlier as neither girl had warmed to her much in the past. A conditional requirement imposed by Nan, the glorified baby-sitter officer had sacrificed much to protect the girls—especially Boomer. Jason's mind flashed back to Captain Stalls and the torment he'd brought into all their lives. He briefly wondered if the psychotic pirate was still locked up within the brig on board.

"I didn't expect to see you again … especially anywhere near *The Lilly*," Jason said, with a sideways glance.

She extricated herself from the girls' arms and readjusted her spacer's jumpsuit. "I had no plans to return to this madhouse, sir. But over time, I became restless. Restless ... and feeling rather guilty. I realized what I did here *was* important. That the now acting president's daughters needed me. That you needed me to be here."

"Whoa ... slow down, Petty Officer ... let's not get ahead of ourselves here," Jason said with a wry grin. He kept moving, heading for the closest DeckPort. He spoke over his shoulder, "You taking control of the little monsters?"

"Yes, sir ... I've got them."

★ ★ ★

After a quick stop at his quarters to drop off his duffle and change clothes, Jason headed into the bridge.

The ship's AI announced, "Captain on the bridge," as he entered the command center of *The Lilly*. The XO, Lieutenant Commander Perkins, stood up from the command chair and smiled at him. "Welcome aboard, sir. I take it your leave was restful?"

"Thank you, XO. It was fine. Where are we at with things?"

More of the bridge crew began filing in and Jason saw Perkins' eyes flash over to Orion as she took her seat at the tactical station.

"We've just returned from the line ... what we now call the outer perimeter of the solar system, where we've set up—"

"I know what the line is, XO ... I haven't been that re-moved from what's going on. The line is where we've set up defenses against the three Craing fleets: Fleet 9, Fleet 173, and Fleet 25—comprised of at least five thousand warships—which have basically been in a holding pattern in space for approximately sixty days."

"Yes, sir."

"Still no communications from them? Still not respond-ing to our hails?"

Perkins shook his head. "No, sir. But they don't seem to

be accepting their incoming hails from command back in Craing space either. That could be important."

Jason chewed on his lower lip and thought about that for a moment. "That is interesting. What else?"

"Well, before that, we were in Allied space. The admiral was with us."

"How we doing, bringing the Alliance back together?"

"Mixed. A few of our old allies are considering rejoining the Alliance ... others, though, are adamant they are better off on their own. In light of the destruction caused by the Vanguard fleet ... the fact that neither *The Lilly* nor the *Minian* were there to assist them ... they just don't see the point."

Jason didn't have an argument for that. He raised his eyebrows for him to continue. Again, the XO glanced over to Orion. "We, um ... made a stop-off at Jhardon." Perkins made a sympathetic expression and Jason understood what his problem was.

"Yes, you dropped Dira off on her home planet." Jason turned toward Orion and then back to Perkins. "I'm not a child. You don't need to pussyfoot around the subject. It's fine. I'm fine."

Ensign McBride turned from his station toward the command chair. "Welcome back, Captain, what destination coordinates should I be configuring, sir?"

"I have a meeting with both the acting president and Admiral Reynolds in Washington, in two hours." That reminded Jason, he needed to check in with Teardrop on his progress with the plasma turret. "Give it another thirty minutes before we head out. I'm having some last minute work done above ground."

"Aye, Cap."

Jason retrieved his virtual notepad and started to review all the messages marked urgent. There were several from Ricket. Jason had been keeping up with him on his and Gaddy's mission to Terplin. Their covert mission had required them to take the *Streamline* back through HAB 12 to Halimar, and then onto the north pole of Terplin. Once there, they were to meet with the revolutionary command. Jason scrolled down to the last message. Apparently, Ricket and Gaddy had met several times with Zay-Lee. Jason had been introduced to the young revolutionary on Halimar and had provided him with some weapons and SuitPacs; they'd obviously made a world of difference for the small band of revolutionaries. Jason noted that Ricket, now traveling under his alias of Nelmon Lim, and Gaddy were optimistic that the new, fledgling, independent government wanted to establish diplomatic ties to both Earth and what was left of the Alliance. This news alone was staggering, considering the events over the past few years. Of course, there was still the problem of the vast Craing force still stationed in space. So far, the now-alienated fleet, what was considered the Imperial Craing military in space, was leaving the Craing worlds alone, not hampering the new, quickening spread of independence—freedom from the old regime ... and the ways of the Emperor.

Jason's eyes scanned further down and caught on the name Ot-Mul. He read the line again:

It is now confirmed—Acting-emperor Ot-Mul survived the attack on Chrimguard. He, along with four battle droids, has escaped. He is now firmly in command of all Craing forces in space.

"Damn it!" Jason spat under his breath. That was one piece of information he hadn't been aware of. He looked up to see Gunny watching him.

"Ot-Mul?" she asked.

"Yeah ... it's like he has nine lives." He scrolled down to see if there were any more messages from Ricket and found none. "Anything else new from Ricket?"

Gunny shook her head. "Last confirmation we had they were heading back to Halimar on board a small shuttle ... that was two weeks ago."

"We've been able to contact the AI on board the *Streamline* ... they never made it back."

"What are our options? Can we communicate directly with Zay-Lee?" Jason asked, concern in his voice.

"Communications have been spotty, at best. He did confirm the two had indeed been loaded onto a shuttle and sent on their way. He, too, is worried. I guess Zay-Lee and Gaddy became close ... she was talking about returning to the Craing worlds permanently, to be with him."

Jason sank back in the command chair and thought about the situation. *What have you gotten yourself into, Ricket?* He didn't want to overly speculate on what may have happened. The truth was, Jason had few friends in life ... real friends. Billy and Ricket came to mind. First Dira, and now Ricket too, lost? The heaviness in Jason's heart must have shown on his face.

"Well, if it isn't our long lost leader."

Jason looked up to see Billy's smiling, concerned face. He returned the smile, stood up, and shook Billy's outstretched hand.

"Tan ... relaxed, probably drank Mai-Tais poolside ... you sure you want to be back here?" Billy asked.

"All good things come to an end ... plus the peovils, what my kids call the zombies, were getting a bit too close for comfort."

"Well, it's good to have you back. It's time we get out there and kick some more Craing ass."

"That's the plan ... but we have some other business to take care of first." Jason's mind then flashed back to Ricket. *What have you gotten yourself into, Ricket?*

CHAPTER 4

The sheer size of the vessel, if that's what you could even call it, was on a scale that rivaled a small planet—certainly a planetary moon. *Dreathlor* prison barge was well over one thousand years old. One of their first bounties of war, some two hundred years earlier, the *Dreathlor's* immense value and potential had quickly been obvious to the Craing. First of all, it was impregnable. With an outer hull hundreds of feet thick, and made from some kind of iron-carbon composite, the prison barge had never been breached. Not even close. The sight of the barge alone instilled fear and dread in all those coming anywhere near it. Dark, rusted, and always moving slowly in space, the prison barge was more than what it functioned as: It was a clear message—no, more like a warning. Go up against the Craing Empire, *or what was the Craing Empire,* and you'll find yourself confined in here—a fate often worse than death.

Superintendent Gettling was not Craing. He was human. A slender man of average height, with a tightly, impeccably trimmed beard, he was fastidious: a quality that was in direct opposition to the chaotic, and all too unpredictable environs around him. *Dreathlor* prison barge was his domain, his purpose in life. And where most beings would find such a dark existence intolerable—exiled, as it were, among the misery and depravity—he relished it. There was a place in the universe for *Dreathlor*. There was a place in the universe for people like him. He would probably never leave the ship. He had no desire for conventional relationships, or to live among his own kind. Here, among the distant moans and screams of the exiled—and routinely tortured—was home.

Deep within the maze of tight, intersecting corridors at the prison's mid-starboard section, Gettling sat at his desk and reviewed the interstellar correspondence one more time. It was short and concise, something he liked about the Craing— always to the point, no wasted sentiment or formalities:

To: Superintendent Miles Gettling

Directive 1: Continue to interrogate prisoners Gaddy Lom, and her friend, Nelmon Lim. It is essential that more information be harvested from both of these dissident traitors.

Directive 2: You will alter course to the new heading provided. Expedite disposal of all non-essential prisoners before reaching the intended destination—Corpus-Lang, within the Orion star system. Make haste. No stops or deviations from provided route.

Immediate commencement of these orders is a directive of Admiral Ot-Mul.

Gettling smiled. He'd been traversing this same quadrant in space for nearly four years now. Time to mix things up. He inputted the spatial coordinates into the terminal on his desk and waited for the methodical, slow-thinking AI to respond.

A heavily accented voice, guttural and menacing, filled the confined office space. "Superintendent Gettling, your course change has been approved by Craing Command. Shall I instigate?"

"Yes, of course you should. Do so now!"

"Course change instigated. Affected departments will be notified. Superintendent, I was told to remind you of the importance of this morning's other directive."

"I'm well aware of the other directive. Mind your duties, AI—I'm quite busy here."

The truth of the matter was Gettling was unable to think about anything other than the two dissidents currently held in pit-11141. He'd never held higher-profile prisoners in confinement, nor had his actions been so closely monitored. Gettling had no family of his own that he was aware of, but he wondered how the late Lom would feel, knowing his niece had been sent to this unholy place—would he be doing summersaults in his grave? Gettling always knew Ot-Mul was beyond ruthless—his exploits as commander of the Vanguard fleet were notorious. But sending Lom's niece here, among these realms of despair and torture—this place of pain … Gettling stood while pondering the question. He spun the cold metal wheel on the hatch and heard the internal latching mechanism disengage. Using both hands, he pulled the two-foot-thick door open, stepped into the corridor and secured the hatch closed behind him. The sounds of *Dreathlor* prison, the sounds of misery, had just increased in his ears by a factor of ten.

Pit-11141 was on the far side of the basically circular, slightly oblong prison barge. He calculated the distance in his head, somewhere around six hundred miles away from his current location. Although the prison was anything but high tech, and for good reason, its transportation system was state of the art. As superintendent of the prison, he was not only afforded a personal transport terminal, but also his own anti-grav railcar. One of his few perks.

The superintendent made his way to the group of terminal buildings and entered the smallest one. His railcar was still there, waiting from when he arrived on it in the morning.

"To the pits, 11141," he said. He sat and felt the car immediately start to move forward—G-forces pushed him back into his heavily cushioned seat. Within moments the anti-grav car was speeding along ten times the speed of sound. Although muffled, sonic thuds resounded off the tunnel walls and vibrated up into his buttocks. A sensation he'd come to appreciate over the years.

The car slowed and came to a stop at a terminal similar to the one he'd left minutes before. He got to his feet and exited the terminal building. He didn't make this trek to the pits as often as he used to. Standing there on the metal catwalk, his breath caught in his chest. The view before him, the spectacle and enormity of what encompassed the *Prisoner Isolation Trenches*, even now, was mesmerizing. Black as obsidian, there were thousands upon thousands of thirty-foot-deep holes—each with a surface smooth as glass. Like well-organized craters on a lunar surface, the hole-pocked landscape stretched out as far as the eye could see.

Adjacent to the crisscross of security catwalks were constantly moving, and stopping, tram-plates. Nothing like the high-tech anti-grav cars, these were nothing more than moving plates of metal, primitive but effective in moving someone from one pit location to another.

Gettling pressed a series of buttons that would take him to Pit-11141. Holding tight to a metal cross bar, the tram-plate jerked forward then changed direction at the first intersection it came to. Gettling swayed as the tram-plate gained speed, his eyes catching movement and then momentarily tracking indecipherable figures along the base areas of several of the pits.

The tram-plate began to slow and changed direction again. Each pit was sectioned to three others, and tied together by a center-hub management station. It was there that the tram-plate came to a stuttering stop. Gettling jumped off and headed for the hub station that managed pits 11140 through 11143. A winding metal staircase led down to the hub management station. The superintendent's soft leather boots made little noise as his feet stepped from one rung to another. Thirty feet below the surface, he entered the clear, cube-like station. Opening the hatch, he was greeted by a familiar smell. Trancus was a Mollmol. And, as far as Gettling knew, all Mollmols smelled the same: like rotting fish. It was quite unpleasant until one got used to it.

"Trancus! I'd forgotten you'd been assigned to these prisoners. Splendid!"

Trancus was standing at one of the clear partitions, looking into one of the confinement pits. At close to eight-feet-tall, and an interesting mix of reptile-serpent, and perhaps some human, components, his muscular system, beneath black, always glistening, wet skin, evoked fear from virtually everyone he came in contact with. Add in his disgusting smell, and Trancus was the complete, fear-evoking, package.

"Superintendent. I didn't expect you for several more hours," he said in a wet, lisping voice. "As I told you earlier, I have yet to retrieve any new information from her."

Gettling stood at Trancus's side and watched the lone pit inhabitant trying to climb the sheer curved walls. It would be impossible for her, of course. Completely open thirty feet above, the top beckoned, seemingly reachable. But, as with the barge itself, the pits were totally secure.

Gaddy, her clothes soiled and bloodied, continued to move in a circular direction around the base of the pit.

"It's always amazed me how prisoners think escape is possible … why they circle around and around as if that will make some kind of difference, evades me."

Trancus did not respond.

Turning around, Gettling walked to the other clear partition. "And this one, the one called Nelmon Lim. What about him?"

Trancus joined the superintendent and both peered across an identical-looking pit inhabited by a young-looking, unconscious, Craing male. Sprawled awkwardly in the middle of the floor, Ricket opened his eyes.

CHAPTER 5

They'd phase-shifted from the subterranean base to two hundred feet above the scrapyard. Jason was on his feet and standing behind McBride. "Hold here a moment, Ensign."

Jason walked around the helm console, not taking his eyes from the overhead, 360-degree virtual display. The large scrapyard property sprawled hundreds of yards beneath them. The impressive newly built house, with its rectangular aqua-blue pool, stood like a sentinel. Perched on a raised hillside, it occupied the southern quadrant of the acreage. But what held Jason's attention was the recently repaired turret gun. Series of bright blue bolts of plasma were spewing from its muzzle. That, in itself, was surprising. He'd instructed Teardrop to reconfigure the weapon to fire only when the peovils physically encroached onto his property. Obviously, the fence was not a determent to their advancement. No less than ten bodies, some still smoldering, lay prone within the confines of the scrapyard acreage. What would the scrapyard look like in a month from now ... two months? How many bodies would be piled up here. Hell, he probably had known some of these people. *This isn't working.*

Jason put a hand up to his right ear and contacted Teardrop via his NanoCom. "Teardrop ... is there a way you can disengage the scrapyard turret weapon remotely?"

"Yes, Captain."

"Do so, now."

Jason watched the turret gun become still. He took one more glance at the house on the hill and turned away. He hoped it would still be there when they returned. "Take us out of here, Helm."

★ ★ ★

The Lilly descended, flying above Washington, D.C. and right over the White House. There, too, a new encircling, steel fence had been constructed. Far more elaborate than the one at the scrapyard, this walled barrier was easily sixty or seventy feet in height and erected at an approximately thirty-degree angle. It seemed to be effective, since none of the peovils presently climbing it progressed any further than halfway up before falling back to the ground.

The Lilly settled onto one of the large landing pads at the back of the property. For the past year, landings by space vessels as large as *The Lilly*, or larger, including light and heavy Craing cruisers, had become commonplace. A painted white Craing cruiser, U.S. flag emblems affixed to its wings, and along both sides of the hull, took up the only other landing pad.

"Want to get some air?" Jason asked Billy, standing near his side.

"In the White House? Sure ... you bet I do," Billy replied.

"You too, Gunny," Jason said, to Orion's obvious surprise. "XO, you have the bridge."

★ ★ ★

They were met at the end of the gangway by a small team of Army Rangers. Jason spotted two other armed teams also patrolling the rear grounds. The threesome were still wearing their spacer jumpsuits, their SuitPacs at the ready on their belts.

With the security team now positioned in front and behind them, they headed into the back of the White House through a small, wood-paneled vestibule where they made a quick right turn toward the West Wing. The presidential seat of government was bustling with activity. Jason had visited here several times in the past and today there were two or three times more people scurrying around than normally.

The security detail stood back at the open doorway of the Oval Office. Orion and Billy exchanged quick glances as they were prompted to follow Jason. Nan was seated in one of the armchairs, positioned across from the couch. Jason's father occupied the other armchair. Jason recognized Secretary of Defense Benjamin Walker, who was seated on the couch. Nan and the men were dressed in casual clothes and stood when Jason and his two team members entered the room.

Nan got to her feet, rushed forward, and pulled Jason into an embrace. He held her tightly and realized she was crying—sobbing onto his chest. He placed his hand at the back of her head and gently held her close. Over her shoulder Jason acknowledged Walker. He was pleased to see that the gruff old Secretary of Defense was still around.

Nan pulled herself away, wiping the moisture from beneath her eyes, and looked up at Jason. "Sorry, must have needed that."

Jason then caught the curve of her belly. She really was showing now. She saw the direction of his stare and smiled. "I guess I'm just a baby-making machine." She shrugged and moved over to Billy and Orion, giving each a quick hug. "I'm so glad to see the three of you ... you have no idea."

It occurred to Jason that Walker actually had seniority over Nan. Shouldn't he be the acting president?

Walker moved a step forward and took Jason's outstretched hand in both of his own. "Young man, you are a sight for sore eyes."

Jason smiled and turned toward his father, who acknowledged him with a wink and a smile. Nan said, "Sit ... let's all sit and get down to business."

Billy and Orion took seats next to Walker on the couch as Jason brought an antique chair over from the wall.

Jason figured he might as well express what was on his mind. "So who is the acting president of the United States?" His eyes looked between Nan and Walker.

"She is ..." Walker hesitated. "They found me ... my cocoon ... several days ago and I seemed to be in relatively good health. Fortunately, I'm type O. Now, even though I am technically the senior government official in line, tomorrow that could change from me to the chief of staff, or perhaps even the vice president ... if either of their respective cocoons are found. But what our country needs today is stability. What we need is a president the country already has faith in, and that person is Nan Reynolds. Keep in mind, nothing about these present times is normal ... this certainly won't be the last break from usual presidential procedure."

Jason caught his ex-wife's eye and saw something there he couldn't remember ever seeing before. More than just confidence—it was more like an emanating force that seemed to be growing. Not only was she the acting president, she was actually owning the position.

She sat up in her chair and looked into each face. "We have no time to waste with chit chat. Our country is on the verge of collapse. With much of the populace infected ... roaming the streets like zombies—medical services, utilities, our nation's whole infrastructure, is barely operational. We're in deep trouble. And that doesn't even address the impending troubles we're facing in space, with three fleets of Craing warships ready to attack us." Nan hesitated, then continued, "I've been talking with the admiral and the truth of the matter is there's very little we can do about the Craing. Steps are being taken to bring the Alliance together again ... but that's a slow, methodical process. We don't know why the Craing have held steady. We can only hope it's a good sign. So, to bring us up to date on the situation here at home, Admiral, can you tell us about the progress being made on the science front?"

Jason turned in his seat to look at his father. His salt-and-pepper gray hair had grown longer, hanging well over his collar. He also seemed to be growing a full beard.

"In Ricket's absence we had to solicit help from that Caldurian, Granger. As you all know, our history with him has not been smooth. None of us are under any illusion about him and his self-serving motivations. With that said, his scientific capabilities are probably on a par with Ricket's. He's agreed to work with our own top-level scientists and to utilize some of the *Minian*'s advanced technology to see if there is anything we can do to treat those infected."

"How's that coming along?" Jason asked.

"Actually, pretty well. Research has started on board the *Minian*. Its lab is holding four subjects."

"Peovils," Jason interjected.

Nan smiled at the word she knew Mollie had assigned to the molt weevil zombies. "Yes," the admiral continued, "okay … peovils … and with a combination of nanites injected into their bloodstreams and specific, programmed, MediPod treatments—the four have made full recovery."

Nan continued, "The problem is scalability. Granger is confident we'll have a full cure within days. But, as of right now, it takes twenty-four hours, and dedicating full use of one of the *Minian*'s MediPods for even one person's recovery. Obviously, that's not a long-term solution for the millions infected."

The admiral jumped in, "It was actually that pirate kid, Bristol, who's come up with the most realistic approach. It still takes twenty-four hours for the treatment to take effect, but it doesn't require a MediPod. I can't even attempt to relay all the science involved, but basically he's modified a multi-gun to fire off a combination of injectable nanite-infused projectiles, along with an energy … some kind of modified plasma pulse … that renders the subject unconscious long enough for the treatment to take full effect."

"So, like … we roam the streets, with these modified multi-guns, shooting all the peovils we come across? And a day later, they wake up perfectly human again?" Orion asked.

"Basically, that's the idea. It still needs to be fully tested."

"Sign me up for that," Orion said, showing genuine interest. Billy looked at Orion with raised eyebrows. "I'm just saying … it sounds like an effective—"

"Just stop while you're ahead," Billy said with a smile.

"So we have made at least *some* progress … some hope of dealing with this catastrophic infestation," Nan continued. "But that's far from being our only problem right now." Nan stopped speaking and took a sip of water. "North Korea is looking to use this calamity as a power-grab opportunity."

"You're serious?" Billy asked, looking skeptical. "North Korea?"

"Dead serious," Secretary Walker said. "They were one of the few geographic locations on Earth relatively untouched by the molt weevil infestation. And areas of Russia, as well, but that still needs to be confirmed. As of last night, midnight, we were given twenty-four hours to recognize the Democratic People's Republic of Korea as the supreme worldwide government. The demand was backed up with both a threat and a demonstration of how serious they are."

"What kind of demonstration?" Jason asked.

A deep sadness came over Secretary Walker. He looked old and defeated. "Until now we've kept this from the public. The President is scheduled to make a statement to inform the American people … the world."

"What … what is it?"

"At 3:30 a.m., a North Korean Soviet-made Golf II class nuclear submarine, in the Pacific Ocean, fired off a missile … one with a single, five-megaton warhead, toward the Hawaiian Islands."

The room became quiet. Walker let out a long breath, his next words barely audible. "There's absolutely nothing left of the islands."

Jason was having a hard time comprehending what he'd just heard. The millions of lives lost in a flash and for what? What kind of monster makes that kind of decision?

After a long silence, Nan leaned forward in her chair. "Jason, I want you to go—have a little chat with Kim Jong Un. "

CHAPTER 6

Jason's directive over the next week was to visit Pyongyang, and from there, on to Moscow. Both governments would be made to understand, by force if necessary, the consequences of any further attacks, nuclear or otherwise. Now was not the time for reciprocity. That, the Secretary of Defense assured everyone, would come about in time. But for now … what was paramount was restraining further escalation—basically, avoiding the total eradication of humankind.

"Captain, we're entering North Korean airspace," McBride said.

"Bring us down, all four of us. I want to be scraping their rooftops."

"Aye, Cap."

Our aerial convoy of goliath-sized warships, slowly moving in unison across the North Korean skyline, must be quite a sight, Jason thought to himself as he sat in *The Lilly*'s command chair. He watched the green agricultural landscape slowly move across the display. It was all about a show of force—one that would inspire fear and awe—from the peasants in the field, on up to the people's assembly—to the premiere himself.

Jason was aware that *The Lilly* and the three massive Craing vessels at this altitude would generate substantial vibration—enough to cause damage to both residential and business structures below. Thunderous waves would course through the populace's bodies and, more importantly, their psyches. The earthshaking started eight hundred miles from Pyongyang—and now, the news would spread like wildfire. Nothing would instill the futility of war, the ridiculousness of fighting the Americans, more than the sight of menacing warships overhead.

"Contacts!"

The display above showed recently scrambled fighters. "Mig 21s, for the most part, Cap; Russian supplied," Orion said. "Looks like they're putting everything they have into the air. Even a reconfigured passenger jet."

"Bring us up to two thousand feet. Shields up."

"Aye, sir," Orion replied.

"Incoming missiles."

Jason stood up from the command chair and watched the display above him. Looking at the high-definition, real-world view, Jason more than once ducked as incoming missiles harmlessly struck, and exploded, against their outer shields. The flurry of explosions dissipated as the fighters exhausted their payloads against the five slowly moving warships.

Jason sat back down and watched as the North Korean air force, like bees, swarmed harmlessly at the fleet's shielded perimeters. He brought up his virtual notepad, wanting to get specific, pertinent information about North Korea. Who, exactly, was he dealing with? What he soon discovered was sobering: The country seemed one of the most miserable places on the planet to exist; most of the population had no flushing toilets and survived on less than ten dollars a month. Meat is considered a luxury item. Children stunted in growth from malnutrition are commonplace, while the ruling dictator has an estimated personal wealth of one hundred billion dollars—of course, all kept in secret accounts outside his wretched country.

Jason continued to read about North Korea. He shook his head. The last thing he wanted to do was cause more deprivation for its citizenry. No, it was its leadership he needed to have a one-on-one with, this Kim Jong Un. "What's the local time here, Orion?"

"Zero five-thirty, Cap."

Jason changed his search parameters, now looking to see where the leader's residence was located. "Huh, well, there's this *Kumsusan Palace of the Sun* ... sometimes called *Kim Jong Un Palace*," he said.

"That looks like quite a place," Orion said out loud. She'd joined him at his side and was reading over his shoulder. There was a picture of the palace. "Wow, no need to worry about finding sufficient parking space for the fleet," she said.

The palace and its grounds were immense.

"Looks like Kim Jong Un has multiple residences ... who knows where the little squirrel is hiding out. We have to start somewhere. Helm, take us to Pyongyang—*Kumsusan Palace of the Sun*."

"Aye, Cap," McBride answered.

"And take us back down to a thousand feet."

"Aye, Cap."

The overhead display zoomed in on the landscape moving below them. Currently, they were passing over building after building of tightly grouped apartment dwellings. All looked the same—in the same state of grimy decrepitude. The landscape opened up and several small farms appeared. Workers began running, scattering in all directions, apparently terrified by what must seem tantamount to an alien invasion. Others, crouching low, stopped working to observe the spectacle above. Eventually, they would notice the U.S. flag emblems on the warships' undercarriages and then know exactly where the vessels came from.

"Pyongyang, sir. The palace is on the display ahead."

Jason was back on his feet and watched as the large, marble-sided and square-ish three-tiered structure came into view. Whereas the image he'd seen earlier, on his virtual note-pad, showed acres and acres of open space at the palace's front quad, now a uniformed army of at least ten thousand green and red coated men awaited. Tanks and batteries of artillery were poised to fire from the structure's east side.

"Nowhere to land, sir," McBride said.

Jason continued to watch in silence. He nodded his head, as if coming to some sort of mental decision. "Have the fleet positioned right over them. We'll need all this space. Make sure the fleet commanders understand they are to bring their vessels down slowly. Those below who are too slow or stupid to move away will quickly find themselves dead."

"Aye, Cap," McBride answered, then began talking on comms to the other ships.

Ground fire below initiated everywhere: from soldiers' automatic weapons, to tank and mortar munitions. In uni-son, the warships began to descend. Even from close to one thousand feet aloft, thruster heat hitting the ground would be extreme. As expected, the regiments of North Korea ran—the soldiers who'd waited too long, or had followed orders not to abandon their positions, came into contact with the vessels' virtually-impregnable lower shields. More than a few soldiers were crushed as the fleet of ships settled onto solid ground.

Jason hailed Billy.

"Go for Billy."

"Got your team assembled, ready to deploy?"

"We're at the forward airlock."

"I'm on my way," Jason said. "XO, keep me apprised of any developments."

"Aye, Cap," Orion replied, taking the command chair.

Earlier, Jason had asked Billy to assemble a ten-man SEAL assault team. Now, as Jason activated his own SuitPac, he ap-proached his friend.

Billy, a wet and disgusting-looking stogie at the corner of

his mouth, nodded as Jason came up. "Hey, Cap."

"Smoking in an airlock, huh? Hell … I bet you smoke in the shower."

Billy gave a half-hearted shrug and disposed of the unlit cigar in a nearby refuse panel. Helmet visors were lowered and a virtual 3D schematic representation of the *Kumsusan Palace's* internal layout hovered before their eyes.

"I have no idea where we're going here. Not much intel on the whereabouts of North Korean heads of state. So maybe someone will stop and give us directions," Jason said.

That evoked chuckles from the team as Jason slapped the airlock's hatch release button. The gangway was deployed; from the top of the ramp Jason couldn't see anyone below, but his HUD indicated there were thousands of Korean combatants moving in. "Let's go."

Multi-guns held at the ready, he led the team down the gangway and out onto the Kumsusan Palace quad. Jason and the SEALs turned and took it all in. *The Lilly* was positioned closest to the palace's front entrance. The other four significantly larger Craing heavy cruisers were spaced evenly throughout the quad area.

They moved away from the ship toward the main building. A slight distortion caught Jason's eye as *The Lilly's* shields came back online. Somewhere in the distance came a screaming command. Gunfire erupted from all sides. Several bullets pinged off Jason's battle suit; then more bullets struck and eventually he, and the others, found it difficult to remain standing.

Billy was the first to be knocked off his feet, as an explosive *something*, perhaps a frag grenade fired from an RPG weapon, erupted directly to his left. Soon, with more explosions coming, one after another, they were either thrown to the ground, or bounced up into the air, or tossed tens of yards in opposite directions. The escalating concussive effects were dizzying.

Jason, sprawled on his ass, had a hard time standing. His mind flashed to a similar situation involving stampeding buffaloes. He brought up his HUD phase-shift settings for the entire team and tried to activate a phase-shift. The pounding vibration was making it difficult for him to think, let alone configure specific phase-shift destination settings.

Billy's voice stammered into Jason's ear: "Great impression we're making, Cap. Real imposing. We look like fucking rodeo clowns out here—bouncing around like this."

"Just give me a second … I'm working on it," Jason replied.

The world flashed white and simultaneously the SEAL team was transported inside the palace. It took Jason several moments to realize he had phase-shifted directly into a suspended glass coffin. The body of a long-dead North Korean man, dressed in a military jacket and obviously a once-important dignitary, had just been split in two. Jason wasted no time pushing the two halves of the body out of his way as he stepped clear of the fragmented glass pieces of coffin, its pedestal, and the withered, newly transected corpse.

CHAPTER 7

Billy and the SEAL team watched Jason with mild amusement. Without saying a word, he got clear of the mess and moved to the center of what looked like a large vestibule, or viewing room. There were surrounding marble pillars that reached up thirty or forty feet to a high-cantilevered ceiling. Everything was marble: the walls, the floor, and an engraved marble plaque that covered most of one wall. An English translation of Korean characters hovered on Jason's HUD. Apparently, Jason had inadvertently catapulted into the lying-in-state remains of one of the recently deceased Jongs.

Angry shouting from an adjacent corridor echoed off the marble walls. Someone was barking out commands in Korean. Three men appeared at the entranceway; they each sported short black hair and wore similarly styled glasses. The threesome tentatively moved into the room, while a cluster of armed soldiers peered around the corner of the entrance behind them.

Jason met them halfway into the vestibule. One of the men—thinner and slightly taller than the other two—took two tentative steps forward. Beads of sweat had formed on his brow. He cleared his throat and began speaking in Korean. Jason waited a brief second and soon his nano-devices began translating. As the Korean continued to speak, Jason raised the visor on his helmet, providing him with some semblance of actual human-to-human contact.

"I am Ri Young, on the Secretary of the General's Staff. You have invaded our country. Desecrated the remains of our most beloved—"

Jason cut him off before he could continue. "Early this morning, or perhaps it was late last night here, your country fired off a nuclear warhead toward the Hawaiian Islands in the Pacific Ocean. The islands were destroyed. Millions of lives cut short in an instant. Needless to say, our two countries are now embroiled, de-facto, in a state of war. I am here to discuss the conditions of your country's complete, unconditional surrender to the United States of America."

The three North Korean dignitaries stared back at Jason, who was not only speaking perfect Korean, but had precisely nailed its dialect and its accented attributes, as well. Again, the Secretary of the General Staff official spoke. "I have no knowledge of a nuclear missile. I am but an official administrator."

"Where's Kim Jong Un?"

The three dignitaries became tight-lipped. The chubbiest of the three, the one to Jason's left, was staring at the grizzly remains of Kim Jong Il on the marble flooring.

Jason's visor closed and he took a step back from the dignitaries. Via his HUD, he set his multi-gun for its lowest-level stun. He brought up his weapon and fired directly into the face of the official. With a blackened scorch mark between his eyes, the man fell to the ground in what seemed a lifeless heap. The other two dignitaries cowered; neither would look Jason in the eye. A dark yellow pool of urine slowly spread across the floor at their feet. Jason wasn't sure from which man it had come.

Turning again to the Korean on his left, Jason brought the muzzle of his weapon up and placed it at the tip of the man's nose. "Think twice before answering my next question. If I even suspect you're lying, or if your information is not particularly useful, you'll join the Secretary's official on the floor. Where, exactly, is Kim Jong Un right now?"

"Ryongsong residence." The dignitary spoke quickly and

nodded his head, a gesture conveying he had no problem sharing the information.

The other dignitary, who had not spoken until now, added: "The residence is located in Ryongsong district, here in northern Pyongyang. Go now and Kim Jong Un will be there, I assure you."

Jason brought up his virtual notebook and projected a virtual 3D representation of northern Pyongyang. "Show me on here—exactly where."

Both dignitaries simultaneously pointed at the same spot on the hovering projection. Jason saw that the area was fairly close by and appeared rural. A forest of trees encircled multiple large structures. It was a fortified compound.

"We'll drop by and see if he's in. Remember, we know where to find you if he's not there. Also, you will make no attempt to warn him; is that clear?"

Both men nodded. Billy, who had been hovering nearby, moved to Jason's side. His visor was up and he was chewing on an unlit stogie. He turned and gestured toward the shattered glass, and the transected body parts scattered on the floor. "I suggest you get this mess cleaned up before we return."

The room flashed white.

★ ★ ★

Jason had set the phase-shift coordinates to a small clearing within a wooded area set back twenty feet behind Kim Jong Un's residence's back lawn.

Jason heard Billy's voice over his comms. "HUD's telling me we have thirty men on active patrol, Cap."

Jason spoke into an open channel: "Split into three groups. Hold fire until my order."

They all moved from the cover of the towering pines out onto a manicured gravel pathway that looked to circumvent the entire property. One team led by Billy moved left while the second team led by Rizzo went right. Jason's team stepped back into the woods and waited sixty seconds. "Billy … Rizzo … in position?"

"Affirmative," came Rizzo's voice.

"We're set," Billy said.

Jason's team moved back out from the cover of the woods and onto the lawn. Keeping low, they hurried forward in the direction of a cluster of Korean soldiers eighty feet away, standing in a circle—all smoking cigarettes. As Jason approached, he heard their hushed voices getting louder. Someone must have said something funny because the group as a whole started to laugh. The soldiers were now flicking their cigarettes to the ground and using the toes of their boots to extinguish them. Two soldiers looked up and froze.

"Take them out," Jason said over the open channel. He pulled the trigger of his own multi-gun four times. Plasma bolts flashed around him as he and his team brought the Korean soldiers to their definitive demise.

Within thirty seconds, the three teams had intersected into one group again. Closer to the main structure, Jason saw that the main house, more like an industrial building, was practically all glass, with brushed aluminum accents. The team approached, skirting three dramatic fountains; each one, square-sided, had four majestic waterfalls pouring into Zen-like pools some fifteen feet below ground.

Little time was spent gawking at the lush surroundings. Not far within the confines of the residence, he noticed something repeatedly flashing: explosions! Faintly, he heard gunfire. "What the hell …"

DeMille, the stocky, friendly-faced Seaman, was pointing into the residence. "I'd recognize that sound anywhere. Call of Duty, sir. Definitely Call of Duty. Looks like someone's got a PlayStation."

Jason nodded. "Why don't you do the honors, DeMille. Give us a back door."

The young SEAL took a step back, made an adjustment to his multi-gun, and fired.

The back of the residence erupted into a shower of glass and metal. The SEAL team rushed in, weapons held high and at the ready. Separating into their smaller teams of three again, they proceeded forward—some scouting out the first floor, others climbing up a thick glass stairway to the upper levels. Jason entered last. Jason heard a definitive *clear* as, one after the other, the SEALs secured the premises. Jason knew, from the singular red icon showing on his HUD, that the only inhabitant here was in the adjacent room.

As Jason entered what must be considered the great room, sitting on a humongous sectional couch was Kim Jong Un. Five SEALs stood behind him, their multi-guns trained on his head.

Sitting in his tighty whities and a black T-shirt far too small for his amply protruding belly, the young North Korean leader looked up at Jason. A bright red bowl, half full of popcorn, was precariously propped on his leg. He turned his attention to the wall-sized flat screen TV and then back at Jason, who noticed the video game was paused, frozen on a combatant figure in the midst of firing some kind of RPG weapon. The figure wore a battle suit remarkably similar to the one Jason and his teammates were currently wearing.

Jason gestured for everyone to lower their weapons, as Billy directed several of the team to secure an outside perimeter. Looking at the young leader, his mouth open and half-full of popcorn, Jason wondered if the Korean leader had any idea what was going on; if he was even aware that his country was now at war. Then Jason noticed several smaller TVs. Four of them hung higher up on the wall, above the game playing on the large TV screen. Two TVs were tuned to North Korean news channels, showing helicopter shots of Kumsusan Palace, and the fleet of Craing warships parked on its sprawling quad. One TV was tuned to an old Gilligan's Island rerun, while another displayed a feed from some high-level meeting; no fewer than ten military officers, clad in dark-green uniforms that were decorated with ornate chest ribbons and gold shoulder stars, stood like wax statues, their faces looking back at him in stunned attention. So, while his country sent a nuclear warhead toward America's fiftieth state, this little shit was playing video games. The absurdity of it made Jason's blood boil.

Kim Jung Un smiled up at Jason and then resumed, slowly at first, to chew on the popcorn kernels still in his mouth.

Jason stepped over a small tower of comic books lying scattered about the floor and sat down next to North Korea's supreme leader.

"As of now, we are taking control of your country. When you learn to play nice with your neighbors, perhaps someday you will get it back."

No one spoke. Jason said something into his comms and then gestured toward the TV, currently showing the fleet of U.S. warships sitting on the quad of Kumsusan Palace. *The Lilly* rose slowly into the air, only five hundred feet or so. Small cannons appeared beneath her underbelly. In a spectacular blaze of plasma fire, *The Lilly* let loose a fire barrage for nearly ten seconds. The cannons then retracted back into the ship's hull and *The Lilly* resettled down onto the quad.

Jason was on his comms; out of habit he placed two fingers to his ear. He nodded and looked over at the North Korean leader.

"There are now none remaining of the few nuclear warheads your country possessed. Even their silos have been eradicated. Your air force and naval assets have also been destroyed. For all intent and purpose, your country is now totally defenseless."

Chatter erupted from the TV feed up on the wall. The military officers, earlier stone-faced and quiet, were now in frenzied states of agitation. One of the officers was standing, screaming at the camera, trying to get Kim Jong Un's attention.

Jason was being hailed.

"Go for Captain."

"Change of plan," the admiral said.

"What's up?"

"We need to get you and *The Lilly*, and your convoy, back into space."

"We haven't quite finished here," Jason said.

"We'll take care of the Russians later. I've dispatched another light cruiser to take up residence in Pyongyang Square. We need you up at the line … The Craing fleet is on the move."

CHAPTER 8

Rain continued to buffet her two, side-by-side bedroom windows. She pulled the curtains further apart and peered upward, toward the sky. The tallest of the six surrounding castle spires disappeared into the dark, menacing clouds above, never seeming to move away.

Dira lifted her arms up to let El, her young handmaiden, pull the silver mesh gown over her head. El gripped the sheer, snug fitting fabric on both sides of Dira's body and, with two practiced hands, pulled the garment down over her breasts and upper torso. The two briefly made eye contact.

"This is ridiculous, El. Seriously ... I don't need a dresser," Dira said, trying to contain her irritation. "And I certainly don't need to be dressed up like this."

El made a resigned expression, which bespoke she'd heard the same complaint a thousand times before. She continued to adjust the bodice until the material lay flat over Dira's belly, then smoothed it around her narrow hips. The full length of the gown blossomed out into shimmering, cascading folds that fell lightly to the floor.

"Nonsense, you're a princess ... soon to be queen."

Dira's eyes shot to the dresser's face. "Watch your tongue, El!"

El stood back and placed a hand over her heart, bowing her head. "I apologize, my princess. That was incredibly callous of me ... heartless."

Dira's thoughts turned to the queen, who was abed, unconscious, in the royal suite two floors below. She was not expected to live through the night. Injuries from the Craing attack had put her at death's door. Even with Dira's advanced medical training, there was little that could be done to help her. What she needed was a MediPod. Requests to her father—to bring this amazing technology to the palace—had fallen on deaf ears. The king's adherence to ancient, out of date monarchy tenants was infuriating.

Dira mimed the dresser's repentant gesture by placing her own hand over her heart. "No ... it's all right. You are just saying the simple truth." She watched El move off toward one of the wardrobes. Continuing to press her hand into her chest, Dira wondering if the pain inside her would ever subside. Leaving *The Lilly*, and Jason, was the hardest thing she'd ever done. Her departure from him broke her heart. Then, upon returning to Jhardon and the palace, her already broken heart was ravaged anew upon seeing the rapidly declining condition of her mother's life force.

Dira stepped in front of the full-length mirror positioned in the corner of her bedroom and appraised her refection. She turned her upper body slightly to the left—then to the right. She was unaccustomed to dressing this formally. Her eyes fell to her exposed shoulders—the neckline that gave the briefest glimpse of cleavage. Again, her thoughts returned to Jason. She imagined him here now, his fingers gently following the contours of her neck—like a whisper; his lips kissing her there, at the nape, where her violet skin flushed—

"You should wear these," El said, holding up a pair of strappy-looking silver shoes.

Dira let out a breath and nodded. "Those will be fine." She reached down with both hands and pulled the hem of her gown up. Kneeling, El fitted first one, and then the other, shoe onto Dira's feet and then stood up. Both turned their attention to the mirror.

"Oh my … A more beautiful vision I have never seen, my princess."

Dira gave El a smile that didn't quite make it up to her eyes. "Thank you, El. Please inform the king that I'm ready."

The dresser bowed her head and quickly bustled out through the bedroom door. Dira turned away from the mirror and slowly walked toward a tall antique armoire, opposite her bed. As El had left its doors slightly ajar a narrow swath of light filtered into the old cabinet. As Dira reached to close the doors, she suddenly stopped. Three shelves down from the top, folded into a perfect square, was the spacer's jumpsuit she'd arrived in. Atop the clothes was the small silver SuitPac device she customarily wore on her belt. She closed the cabinet doors.

★ ★ ★

The King and Queen of Jhardon were far more than their monarchy titles implied. No, here they reigned and ruled with full authority in their titled positions. For one thousand five hundred uninterrupted years there had been a ruling monarch—either a king or a queen—or, sometimes, both. Dira walked along the wide cobblestoned hallway that bordered the open palace courtyard to her left. Every fifteen feet she passed another magnificent fluted column, which reached hundreds of feet into the air. Rain continued to fall into the courtyard; the koi ponds had overflowed their banks weeks ago and the intricately patterned formal gardens, formerly lush with colorful flowers, were now nothing more than sodden rows of sagging, flowerless, stalks and vines.

As Dira approached the king's antechamber she slowed her pace. Her mind was reeling. She was debating with herself whether to avoid their discussion entirely. Her head down, the intersecting hallway loomed ten paces in front of her. She made a quick left and then stopped. *Shit! What's wrong with me?* She'd already had days to prepare ... no, a full week now. *Why is this so difficult?*

"Dira!"

She turned back toward her father's antechamber.

He stood there, looking around the half-opened door. "Come in, Dira. Join me for a hot *sangerine.*"

She smiled and joined her father as he widened up the doorway, and entered into what she knew was his favorite refuge. She eyed the leather couch, and the two matching leather chairs in front of his desk, but didn't sit. She watched the King of Jhardon walk to a credenza and pour two steaming cups of the bittersweet sangerine. He handed her a cup and waited for his daughter to speak.

She took the cup and sipped. Finally, she met her father's loving gaze. That was all it took for her eyes to brim up with tears. Her father's thick arms surrounded her—pulled her into his chest. "This is what you were destined to be, my sweet daughter. I have never known a more capable person than you, Dira."

She pulled herself away and looked into the king's heavily lined face. "I don't know if I can give up my life—"

"Yes, you can ... and you will. Because this involves much more than simply you and what *you* want."

"But why now, father? Why not in a year, or five years?"

"Because when your mother dies ... I'll die. We are one. It is the Jhardon way, Dira. Husbands and wives ... kings and queens, we have always had this choice. Our ultimate commitment is to one another. You are our sole heir, my daughter. In less than a week ... you will be queen. You will rule Jhardon, and those who live here ... our good, wonderful citizens ... you'll rule all the land, and the space around our still spectacular planet."

Again, Dira's hand found its way to her heart. Every beat ached for the love she would never realize. Every beat pounded, like a distant drum—echoing her shattered dreams. And then she thought of Nan and her unborn child. Jason's un-born child.

"Yes, father. I will do as you ask. I will make you proud. And when you lie down next to mother ... next to the Queen. When you go ..." tears were now streaming down Dira's cheeks, "I will send both of you on your way ... back home ... to the heavens of *Calime*. I will then proudly take my rightful place on Jhardon's throne."

Yes, she'd said the words. With them went any chance of a future life with Jason. The Queen of Jhardon could never marry outside her Jhardonian bloodlines.

CHAPTER 9

With the fingertips of his hands touching—as if in prayer—Jason sat quietly in the command chair as they approached the line. It was six hundred thousand miles of nothingness—a mere stone's throw away, considering the vastness of space, between the U.S. fleet of about one hundred ships and the three Craing fleets—about five thousand strong. Jason stood and looked up at the display and what comprised the entirety of the U.S. fleet. Even with their recommissioned Craing meganaught added to it, the small U.S. fleet seemed ridiculously outmatched. But the advanced technology of *The Lilly* and the *Minian*, both Caldurian vessels, put things on a somewhat more level playing field.

Jason watched as they approached the *Minian*. Nearly identical looking to *The Lilly*, she was almost twenty times her size, and significantly more advanced. They'd had two full months to complete the *Minian*'s repairs. Ricket, Bristol and Granger, an impressive combination of intellect and talent, revived the ship to her former glory; after having been technologically gutted, thanks to the Craing, she was now operating at full capacity.

"XO, you have the bridge."

"Aye, Captain," Perkins replied, taking the vacated command chair.

As Jason left the bridge and passed by his officer's quarters, he thought about his priceless cargo, Mollie and Boomer, still asleep in their bunks. Would having them on board affect his decision-making? He didn't think so … at least, no more than usual. But the battle that was coming would be like none any of them had fought in before—he knew that. He also knew losing to the Craing would ensure Earth's demise. There simply wasn't a safe haven for anyone … especially the children of Captain Jason Reynolds.

Off in the distance, down the corridor to the left, Jason's eyes locked on the entrance to Medical. How many times had he taken these same steps only to see Dira emerge, coincidentally, fifty feet in front of him? Their eyes would meet and neither would be able to keep themselves from smiling. But today the corridor remained quiet—Dira didn't emerge from Medical … she probably never would again.

He made his way to the DeckPort, stepped in, and emerged from the DeckPort closest to the flight deck. He still had forty minutes before he was due at the command meeting taking place on board the *Minian*. He could simply phase-shift over, but he needed to think and he knew the best way to do that would be getting behind the stick of the *Pacesetter*.

The flight deck was relatively quiet, with only a few droids moving about, conducting general maintenance on the varied selection of shuttles and on the six Caldurian fighters. The dark red *Pacesetter* sat on the open deck; she'd been prepped and seemed to be waiting for him—beckoning him to hurry up and climb on board. Jason felt his pulse quicken. With her gentle curves and slightly backswept wings, the fighter could best be described in one word: *sleek*. Everything about this fighter said fast—fast and dangerous. Jason climbed up the inset ladder and climbed into the forward cockpit. The canopy slid silently into place as Jason went through his pre-flight checklist.

Within a minute's time, he'd brought the *Pacesetter* off the flight deck and was heading into open space. He banked right, giving himself ample clearance of *The Lilly*'s two powerful drives, and accelerated. Jason moved away from the fleet of U.S. warships and headed into open space. With his HUD synced to the fighter, he placed the *Pacesetter* into training mode and started with some simple Basic Fighter Maneuvers, BFMs. Some of what he was seeing now was simulation and Jason marveled at the complexity of it all … how reality, such as the contours of the adjacent ship, was integrated into this new battle scenario. He scanned his surroundings—the brightness of distant stars—a giant nearby planet with its amber continents and blood red oceans. Four silvery moons … all of it transported Jason to another place in reality. This was the ultimate video game and he couldn't help but smile. He heard the soft voice of the AI in his ear, "Three bogies are approaching at sub-light speeds. All three have detected your presence and have locked on to your coordinates."

"Who are they?"

"Caldurian RAM fighters, Captain."

Jason saw the three fighters, approaching in a V formation, on the center 3D virtual display. Another smaller display to his right showed a wire-frame depiction of a RAM fighter, along with the vessel's impressive stats. More compact than the *Pacesetter*, these little beasts were fast and highly maneuverable. They also possessed a generation newer tech.

"Let the games begin …" Jason said, adjusting the position of the stick. Masses of information streamed into his mind—information he'd acquired through the hours of HyperLearning spent within a MediPod. Within this realm, the BFM program would push the pilot to the limit … his understanding of the mathematics of pursuit within a three-dimensional arena, where different angles of approach equated to different rates of closure. He needed to use this geometry now—to not only get within firing range, where the *Pacesetter*'s weapons could be used, but also to avoid common mistakes, such as overshooting, which consisted of flying in front of the opponent, called a "wingline overshoot," or crossing the enemy's flightpath, called a "flightpath overshoot."

The three bogies separated and the *Pacesetter* was almost upon them. In space, at the incredible speeds vessels could achieve there, virtually all flying was managed via the on-board AI. That's not to say all pilots simply sat back and let the advanced computer do the fighting for them. What Jason had come to understand was this was a melding of man and technology that was almost supernatural—the way one would anticipate the actions of the other. Jason had come to learn that not all AIs were the same. This *Pacesetter*'s artificial intelligence had seemed to become one with his own thoughts … his own intent.

"Incoming!"

Jason saw the crisscrossing vector lines on the display—each constantly altering to the relative positions of the three enemy crafts, each of which had fired off two fusion micro-missiles. He searched his mind for a solution and quickly came to the realization it wasn't a part of any past Hyper-Learning session.

"Any suggestions, AI?"

Jason reflexively jerked back in his seat as one of the Caldurian fighters crossed mere yards in front of the canopy. "You ballsy shit!" Jason said aloud. He banked right in pursuit of the fighter as his fingers moved to the trigger. The *Pacesetter*'s primary plasma gun came alive with rapid-fire bolts of energy. The virtual display showed he was actually gaining on the smaller craft … but it also showed he now had six micro-missiles quickly closing in on his ass. He pulled the stick back and then to the right and felt the crushing G-forces against his chest as the *Pacesetter* initiated a backwards loop. "You're going to have to do a better job compensating for those Gs, AI."

"Yes, Captain. I've already modified settings."

Jason pulled up a new menu on his HUD and made a quick scan of his available munitions. "Ah … there we go.

Old school." He deployed the rail gun and selected rail gun munitions, with tracking explosive rounds.

The trick was to instigate enough quick maneuvers to get in behind the missiles, while still evading the three fighters. They were firing their own plasma weapons now and over the past thirty seconds Jason saw that his shields were dropping—fast.

"Shields are at twenty percent, Captain."

"Yep ... see that."

He rolled the *Pacesetter* into a forward roll, and then back out into a backward figure eight. The superior speed of the *Pacesetter* put her in behind two of the Caldurian fighters and he let loose with the rail gun. In a flash, both fighters exploded, leaving fragments behind no larger than a pencil's eraser.

He banked and banked again. He saw the six missiles out through his canopy, moving in the opposite direction. He didn't need to get in behind them. As she'd done many times before, the AI was anticipating his commands.

"Acquiring lock."

The *Pacesetter's* turret-mounted rail gun spun, firing backward at close to a forty-five degree angle in the direction of the now-tightly-clustered grouping of missiles. Out of visual sight, Jason watched as the missile icons faded away, one by one, on the virtual display. Unfortunately, within that same fraction of a second, the one remaining Caldurian fighter was upon him. Close range plasma fire took the *Pacesetter's* shields down to five percent ... two ... zero.

"You have been destroyed. Simulation complete," the AI said, without a trace of sympathy. Jason let out a deep breath, allowing the tension in his shoulders to unwind. He was being hailed.

"Go for Captain."

"So if you're done fucking around, you might want to get your ass back here ... we're all waiting for you."

"Aye, Admiral. I'm on my way."

CHAPTER 10

Jason entered the admiral's ready room and took a seat in the one remaining chair at the far end of the table. With a quick glance around the room, he nodded to the others. The admiral was seated directly across from him, at the other end of the table; to his right was his brother, Brian; next to him was Perkins, then Bristol, Billy, Gunny, and the Caldurian, Granger. On the other side of the table was young Captain Curtis Pollard, who'd been promoted to skipper of the *Anvil*, one of the Craing's heavy old cruisers. Next to him was Commander Dolm Mo Huck, a representative of the now-collapsed Alliance. And directly to the admiral's right, surprisingly, sat Secretary of Defense Benjamin Walker.

"Thank you for joining us, Captain," his father said, making no attempt to hide his annoyance. Jason glanced around and noticed that each of the inset displays in the ready room had active live feeds, showing at least another twenty attendees. Now Jason did feel some guilt at holding things up ... especially seeing Nan, the acting president of the United States, looking back at him with obvious irritation.

The other, virtual, attendees were mostly unknown to Jason, but judging by many of their non-human physiologies, it was evident that they also were, for the most part, past Alliance dignitaries and command personnel. Jason took the next few moments to acknowledge each of the virtual attendees. His focus abruptly stopped on the display on the bulkhead directly to his left when he recognized the king. An imposing figure, with wide, muscular shoulders, and wearing some kind of animal hide robe, was King Caparri, whose striking violet skin first caught Jason's attention. So did the unmistakable female beauty, sitting just slightly behind him. Like the Jhardonian monarch, she was also attired in formal, royal vestments. So striking was Dira's appearance, Jason realized she'd purposely downplayed her looks while serving on *The Lilly.* Their eyes met and held—locked on each other for several moments.

The admiral cleared his throat. "I'm going to move things along. We have four key developments or issues we need to address, one by one."

Jason brought his attention back to the meeting. He consciously willed his heart rate to slow—to concentrate on the words his father was saying.

"Issue number one: The ongoing revolution within the Craing worlds has culminated in what appears to be a fortuitous end; they are becoming an independent and free society that is separating itself from its former Craing dominion warring ways of the past. With the death of the emperor, and the scattering of their remaining high-priest overlords, all the Craing worlds are on the precipice of true change. We have been in direct contact with the interim revolutionary government there and Earth has agreed to further peace discussions."

"*Pssst* … they're sitting ducks," Bristol interjected. "They're living in a fantasy world if they think that Ot-Mul, and his Craing forces in space, will allow them to continue."

The admiral looked irritated at Bristol's unsolicited comment. "We'll get to Ot-Mul in a moment. Moving on to issue number two … it's been confirmed: Both Ricket and Gaddy have been taken prisoner and are confined on something called the *Dreathlor* prison barge. Unfortunately, from the intel we've been able to uncover … the damn thing is impregnable. The vessel has never been breached. No escapes … no successful incursions." The admiral looked like Jason felt …

totally disheartened. His father had spent many a year with Ricket by his side. It was the admiral who had discovered the then-cyborg, buried far beneath the scrapyard, within an ancient, dried-up aquifer. As close as Jason had become to Ricket over the last year, his father was equally close, perhaps even more so.

"There will be no rescue operation. Not with what we're up against—"

Jason wasn't sure he was hearing him correctly. He cut him off, "After what he's done for you ... for all of us ... how can you sit there and casually relegate him to a miserable life on a Craing prison barge?"

All eyes were on Jason. He hadn't realized he'd stood—his fists clenched white in anger.

"Sit down, Captain, and let ... me ... finish!" the admiral barked, fury smoldering in his eyes. He waited for Jason to sit back down before continuing, "There will be no rescue operation, not with what we're up against ... until ... we first deal with the three Craing fleets sitting on the other side of the line. If that is acceptable to you, Captain Reynolds."

Jason kept his expression neutral and said nothing. It was obviously a rhetorical question, anyway.

"Captain Reynolds, you will put together a plan of attack and assemble your best-of-the-best Special Ops forces to bring about the successful retrieval of both Ricket and Gaddy. When the time comes, if ... it comes ... be ready to roll."

"Yes, sir ... we'll be ready," Jason said, briefly making eye contact with Billy.

"Issue number three: As we can all see by the attendance of many of our past Alliance dignitaries on virtual display, there is an interest in rebuilding the Alliance. If we can make that happen, our fleet of one hundred warships will more than double. It's a start. By the end of today, we will attempt to ratify a new, unilateral declaration. One that reestablishes our commitment to one another."

"I don't mean to throw a wet blanket on such positive talk, Admiral ... but what's different now?" Nan asked, looking mystified. "I'm sorry, but it wasn't that long ago when Earth was on the brink of destruction at the hands of a Vanguard fleet, when many of the leaders at this same meeting refused to come to our aid."

"Just as you refused to come to our aid when the Craing set our sister planet ablaze, only days prior to that," countered the green alien, wearing a black turban. He looked indignant, as he looked left, and then right, in an apparent attempt to garner support from the other live-feed individuals in attendance.

The admiral held up an open hand and nodded in agreement, "Our friend, the esteemed Sultan of Ali Cafrica, makes a valid point ... just as you do, Madam President. And this brings us to issue number four: Ot-Mul's combined forces in space. No longer can we refer to him and his kind as the Craing. He's the rogue leader of an incredibly powerful, far-reaching military force. Gaddy, in the past, commonly referred to him as the Drac-Vin ... the evil one. So, for no better terminology, we've designated Ot-Mul's forces as Drac-Vin. The truth is, we're not entirely sure how many warships are at his disposal. It could be a hundred thousand ... it could be more. What we do know is there's much contention. Thousands of Craing, sympathetic to the revolution back home, have gone AWOL. No less than two hundred warships have either returned to the Craing worlds or fled away into open space."

"Where does that leave us with Fleet 9, Fleet 173, and Fleet 25—the five thousand warships sitting on the other side of the line?" Jason asked.

For the first time Jason saw a smile on his father's face. "For the last ten minutes I've been getting NanoCom updates from the *Minian*'s bridge. I wasn't going to read too much into this, but indications are ... well, quite promising."

From the looks around the room, and from the live feeds,

the admiral knew he'd better get to the point fast. He sat up straighter in his seat and gestured for everyone to look at the display just over his left shoulder. As if on cue, the feed changed to open space. They were looking at a single, painted white Craing light cruiser.

"Okay ... a U.S. fleet light cruiser. Big deal," Bristol said, dismissing the feed with the wave of his hand.

The feed widened to show no less than five hundred ships.

"Um, we don't have that many warships ... not even close," Jason said, not fully understanding what he was seeing. Then, under closer scrutiny, he realized not all the ships were white. Some were only partially painted, others not at all. The feed changed to another, close-up, view—this one showed a gleaming white Craing destroyer. Everyone around the table leaned forward.

"There's something wrong with the flag," Billy said.

Jason counted the bright red stripes of the U.S. flag emblem on the side of the vessel. Sure enough, there were eight red stripes instead of seven. Chuckles erupted around the table.

"Good intentions. But their message to us is anything but subtle. Why it took them two months to convey it is anyone's guess," the admiral said.

Jason shrugged. "That's a hell of a lot of white paint. Probably had to bring it in from somewhere else. Another planet somewhere." Jason smiled at his father. "Are we to surmise our fleet has increased by five thousand warships?"

"It's certainly an unconventional way to convey the news." The admiral raised two fingers to his ear. He raised his other hand at them as he listened. He nodded twice and said, "Understood. Admiral Reynolds out." He looked around the table, then to the feeds on the displays. "As of three minutes ago, we received an unconditional surrender from the 9th, 173rd, and 25th fleets. Apparently, they wanted there to be no doubt about their intentions."

Cheers erupted from all around the room. Those on live feeds were just as vocal as those sitting at the table. Jason saw Nan smiling, wiping tears from her eyes.

"All right, settle down, everyone. It's about time we've had some good news. Obviously, we need to sit down with the fleet commanders. Captain Reynolds, assemble a security team and prepare to join me on board their command meganaught."

Jason sat back and watched as those at the meeting quickly dispersed. So much had changed within a matter of minutes—everyone needed to make new preparations. One by one the live feeds flickered off. The admiral left the compartment, talking to Walker.

Jason eventually stood and stepped away from the table. To his left he noticed one of the display feeds was still active. There, standing alone, was Dira. Her eyes ... those incredible, violet eyes, were watching him. A full minute passed—neither spoke—neither moved. The sadness Jason felt was also mirrored on her face.

"I've missed you, Jason."

"Come back ... come back to me."

She shook her head with barely any movement. "I'm needed here. My parents ... Jhardon needs me."

"There's no way I'm giving up on what we have."

Her expression changed from one of sadness to cynicism. "I think Nan might have something to say about that, Jason; she's carrying your child."

"Listen, you and I weren't ... well, we weren't together then. Not really. Hell, it was one night. A mistake. It took place over six months ago. Neither Nan nor I have any intention of getting back together again. How could you not know that my heart belongs to you?"

She seemed to take that in and the sadness returned to her face. "Well ... then. This truly is a bitter goodbye, isn't it? I need to go. My life is no longer my own. One week from now I will assume the title of Queen of Jhardon. Nothing can change that. Goodbye, you will always have a special place within my heart, Jason."

Jason's mind reeled. He wanted to reach through the display and pull her into his arms—to hold her tight and make everything perfect between them again. She tilted her head and smiled—the kind of sad smile that conveyed all the pain and regret that a person could possibly endure. She turned then and slowly walked away. The display flickered twice and went black.

CHAPTER 11

Apparently word had quickly spread throughout the remaining Allied worlds that three Craing fleets had been dropped off at Earth's doorstep, all tied up with a pretty red bow. Jason and his team waited on the flight deck outside the *Perilous*. The admiral was soon inundated with interstellar communications—it seemed everyone now wanted to be friends. Jason himself had been contacted by a constable, a premier, and an empress when they couldn't directly reach the admiral.

Moving with haste, the admiral emerged from the Deck-Port.

"Sorry for the delay. Seems we're the *belle of the ball*, today." Jason's team came to attention and saluted the admiral as he came to a halt at the back of the shuttle.

"Billy, Gunny, Rizzo ... good to see you," the admiral told them.

"You remember Sergeant Toby Jackson, Delta Forces?" Jason asked.

"Yes, good to have you along, Sergeant," the admiral said, nodding.

Muscular, and over six and a half feet tall, Jackson grinned, revealing a white smile with a gold front tooth. "Good to be here, sir."

"The rest of the team are on board, Admiral," Jason said.

The admiral strode up the ramp and acknowledged the five other SEALs, already seated. Jason and Billy, bringing up the rear, sat at the back of the shuttle. Jason used his Nano-Com to let Lieutenant Grimes know everyone was on board and they were ready to go.

Once the shuttle was off the deck, had cleared the *Minian*'s starboard flight port, Jason stood and moved to the seat next to his father. Billy made a face. "Was it something I said?"

"Talk to me about Walker, Dad. What's he doing here?"

The admiral looked as if he knew the question was coming. "Look … Walker's not only a politician, he's also a master strategist. The country's made mistakes over the last few years … Hell, I've made mistakes over the last few years. I'm military. I think like a soldier when sometimes I should be thinking like a politician. Earth is entering a new phase. A phase where strategic alliances will become even more important. Can you think of anyone you'd rather have at the table than Secretary of Defense Walker?"

Jason thought about that for a moment. "No … he's smart, cunning, and loyal to his country. I'm sure he'll represent Earth from space with that same tenacity. I guess what I'm getting at … we've always had a clear delineation between the two. Now who'll be in charge of space command?" Jason shrugged. "It's hard enough taking orders from my father. Will I … will we now be marching to the drum of the president? My ex-wife … or through her proxy, Walker?"

The query brought a smile to the admiral's face. "I don't know what to tell you, Jason. I've offered you my position several times now. I'm getting too old for this bullshit. You should have moved up the leadership rung last year."

"This isn't a plea for a promotion. I'm just getting the lay of the land, seeing it the way you see it."

"I see it the way I've always seen it. Only now, the stakes are much higher. I'm not prepared to make decisions that not only affect the Alliance, but Earth … hell, all human kind."

He raised his hands in a gesture of surrender. "Look at what we're up against. Ot-Mul ... his Drac-Vin forces make anything we've gone up against in the past look like child's play. Think about one hundred ... two hundred ... hell, it might be three hundred thousand warships. Nothing gets in the way of that kind of military prowess."

"So why bother?"

"You know why ... it's not over till the fat lady sings. And from where I'm sitting, she may be singing a different tune than Ot-Mul is counting on." The admiral turned in his seat and looked into his son's eyes. "Jason ... I'm putting through the paperwork for your admiralship. You're what, forty now? It's time for you to take the next step in your career. Grow the hell up!"

"I'll think about it ... if we even survive the next few days," Jason said, wondering how the conversation got so turned around.

"Well, don't think about it too long. I'm getting goddamned tired of making this same offer to you."

★ ★ ★

The four dreadnaughts coupled together made the vessel, by default, a meganaught. As the *Perilous* approached the massive vessel it became evident it too had been painted a brilliant white. Five miles long, over a mile high, the Craing ship looked as if it had just come off the assembly line.

"Cap, I've been given clearance to approach. Looks like they want us to move to the forward dreadnaught."

"Proceed, Lieutenant. Keep your finger close to the trigger, Miller. Just in case."

"Aye, Captain."

Jason stood and the rest of the team stood with him. "Lock and load, boys and girls, I'm not expecting any trouble, but ..." he let the words hang in the air. One by one the team triggered their SuitPacs. Jason saw that his father had one of the small devices on his belt, but hadn't initialized it. "You going in there bareback, Admiral?"

"Show of confidence and respect. And if I'm not safe with this team surrounding me, we're all in trouble anyway."

"Your choice, Admiral."

The shuttle rocked as it settled onto the Craing vessel's flight deck.

"A-Team ... move out. I want a perimeter around this ship," Jason ordered as the ramp was deployed from the stern of the *Perilous*. B-Team consisted of Billy, Gunny, Rizzo, and Jackson, and, along with Jason, tasked with the security of the admiral. As the admiral moved toward the shuttle's exit, B-Team fell in around him.

Jason brought up the rear. Halfway down the ramp he hailed Wilson.

"Go for pilot."

"Hang tight here. I want to know if anything starts to smell fishy ... keep both eyes open, Wilson."

"Count on it, Cap. I'm already on edge."

The size of the flight deck was par with the one on the *Minian*—huge. But that wasn't what had Jason's undivided attention. It was row upon row of Craing crewmembers standing in formation ... easily one thousand of them. They were wearing what looked like U.S. issue spacer's jumpsuits.

Jason's father made a quick look over his shoulder and caught Jason's eye. His expression said it all—*what the fuck?*

A small contingent of four Craing officers approached, marching in lockstep. When both groups converged, the four officers bowed their heads and lowered to one knee. Jason, still at the back of the pack, had to peer around Jackson's wide back to see what was going on ahead. He moved up through the group and stood at the admiral's side.

One by one, the four Craing officers removed medallions, all gold, from around their heads, and held them out in their hands as they lowered their heads.

The admiral looked over to Jason with an inquiring look. Jason took a step forward and took one of the medallions, held it high over his head so all could see it, and placed it back over the officer's head. He repeated this same action three times.

All four officers stood. Jason could see the obvious relief on their faces. "I would like to introduce you to Admiral Perry Reynolds, commander of all U.S. forces in space. I am Captain Jason Reynolds."

The admiral stepped forward and held out his hand. "Who am I addressing here?"

The four Craing officers exchanged quick glances. The officer closest to the admiral stepped forward and took the admiral's hand in his own, and they shook. "I am Admiral Jo. This is Captain Pen, Captain Gee-Shi, and Captain Mar-Lee." The three captains bowed their heads.

"I am honored by your presence on our command ship," Captain Pen said. "We have been preparing for this event for fifty-eight days. I apologize—not all preparations are completed yet. We ran out of paint and only today were we able to redeploy our droids to start work again."

The Craing admiral looked to be at a sudden loss for words, so Jason piped in, "You wish to join our fleet? Am I correct in this assumption, Admiral?"

Admiral Jo's expression turned perplexed. "Have you not received our unconditional surrender?"

"Oh yes ..." Admiral Reynolds replied quickly, "it's just that we were not expecting the ... um ... fleet alterations and ..." the admiral spread his hands out, encompassing the Craing crewmembers standing in fixed formation, "the matching uniforms."

"It's a fine gesture. A welcome one, indeed," Jason added, looking at his father accusingly.

"Yes, a fine gesture," the admiral repeated with a forced smile.

"We will adjourn to the proper meeting room, but first, nourishment and refreshments. Please follow us to the Grand Sacellum."

Jason and his father spoke up at the same time, "Please …"

Both of them were well aware of what went on within a Craing vessel's Grand Sacellum. Jason's mind flashed back to a time when he saw human remains sizzling atop red hot caldron grills.

"If it's all the same, we would prefer to get down to business right now."

Again came more bowing. "As you wish, Admiral Reynolds."

That reminded Jason of something else. "May I ask you a question, Admiral Jo?"

"Of course, I am here to serve."

"I am familiar with the configuration of these vessels … dreadnaughts. What is the disposition of your holding cages? Is anyone being held … currently?"

Jason was unsure if his question would be taken as an insult, but apparently it was not.

"Oh, yes, each of the dreadnaught holding cages, as well as others within the three fleets, are fully occupied. You're free to inspect our cages. Perhaps a special meal could be prepared for your officers?"

This needed to be nipped in the bud from the get-go, Jason figured. "Are there any humans being held?"

The Craing admiral hesitantly nodded. "Some."

"Rhino-warriors?"

"Quite a few …"

Jason fought to keep his ire down. His father placed a hand on Jason's shoulder and intervened. "That is not a practice we embrace, Admiral Jo. We have many cultural differences, which will take time and patience for both sides to adjust to." He looked from Captain Pen to Jason. "I suggest we separate. I'll continue on with Captain Pen and get the surrender formalized … have various fleet assets itemized and moved over.

How about you, Billy, and Rizzo get started with the holding cages? Obviously, not all captives can be released … I'm sure there's more than a few dangerous species being held."

Jason continued, "We'll need all humans, as well as the rhinos, out of their cages as soon as possible. And figure out exactly where, upon their release, they can safely be taken to on board these Craing vessels—it'll be a big job."

Captain Mar-Lee said, "I will accompany you to this vessel's holding cages. Come with me."

CHAPTER 12

Captain Mar-Lee had been designated their chaperone. Jason, Billy and Rizzo stood with the Craing dreadnaught captain aboard a flatbed hovercraft, now speeding its way through the long corridor of holding cells that spanned the full length of the meganaught. The air was thick with soot—tasted like char.

Jason indicated the best place to start would be cage one, on deck one—they would proceed from there. The Craing pilot, the only one of them seated, brought the hovercraft down eight decks, slowed, and made a wide U-turn. The craft came to a gentle stop, twenty feet out from the first cage. Standing in the center of the cage was a human male. With long, stringy black hair, and a full beard, the man stood, arms crossed over his chest.

Jason signaled to the pilot that he wanted him to move closer to the catwalk. As they neared Jason called to the unkempt prisoner, "Do you understand what I'm saying?"

The prisoner blankly stared at Jason, then tilted his head. "Yeah … I understand what you're saying."

"You're from Earth?"

"Born and raised in New Orleans, Louisiana."

Jason gestured to his surroundings, "How long?"

The prisoner shrugged. "Hard to tell. I'd guess two years … maybe two and a half. That's when our convoy was overtaken by the Craing, in between Solgorn and Gamia 55."

Jason thought about that for a moment. "Allied space … you were among the admiral's fleet en route to the—"

The prisoner cut him off, "The Drunsdin System unification talks."

"I'm Captain Jason Reynolds. Sorry it took us so long to rescue you."

For the first time, the man's expression changed. Although most of his smile was hidden behind two years of beard growth, his eyes were all the indication Jason needed to see he was exuberantly happy.

"We need to get this cage open," Jason said to the Craing captain. Several Craing guards were nearing down the corridor. Captain Mar-Lee spoke quickly in Terplin and within seconds, the cage door was clanging open. Jason and the others jumped from the hovercraft onto the catwalk. They stood by as the prisoner slowly stepped out of his cage.

Jason stepped forward with his hand out, ready to shake. With surprising speed, the prisoner darted forward, knocking Jason aside, into the railing. In a blur, the prisoner fired off a low, right cross to Mar-Lee's left cheek. The little Craing captain, sent airborne, was transported several yards down the catwalk.

Rizzo and Billy moved in, both taking ahold of the freed prisoner's arms. The Craing guards brought their weapons up and pointed them at the prisoner.

"Everyone hold on!" Jason yelled. Straightening up, he approached the prisoner while the two guards helped Mar-Lee to his feet.

"Are you all right, Captain?"

He rubbed at his cheekbone and stared at the prisoner. The look was one of pure hatred. "I am fine."

Jason turned his attention to the prisoner. "I hope you've gotten that out of your system. We don't want to put you in restraints."

"Out of my system? Are you serious, Captain?" He shook his head and pointed with his chin to the empty cage next to his own. "Last week, Petty Officer Arlene Braden occupied that cell. Why don't you ask the captain here if he enjoyed having her body dismembered and thrown onto a caldron? Ask him if he liked the taste of her grilled flesh?"

Jason nodded at Billy and Rizzo and they released his arms. "What's your name?"

"Captain Dwain DeMille, skipper of the EOUPA ship, *Tungsten*."

Jason spoke in a low tone, "We've all lost people to the Craing, Captain. In the years you've been incarcerated here there have been atrocities committed on a magnitude that's hard to fathom. It's touched us all ... we've all lost people we care about. So, if you still want to take a swing at every Craing you come in contact with, I can't really blame you. But we have a job to do here. The only question I have for you is this ... do you want to spend the next six months in the brig or do you want to get back to work? Perhaps see your family again soon?"

"I'm done throwing punches for now, Captain. But it sure felt good."

"I'm sure it did," Jason said.

"So what are you doing here? Why are they helping you?"

"As of this morning, this meganaught, and the five thousand other Craing warships within this proximity of space, are now the property of the U.S. space command."

"You mean EOUPA ...?"

"No ... the United Planetary Alliance disbanded a while back. Earth, under United States' leadership, has taken a more aggressive role in the protection of herself and her neighbors."

DeMille raised an eyebrow. "I like the sound of that."

Jason turned and looked at Mar-Lee. "Again, I'm sorry you got knocked off your feet, Captain." Looking over the Craing's shoulder Jason took in the thousands of prison cells they still needed to explore; they'd just spent ten minutes on the first cage. This was going to take some time.

"Captain, I'm guessing you have a rough idea whether other humans are being held here?"

DeMille looked down the misty corridor and slowly nodded. "We have ways of communicating between one another. There's quite a few of us … humans. More than a few are from Earth. My guess … close to three or four hundred humans are held in this meganaught alone."

"You good to lend a hand in setting them free?"

Again, his eyes came alive. "It would be an honor, Captain." He made no attempt to wipe away the moisture from his eyes.

Jason brought two fingers up to his ear and hailed his XO.

"Go for XO."

"Perkins, we're going to need your logistical expertise."

"I'm ready to help, sir."

"Good … here's what we're going to need. Get all our shuttles, those on board the *Minian*, as well as those on board *The Lilly*, fired up. Then get our hotshot pilots off their butts. We'll also need a five-man SEAL team assigned to each shuttle."

"Understood."

"Good. Let's see … we're going to need temporary barracks set up for the freed prisoners. Hold on a sec, XO," Jason said, bringing his attention over to Captain Mar-Lee.

"Captain, you do understand you're taking your orders from me now, correct?"

The small Craing officer reluctantly nodded his head.

"You have one hour to move your chief personnel off this meganaught. Also, you will assign one hundred crewmembers to assist us with the transitioning."

"Transitioning?"

"The humans, those who are healthy enough, will be taking over the crew and officer quarters on this ship. Have them cleaned and ready for habitation at once. I want you to assign another one hundred crew to assist us with other duties that we deem necessary as we begin clearing out these cages."

The captain looked agitated. "Not all prisoner species are … suitable for crew quarters. Some are wild … very dangerous."

Jason had already spotted several Serapins moving along the catwalk on the other side of the open, wide corridor. He was well aware how dangerous some species were. "We'll make that determination as we go. Obviously, we're not going to open every cage door without checking first. You understand your orders, so please get started."

Jason returned to his conversation with Perkins: "You got all that, XO?"

"Yes, Captain. Are you sure the Craing admiral will go along with having one of his dreadnaughts' entire quarters re-appropriated for prisoner use?"

"I don't particularly care what he *wants* to go along with. It's happening. Move on this now, got that?"

"Yes, Captain."

"One more thing. Send someone into HAB 17. Locate Traveler and ask him to join me here."

"Yes, Captain."

Jason cut the connection. "Captain DiMille, how about you show us where we can find other human prisoners?"

They all boarded the hovercraft and moved on down the corridor. Jason figured about half of the cells were empty. There were a wide assortment of alien species; one looked liked a giant ameba; another looked like a fish with legs. It occurred to Jason that only prisoners who could breathe oxygenated air were kept in these cells.

"Captain Mar-Lee. Are there other … special-environment cages? Ones that can support a different world's atmosphere?"

"We only take on those that are compatible to our own environment."

Rizzo looked surprised at that. "So what do you do if they're not compatible?"

The Craing captain didn't answer. Up ahead, the first group of shuttles phase-shifted into the corridor. Jason watched as the captain spoke into a headset device. *Good.* He was making preparations for the released prisoners. Jason continued to look at the thousands of cages and dread washed over him like a shroud. He needed to get to Ricket—he needed to save his friend.

CHAPTER 13

It took an hour for Traveler to actually arrive within the corridor. Jason spotted him on the same flatbed hovercraft he and his team had arrived on earlier. As the little craft approached, Traveler, the lone passenger, stood in the middle of the deck. Big and foreboding—like some mythical creature … Jason was glad he was his friend and not his enemy.

The hovercraft U-turned and moved alongside the catwalk. Traveler eyed the metal banister. He was too large to jump across and straddle the outside of the railing as Jason and the others had earlier. The rhino-warrior threw his substantial weight into a swift forward kick. The metal railing pulled away from its anchor bolts and clanged loudly against the bars of the cages behind it. Traveler, heavy hammer in hand, leisurely stepped onto the catwalk and approached Jason.

"Sorry to disrupt your solitude, my friend," Jason said.

The rhino grunted and gave Jason a sideways glance. Jason was well aware of his friend's growing boredom within the confines of HAB 17. It wasn't the environment; it was the total lack of any conflict there. Traveler was a warrior at heart. Simply put, there was no one to war with in that desolate habitat, which he and several hundred other rhino-warriors now cohabited.

"Not sure how much you've been told. The short story is, fifteen hundred Craing warships have willingly joined our side and have been added to the U.S. fleet. There are multiple dreadnaughts ... and, as you know, inside dreadnaughts, and even some heavy cruisers, come confinement cages."

Traveler's deep voice filled the space, "Rhinos are here. We need to free them."

He looked agitated. Jason nodded and said, "I wanted you here before that process began. They don't know me ... as far as they're concerned I'm the enemy. So you'll be their ambassador. That work for you?"

Again, Traveler grunted. "Take me to their cages."

"The first one's this way." Jason headed down the catwalk at a brisk pace, knowing Traveler would easily catch up and overtake him in seconds. He stopped, turned around, and nodded toward the cages on his right.

Traveler, coming up, turned toward the cages holding three immense rhinos. The reaction from the three caged rhinos was one of obvious agitation. Bursts of snot vapor filled the air.

The truth was, Jason had expected an even more volatile reaction. These were Reds. He'd dealt with this breed of rhino-warriors, from the planet Mangus, before, and was well aware the Greys, like Traveler and his kind, had been at war with the larger Red species for millennia.

One of the Reds moved closer to the bars. "A Trumach Grey ... have you come to gloat? Perhaps you and the Craing and this other disgusting breed fornicate together like desert Wilbies."

Traveler didn't answer right away. He stepped forward, bringing his own face close to the bars. He had to look upward to make eye contact. "Trumach no longer exists. Destroyed by the Craing."

His words had an immediate effect on the three Reds. Their shoulders dropped—an eerie silence filled the space around them. Traveler continued, "The Reds and the Greys, at the end, fought and died together."

"And what of Mangus? Was our home also destroyed by these barbarians?"

Traveler did not answer right away. "In the end … yes. The Craing returned to our home space … destroying many planets. Mangus was one of the worlds destroyed."

The three Reds stood and let the devastating reality of what Traveler had conveyed sink in. Jason weighted the reaction. Rhino-warriors were a proud species, they would not show their pain … at least not now in front of Traveler and Jason.

"And what now? What do you want with us?"

"I want to release you, and all the other rhinos … Reds and Greys. But there is no place for war here. Not anymore," Traveler told them.

"Where will we go? What is to become of us?" the tallest of the Red rhinos asked.

Traveler first looked to Jason, then back up at the tall Red. "This breed … humans. They have given us a home. It is not Trumach, or even Mangus, but it is adequate. There is quarry to hunt and much more open land to explore. You could live there."

"Why would you do this for us … for the Reds?"

"I told you, the days of war between us are gone. We are few in number now; we must become brothers." Traveler gestured toward the latch. "Open their cage, Captain."

Jason had been given the master key—a long metal rod having an oblong electronic pod at one end. He inserted the pod into an opening and turned the rod. There were the sounds of internal mechanical workings before the cage door sprung open. Jason and Traveler stepped aside as the three Reds hesitantly stepped out onto the catwalk.

"We need to free the others … Reds and Greys. You will help me keep order. You will help me transport all freed rhinos into HAB 17," Traveler told them.

Jason wasn't sure this was going to work, but he knew there could be just as much friction coming from the human prisoners, as they were released. A small part of him wanted to keep them all locked up, and deal with the shit later on.

"I need to handle some things. Let's meet up later. Traveler, you need to find another rhino … either one here in the cages, or back on HAB 17, who can take over this task for you." Jason handed him the key.

"Why? I will handle this task myself."

"Ricket and Gaddy have been captured. They're in a far worse place than this."

Traveler snorted and stood up taller. "We will leave now. We will rescue my friend Ricket."

"Soon. I need you first to find someone you trust to manage the relocation of all the rhinos, both Greys and Reds. In the meantime, I need to put together the rest of an assault team. I also need to find us a ship."

More and more cage doors were clanged open by SEAL teams in the distance. Jason noticed Craing crewmembers were now integrated into each SEAL team. A necessary move as Serapins still wandered up and down the catwalks. Jason couldn't figure out what the exact power was the Craing wielded over these deadly, blue raptor-looking beasts. At seven feet tall and with massive razor teeth, they were one of the deadliest creatures Jason had ever come up against.

Traveler snorted his agreement and headed off down the catwalk, with the three Reds in close pursuit. Before phase-shifting away, Jason noticed a scuffle up ahead. One of the Reds was lifting something over the railing. Jason watched with curious astonishment as a Serapin, his screeches echoing off the corridor walls, was dropped, falling five decks below to its death.

★ ★ ★

The integration of the three Craing fleets was an all-encompassing undertaking. Jason caught up with his father, along with Secretary of Defense Walker, once back on the *Minian*. Short tempered, the admiral looked up as Jason entered the bustling ready room.

"What the hell are you doing here? I thought you were dealing with the rhinos?"

"They've been dealt with … it's all in good hands."

The admiral turned his attention back to a Craing officer Jason hadn't seen before. "No! What I said is, you all need to stop that shit completely … send out communication right now, to all fleet commanders, that the next Craing crewmember who fires up a caldron will get thrown out a fucking airlock. Meals come from only one place … a food replicator. Go!" The admiral looked back to Jason, exasperated. "What is it you want? A bit busy here."

"I'm leaving."

"Like hell you are."

"I'm going after Ricket and Gaddy."

"With everything going on here—"

"This will be crazy for weeks, if not months … I need to get out there before we completely lose track of that prison barge."

The admiral sat back in his chair. "What do you need from me?"

"A ship."

"You'd need a fleet of ships to crack that damn prison barge, Jason."

"That's why I'm taking a different approach. A small ship … a small team. I'd take the new one, the little transport ship Ricket designed, the *Streamline*, if we still had it."

The admiral shrugged. "I don't know what to tell you, Jason."

"Actually, thinking of the *Streamline,* if I get Bristol involved … he should be able to output a comparable duplicate vessel via the *Minian*'s phase-synthesizer."

"So do that. You've never asked my permission before. Sounds like it would be perfect for your purposes."

That was true, he hadn't. The truth was, Jason wanted to say goodbye. He didn't feel particularly confident he'd be returning from this mission. He knew the odds weren't in their favor. "All right … I'll get back here as soon as I can. It may take a few days."

The admiral's face was taut, his smile forced; he too was well aware this could be the last time they would see each other. "Just get back as soon as possible. If you hadn't noticed, we have a shortage of qualified command personnel around here."

Jason stood tall and saluted his father. The admiral stood and returned the salute. Neither spoke further as Jason headed out of the ready room.

CHAPTER 14

Ot-Mul was pleased with himself. He'd maintained a level head and he'd stayed the course. There hadn't been a defection by a crewmember, or by a warship, in over a week. The truth was, he was almost disappointed. He'd come to enjoy the carnage his four amazing battle droids exhibited when in full-action mode. Looking at them now in their holding berth, standing motionless against the bulkhead, he pondered if somehow they too missed those ruthless encounters—if something hidden deep in their advanced droids' psyches had achieved a small level of consciousness, and that they were now restlessly awaiting their master's edict.

"Soon, my friends … I assure you, it won't be long." He waited several more moments, almost expecting one of the droids' gun-turret heads to nod its assent, but no … he was sure they were far too disciplined for that.

★ ★ ★

Ot-Mul arrived on the bridge exactly seven minutes later. He made his way to the raised platform, ignoring the other three bridge commanders as he sat in the number one command chair. While he kept perfectly still, he let his eyes roam the wide expanse of what was considered the Craing's most quintessential warship bridge. An assault class destroyer, the ship was far and above anything the Craing had produced at any of their many deep-space shipyards, spanning out to multiple distant sectors. The assault class destroyer, appropriately renamed the *Assailant*, hadn't been manufactured by the Craing—they'd absconded with her. One of the few alien races the Craing could never quite defeat, even with far greater numbers of warships, the Korlm, even to this day, were able to thwart whatever the Craing threw at them.

Seizing the *Assailant* was more good luck than strategic battlefield prowess. The Craing had stumbled upon the Korlm shipyard when fleeing a devastatingly powerful small Korlm armada. Now, six months later, Ot-Mul had an excellent opportunity to battle-test the destroyer ... and against one of his own Craing meganaughts, no less. As the Craing's most formidable warship fled to open space, another important asset attempting to desert, Ot-Mul commanded the fleet to hold back. He took up the pursuit himself in his newly acquired *Assailant*. Easily overtaking the fleeing meganaught, they were soon going head-to-head against each other. The *Assailant* withstood a relentless pounding—fusion missiles, plasma cannons, as well as hundreds of fighter droids—everything the four coupled, heavily armed dreadnaughts could throw at the smaller vessel. But it was the *Assailant*'s own formidable DMEWs, Dark Matter Energy Weapons, that decisively won the day. The *Assailant* had taken less than twenty minutes to completely *gut* the combatant meganaught. Obliterated it. Yes ... many thousands of Craing crew died—but they hadn't died in vain. Not with the knowledge Ot-Mul had acquired. Now, as he sat back in his chair, he was sure he had a vessel that was more than capable of battling his hated enemy *The Lilly*. Perhaps, even the *Minian*.

"Admiral, we have reached our final convergence coordinates. We are being hailed by the ChorLok," Ot-Mul's second-in-command announced.

"On the screen."

An elderly, round-faced, Craing officer appeared on the holographic display.

"Admiral Too. Report," Ot-Mul said, with a cold stare.

"Welcome to the Orion system, Supreme Commander. All fleets stand ready for your command."

"Still no more desertions?"

Nervously, Admiral Too took in a breath before answering, "There have been … several ships. We dispatched four heavy cruisers in quick pursuit."

"Let me guess—no sign of the deserters, or the four heavy cruisers in pursuit?"

"Unfortunately … that is correct, sir."

Ot-Mul was tempted to make an example of Admiral Too's ineptitude. Perhaps he'd let his battle droids loose into that old admiral's dreadnaught, currently sitting less than two hundred miles off the *Assailant*'s bow. He stared at the old idiot, someone who'd risen far beyond his true capabilities. But then again, Too had demonstrated loyalty over the past year. Something Ot-Mul valued more than intelligence, at least at this particular moment in time.

"What is the measure of your assets?"

The admiral looked relieved the subject matter had changed. "One hundred and sixty-two thousand warships, Supreme Commander."

That number was somewhat less than Ot-Mul had figured it would be. Still … formidable. And, added to the two hundred and twenty separate fleet assets he'd just arrived with—approximately one hundred and ten thousand warships—they had now amassed the entirety of the Craing forces in space: Two hundred and seventy-two thousand battle-ready ships.

Ot-Mul stood and took in the other active visual feeds around him. At first glance, they looked more like distant star systems than the twinkling lights of thousands upon thousands of warships. His plan was wonderfully simple. Bring back every Craing vessel—those from the farthest reaches of the universe—into a convergence of the most powerful phalanx ever assembled. Moving forward, there would be no more defeats. No more surprises. Tomorrow, when his combined forces moved out, they would clear a swath of destruction that would, finally, end all resistance. He'd start with the biggest thorn in his side, the Allied worlds. And, of course, Earth. He'd destroy their insignificant fleet, along with their two Caldurian vessels. Once and for all, he'd quell the Allied influences that had recently plagued his people. Then, he'd return home to the Craing worlds where, without influences from the outside, their pathetic quest for independence would wither and die.

"Be ready, Admiral Too ... we move out first thing in the morning."

"Yes, Supreme Commander. I will alert the fleet captains."

The visual feed disappeared. Ot-Mul left the bridge, still feeling uneasy. *Why?* He should be elated at what he'd accomplished. Everything was coming together. Ot-Mul headed in the direction of the battle droids' holding berth. Their small compartment had become his refuge ... his sanctuary. He tried in earnest to avert his thoughts from Captain Reynolds. But soon the hatred he felt seethed and slithered up from the darkest recesses of his mind. The face of the repulsive human soon dominated his consciousness. *I'm coming for you, Captain Reynolds. First I will destroy all you care about, and then ... only then ... I will watch you die.*

CHAPTER 15

Ricket could barely make out what was happening in the adjoining cell. The quasi-transparent, cube-like observation compartment distorted his view. He saw movement. More like wavering shapes than anything having real detail. He was sure that was no accident … it was all part of the intended psychological imprint this place made on its inhabitants.

Ricket sat cross-legged in his cell and stared at what was happening, he surmised, within an enclosure identical to his own. He was quite certain who was who. There were two shapes, one small and one large—Gaddy and the guardian. Although he hadn't actually seen a shape other than Gaddy's moving about within the cell, her voice—and later, her screams—were unmistakable. As for the guardian, Ricket had endured, first-hand, experiences with that most unpleasant alien being.

Three separate visits now—each one progressively more invasive—more painful. Aside from the guardian's proclivity to cause pain, Ricket found the creature fascinating. Easily as large as a rhino-warrior, he was an interesting amalgamation of serpent and reptile. And then there was the smell. A strong, fishlike odor. Fish and something else … *chloride?*

Thus far, their keepers were unaware of either Ricket's, or Gaddy's, internal nano-devices. Their inset devices had been their one saving grace. As the torture sessions began, both

Gaddy and Ricket had come to the other's aid; not physically, but emotionally. This, the two had worked out, allowed them to go into something akin to autopilot mode. The ability to turn inward and deal with the misery—misery that inevitably turned into extreme agony.

Now, listening through Gaddy's open NanoCom channel, Ricket concentrated on what the guardian was asking her.

"And how did you return to Halimar? How did you skirt the thousands of warships that surrounded the Craing worlds?"

Calmly, Ricket told her exactly what to say: *A small shuttle. We weren't noticed.*

Ricket listened to Gaddy's raspy voice repeat his words. "A small shuttle. We weren't noticed."

Ricket let out a breath. Any mention of HAB 12 and their ability to move between *The Lilly's* Zoo and the Craing world of Halimar could have dire consequences in the future.

The guardian's frustration instigated a quick reaction and the progressive turning of a small dial. Frustrated with his lack of any real progress, the guardian resorted to a new variety of devices—each designed to produce the highest levels of pain, with minimum actual physiological damage. It made sense. The guardian wanted to extend his torment session time-frames as long as possible—a totally incapacitated prisoner, or worse, a dead one, would be of no use.

Ricket also experienced this particularly terrible device just hours earlier. He heard Gaddy scream out in pain as this same device, now attached to her toes, came alive. Red hot heat, indistinguishable from the sensation of an open flame, first blisters the soles of the feet, then the flesh begins to char, and exposed nerves start sending excruciating, white hot jolts of pain up the leg, and the body goes rigid—to the point leg bones are on the verge of shattering.

Ricket's eyes filled with tears as he heard Gaddy's heightened shrieks of pain. And then, finally, there was quiet.

Ricket heard the wet, lispy, voice of her tormenter say, "I want you to imagine something for me, Gaddy. I want you to imagine having a long life. Many more years. Imagine those years spent right here. Spent right here with me. Did you know my species has a remarkable lifespan? My father survived close to two thousand years. I am a mere three hundred years old, so I will be here long after you take your last breath. If you don't start cooperating, we will be spending decades together ... right here in this little cell. Understand, you will not be rescued ... there is no hope of that. No one has ever escaped the confines of *Dreathlor prison barge*."

Ricket continued to speak into Gaddy's NanoCom, *Gaddy, we will be rescued. Nothing will stop Captain Reynolds from getting us out of here. We just need to hold on a little longer. Can you do that ... can you hold on?*

Ricket listened to the silence and wondered if he was making any impact at all on her, or if she was on the verge of giving the guardian everything he wanted. Then he saw her distorted shape rise up—her head looking up at the towering form standing before her. When she spoke again, her voice was weak and barely audible. "Has anyone ever told you ... you smell like shit?"

★ ★ ★

Superintendent Gettling stood thirty feet above them on the catwalk and watched the Mollmol conduct his trade. In all the years he'd known Trancus, to his knowledge, he had never let a subject get under his slimy, black skin. And now there were two of them. Both, somehow, able to withstand anything and everything the guardian attempted. A part of Gettling took delight in seeing the foul creature bested. Gettling was basically ambivalent about the various methodologies used in acquiring information from Dreathlor's populace. There was a place for torture. He, too, had been the harbinger of such practices for many years. But the Mollmol ... he possessed a level of cruelty Gettling had never encountered. The creature was evil incarnate. There did not seem to be a separation between the heinous acts he performed, and the creature himself.

As if reading his thoughts, Trancus looked up and held Getting's stare. The superintendent took one last inhalation of breathable air and descended the stairs.

Both Gettling and Trancus approached each other within the station. Gettling took the opportunity to observe the Craing male, the one named Nelmon. He was sitting at the middle point of his cell and looked to be no worse for wear. Certainly hadn't the look of a prisoner who had been subjected to one solid week of unimaginable pain. Gettling turned and looked into the adjacent cell. The female, Gaddy. Although not looking quite as unaffected as the male, she too didn't look particularly ill-treated. Was the Mollmol losing his touch? Perhaps he'd grown a conscience and had lightened his methods. No. One look at the brooding creature at his side and Gettling was assured it must be something else.

"Perhaps it's time you took a short break. Let me bring in Drak. Although he's not you, he's always been quite effective pulling out information. It's always best to mix things up, anyway."

"No. That is not an option. I will be the one to break them. It is only a matter of time. There is something ... I'm missing here." Trancus tilted his large, snake-shaped head and turned back toward the Craing male, then turned toward the female. "It is almost as if ..." He let the words hang as he came to some kind of conclusion. "We need to test for energy harmonics. Both of them need to be tested. I think they're communicating with each other."

Gettling let out a long breath and shook his head. "That's impossible. That would have been detected on the transport ship over here. Anyway ... that type of equipment does not reside on this vessel. We're lucky to have flushable toilets on this old barge. But it's more than that. Devices, such as the one you speak of, can be used against us. We have strict rules concerning the use of wireless devices."

"Get me the energy harmonics detector and I will break these two within an hour."

Gettling also knew the importance of achieving their interrogation goals. Hell, his position as Dreathlor prison supervisor could be at stake.

"It will take a few days, and only if one can be obtained on a nearby cruiser. In the meantime, try to be more effective."

Gettling watched as Trancus moved purposely across the compartment and out into the Craing male's holding cell. Gettling's eyes fell to a wet swath of slime left behind on the deck plates.

Turning his attention to the Craing called Nelmon, Gettling watched the small Craing's eyes. Those were not the eyes of someone fearing his captor. At that precise moment, Gettling realized he'd underestimated this one.

CHAPTER 16

It took Jason several minutes to track down the location of Admiral Pen. Ensign McBride relayed him the fact that he was back on his meganaught, along with Perkins. Apparently, the logistics of moving thousands of human and rhino prisoners, not to mention the relocating of just as many Craing crewmembers, was a colossal undertaking. And one, evidently, requiring his on-site supervision. Once Jason determined the Craing admiral was with Perkins, his XO, it was a simple matter of phase-shifting to their location, inside one of the ship's larger mid-ship holds.

Typically, Jason discouraged the crew from phase-shifting into the confines of *The Lilly*, or any other U.S. ship. Even with safeguards, he always felt the risk, though small, of phase-shifting into a bulkhead, or on top of another person, wasn't warranted. Today, though, he was ignoring his own regulations. He flashed into the meganaught's hold, thirty feet away from Perkins and Admiral Pen. Both, startled, looked up at his sudden appearance. Jason took a quick look around the expansive space. He could park two *Lilly*'s in here and still have room to spare.

"Sorry to startle you, Admiral Pen. I require your assistance."

"Not a problem, Captain Reynolds. We're trying to figure out where to put everyone."

"You're putting people here … in this hold?"

"The Craing crew. There's insufficient space within any of the other dreadnaughts. I suppose we will have to make do with a less than adequate solution … we will reconfigure this space accordingly."

Admiral Pen's attempt to guilt Jason into letting his Craing crew remain in their own quarters had not gone unnoticed. "Good. I'm sure you'll make excellent use of this space. Listen, I need to locate a specific Craing vessel."

"Here? One of my fleet ships?" Pen asked.

Jason was tempted to correct the Craing officer; the fleet ships were no longer Pen's. "No, Admiral, it's a prison barge. *Dreathlor prison barge.*"

The admiral's expression turned serious. "Why would you want to find that old prison barge? No one goes near that vessel … at least, not willingly."

"Nevertheless, can you help me locate it?"

Admiral Pen looked uncomfortable with the request. He looked at Perkins: "Can you continue on your own?"

"I think I can handle it," Perkins said, nodding to Jason.

"We'll need to return to the bridge," Pen said. "It seems obvious we've been cut off, from proprietary fleet information, or from communications to Craing High Command. What I can get for you is *Dreathlor's* last known coordinates. The AI should be able to piece together the vessel's intended destination, as well as a best-guess estimate on her current whereabouts."

"That sounds promising," Jason said, feeling encouraged. "As for communications, we've been able to decipher Craing fleets' interstellar communications for some time now."

The Craing admiral looked surprised by this comment. "You can tap into fleet comms? Transmit as well?"

Jason nodded, and left it at that. He wasn't ready to give him further information on what they could, and couldn't, technically achieve.

Admiral Penn continued, "As I'm sure you are aware,

very little time is actually spent traversing open space. Craing vessels, even the prison barge, will be en route to a loop wormhole. Tracking the prison barge, once it has entered the wormhole, will be far more problematic."

"Understood," Jason said. What the admiral didn't know was that both *The Lilly* and the *Minian* were now equipped with a *probability matrix*. They would need very little information for the technology to work finding the prison barge. Jason wondered if this same technology had been implemented into their small barebones *Streamline*.

★ ★ ★

Jason's next task was to assemble a small, effective, assault team. As he'd pointed out to his father, coming at the vessel with heavy, brute force would be more trouble, less effective, than going in covertly. Yes, *Dreathlor* had never been breached … but how many of its would-be assailants had phase-shift capability? From what Jason learned over the last few hours, the old prison barge, never modernized, was purposely kept low-tech. Its heavy, nearly indestructible outer hull and inner bulkheads were so thick even a multi-gun would be depleted of energy packs before causing any substantial damage. And the absence of anything wireless on board kept everything very old school. Thick, hardwired cables encased in thick metal constructs made unwelcome outside access virtually impossible. New, evidently, was not always better.

Jason, deciding on a ten-man team, phase-shifted back and forth from *The Lilly* to the *Minian*, then over to the Craing meganaught, and then back to *The Lilly*. So much for phase-shift safety concerns—but time was a factor. He wanted to speak with his new team one-on-one, and Jason made no attempt to hide the fact that their attempt to rescue Ricket and Gaddy could be a one-way trip. For that reason, the mission was one hundred percent voluntary. Billy and Rizzo were on board, no questions asked. Same with Lieutenant Grimes, who'd be piloting the *Starlight*, which was what they'd christened the *Streamline*'s replacement. Traveler had already made it clear to Jason he was going. That left Bristol. As difficult as the young crewmember could be, he was a technology genius and had gotten the crew of *The Lilly* out of more jams than Jason could count on two hands. Jason tracked him down to the *Minian*'s engineering section.

"Bristol ... can I talk to you for a moment?"

The skinny, awkward twenty-something was lying on his back, peering into the dark recesses of a power distribution interface. He didn't look up from his work. Jason watched him take measurements with a hand-held device. "You're the captain ... you don't need my permission. Talk all you want."

"We're going after Ricket. You want to come along?"

"Not really."

"That's it? That's all you have to say? I thought you were ... friends."

"Ricket's okay. But it's not like we hang out or anything."

Jason stared down at Bristol, who'd yet to look up at him. He shifted to a new drive coupling and began taking measurements there. Then it came to Jason.

"So, what do you want?" he asked.

Bristol finally looked up and shrugged. "Well ... if I did go along on your one-way suicide mission, my brother would have to be released from the brig."

"That's not going to happen. He's a murderer ... not to mention he tried to kill the president of the United States more than once."

"She wasn't the president then. And he wasn't trying to kill her. Sure, he's got a hard-on for her ... and, no offense, I don't get it ... but anyway, send him off to a deserted planet somewhere; drop him off someplace where he can't get himself into any more trouble. That's what I want."

Truth be told, Jason wanted Captain Stalls, the psychopathic pirate, off *The Lilly* for good. Preferably, he'd want him dead. Thinking about it, he still wanted to kill the bastard with his own two hands. Bristol's suggestion to drop him off on a deserted planet just might have some merit, though. He'd have to make sure it was someplace remote enough that he'd have zero chance of escape, and zero chance of another vessel coming anywhere near his location.

"HAB 12," Jason said, finding it hard to keep from smiling.

"That's a bit harsh. My brother wouldn't last a day in there. He'd be Serapin chow."

"It's that or he gets transferred to a federal pen back on Earth. Let him live there among the other maniacs in a high-security ward. I'm sure he'll make some nice friends. Bunk buddies."

Bristol seemed to be mulling the idea around in his head.

"Out of the kindness of my heart, I'll send him on his way with an RCM—retractable camp module," Jason said.

"And a weapon," Bristol added.

Jason shook his head, "No way."

"Then no deal. He'll need to defend himself from those fucking lizards."

"Small plasma hand gun," Jason said reluctantly. The truth was, there was no way Stalls could survive on HAB 12. This was the death sentence for Stalls he'd been waiting for. He watched Bristol pull himself up from the deck and dust off his jumpsuit. He placed the small tester into a toolbox.

"I have everything I need. I'm ready to go."

Jason watched as Bristol retrieved a pack from the deck and slipped it over a shoulder.

"You knew I was coming here? Knew I was going to ask you to come along."

Bristol shrugged again, "You popping up all over the ship … doesn't take a genius to figure out you'd find your way down here, sooner or later."

★ ★ ★

Bristol had Ricket's ridiculously long code for accessing the HAB 12 portal and was in the process of entering it at the small access panel on its left.

Captain Stalls, hands bound in front of him, stood at the Zoo window, looking at the desert landscape beyond. The calm, arid environment looked no more dangerous than any other desert back on Earth. That is, if it weren't for the old disabled utility vehicle sitting in the near distance, and the hundreds of Serapin bones scattered all about on the ground. Hell, except for those things, he could be looking into the Mojave Desert.

Three beeps and the portal window disappeared. Jason moved in front of Stalls and stood eye-to-eye with him. "We'll know exactly where you are at all times. The security bracelet on your ankle provides precise location coordinates. Mess with the device and it will blow your leg off. Understand?"

Stalls didn't answer, his expression one of exaggerated boredom.

Jason cut the plasti-cuffs from his wrists. Rizzo, standing to Stalls' left, raised his multi-gun.

"As promised, here's your RCM … they're actually fairly comfortable. Don't lose it." Jason placed the paperback book-sized device into a rucksack. "In here is a change of clothes, thirty meal bars, a water distillation kit, canteen, and a plasma gun. I've included three extra power packs. When they're used up, well, that's it … hope you're a fast runner." Jason thrust the rucksack into Stalls' chest.

Stalls took the rucksack and looked inside. He latched the top flap and pulled the rucksack over one shoulder. Bristol stood at the portal. "You have less than a minute to get inside."

Stalls smiled and approached his brother. He gave Bristol a hug and said something into his little brother's ear that Jason couldn't make out. Stalls glanced back once, smiled, and stepped into Habitat 12.

CHAPTER 17

Jason walked with Mollie and Boomer—one on each side—toward the DeckPort. Petty Officer Miller walked several paces behind them.

"When will you be back?" Mollie asked.

"Not sure … probably in a few days." Jason thought about his answer. He wanted to be honest with the girls, without scaring them. "Listen, I'm not going to sugarcoat this … you've both seen enough craziness to know the truth about these sorts of trips. Where I'm going … what I'll be doing, will be dangerous."

Boomer looked up at her father, but stayed quiet. He read the expression on her face.

"I just want you both to be prepared. I have no intention of getting myself hurt … or worse. Just be aware that it will be dangerous."

"You're scaring them, Captain. I think they get the idea," Miller said from behind.

Boomer turned on Miller. "I'm not scared. Not even a little bit. My dad always comes back safely. So why don't you stop butting in?"

Jason wasn't overly concerned with Miller getting her feelings hurt by Boomer's lashing out. By now, she was used to his highly expressive, girls … and she'd signed up for this post anyway. He pulled both girls close, one-armed hugs around each girl's shoulder, and said, "Do me a favor. And I want you both to promise me this … that you won't get into trouble while I'm gone. Your grandfather will be extremely busy. He'll have no time for any of your shenanigans. If you have a problem, bring it to Petty Officer Miller," Jason told them, looking over his shoulder at Miller and giving a quick wink and smile.

They reached the captain's quarters on the *Minian*, which, in addition to its ready room, contained a five-bedroom suite. "Okay, here we are. Grandpa's not here … he'll be back later this afternoon. In the meantime, be good." He knelt down and gave both girls a hug and a kiss on the forehead. Standing, he looked at Miller. "Thank you for watching over them. Try to keep them from getting into too much trouble."

★ ★ ★

The full assault team was present and waiting together for Jason's arrival. He hurried over to the team and apologized for being late. He looked up to see a flash. The *Starlight* was hovering, twenty feet above, in the air. It slowly descended onto the *Minian*'s flight deck.

Jason did a quick headcount: Billy, Rizzo, Traveler, Sergeant Jackson, Powell, Hansen, and Bristol. Jason knew Grimes was inside, piloting the *Starlight*.

When the back hatch opened everyone began to file in. Jason caught Bristol's eye: "When you and Ricket first developed this ship, were you able to include the latest tech … like the *probability matrix*, and the ability to decode and transmit Craing communications?"

Bristol stopped and thought about the question. "Yes."

Jason waited for further explanation but none came. Times like this Jason really missed Ricket. Bringing up the rear and about to close the back hatch, Jason saw Perkins run into the flight deck.

"Captain!"

"What is it, XO?"

"Glad I stopped you before you left," Perkins said, out of breath.

"You could have simply contacted me via comms. What is it?"

"Admiral's orders … he wanted me to get this to you in person."

"Well, what is it … we're on a schedule—"

"You can't go. At least not right now. Multiple communications are coming in. The Craing are on the move."

Billy joined Jason's side and immediately took advantage of the opportunity to light a cigar.

"Some fleet or other of theirs is always on the move. Tell the admiral we'll be extra careful."

"No, that's not his concern. He wants you here. It's not one fleet, or even ten … it's all of them. From our latest intel, it's hundreds of thousands of warships, Captain. Ot-Mul's amassed his Drac-Vin forces in their entirety and they're on the move … headed toward Allied space … including Earth."

Jason let that sink in for a moment. Hundreds of thousands of warships? Ot-Mul was either totally batshit crazy or a lot smarter than any of them counted on. In retrospect, his move made sense. Without having the support of his home— the Craing worlds—Ot-Mul had nothing to lose. Why not make the ultimate power play and show everyone up?

"What do you want to do, Cap?" Billy asked.

Jason's eyes were still on Perkins. "What's the time frame? How long before they reach the first Allied star system?"

"Two days … maybe two and a half before they exit the closest loop wormhole. The admiral wants you back on *The Lilly* when they arrive. Here, within the sector. He told me to shoot you if you even think about leaving."

"What the admiral isn't comprehending is when you're talking hundreds of thousands of warships … it's all moot, anyway … it's game over … we're totally fucked," said Bristol, chiming in. Standing next to Billy, he looked pissed off.

Bristol was right. It was ridiculous to even hope for a positive outcome with that massive war machine headed their way. Jason's thoughts returned to Ot-Mul and he tried to think of a way—something to slow his progress. It sure wouldn't be going head-to-head with him in space. "Do we have the coordinates where that loop wormhole's located?"

Perkins shook his head and shrugged. "I don't know, Captain. I'm sure we can find out."

"Why are you asking him? Why ask him anything?" Bristol queried matter-of-factly. "I can have those coordinates for you in thirty seconds. Even the *Starlight's probability matrix* can offer you up that information."

"What are you thinking?" Billy asked, flicking a long ash off the tip of his stogie.

"Theoretically speaking, can a wormhole be destroyed? Or made impassible?" Jason asked Bristol.

"Theoretically, yes."

"What would we need to do to bring down Ot-Mul's intended loop wormhole?"

Bristol laughed out loud. "The Craing use naturally occurring loop wormholes that were discovered, then mapped, over hundreds of years' time span. Keep in mind, these wormholes aren't the same as the little interchange wormholes we're used to, which can be turned on and off at will."

"So, there's no way—"

"No. Well, I guess anything's possible … if it falls within the laws of natural physics. But here's your problem: Depending on the size of this particular wormhole, and I'm assuming it's a big ass mother, like most of their loop wormholes are … you'd need a comparable mass. You'd need a small planet, or moon, and, from what I know, it's impossible to maneuver …" Bristol stopped mid-sentence and stared back at Jason. "Wait. You're not thinking …?"

Jason continued to stare at the pimply-faced genius. Bristol looked away and began chewing on the inside of his mouth. No one wanted to interrupt his thought processes, and what might, potentially, save their bacon.

"If the wormhole is small enough, relatively speaking, in size, and the prison barge has adequate mass ... we might have something to work with. It's all conjecture at this point ... basically fart-matter."

"What do you need to be certain? How can we help you?"

"You can stop talking for two seconds while I think," Bristol snapped back. He squatted down where he'd been standing. Then, sitting cross-legged, he rested his chin on two fists. He closed his eyes. No one made a move. No one spoke.

Two minutes later, movement caught Jason's eye. The admiral emerged from the flight DeckPort and, by the expression on his face, he was fuming. He strode up to Perkins, who remained silent.

Jason held up an index finger, a gesture indicating for his father to stay quiet.

"I'll snap that finger right off at the knuckle. Now tell me what the hell's going on here?" He turned to Perkins. "I told you to hand-deliver my orders and get your ass right back to the bridge." He looked at Jason. "This mission is scrubbed. Why I'm having to explain my orders is beyond me."

"Your orders are stupid," Bristol said, getting to his feet. "You need to listen to the captain ... he's come up with a ridiculous idea that might just save us all ... at least for a while."

CHAPTER 18

It took another ten minutes to get the admiral fully on board with the possibility, the prospect, of turning their intended rescue mission into becoming more than that. Jason suspected the admiral had already come to terms with the coming space battle's inevitable dire end; the futility of making any kind of stand against the Drac-Vin forces. So changing gears—allowing hope to resurface—took him some time.

They called up an interchange wormhole within five minutes after leaving the *Minian*'s flight deck. Jason and his handpicked team found themselves transported thirty-two light-years into deep space in less time than it took for a thought to fire across the synapses of a brain. Now less than a light-year from the best-guess coordinates supplied by the *Starlight*'s probability matrix, they were pushing the technological limits of the *Starlight*. After a series of deep space phase-shifts, each one to the farthest parameters the little ship would allow, they let the *Starlight*'s internal, micro phase-synthesizer components cool back down to minimally safe levels. In the meantime, Grimes pushed the little ship's antimatter drive to its limits, and probably well beyond.

Bristol sat next to Grimes in the cockpit, while Jason knelt between their seats. Hunched over a virtual display mere inches from the tip of his long nose, Bristol shook his head.

"What ... what's wrong?" Jason asked.

"We just got close enough to acquire a lot more data. Here's the *Dreathlor prison barge*, meandering along at a snail's pace." Bristol leaned back to let Jason look over his shoulder. Sure enough, there was an oblong vessel, in the middle of the holographic representation, in that section of space. Bristol adjusted the view's dynamics and they could now see a wider-scale perspective of space. An undefined blob of solid red took up the top third of the display.

"What is that?" Jason asked, leaning in.

Bristol used his fingers to zoom in on the blob. What first seemed solid was an illusion: They now saw, instead, thousands of smaller dots that were actually warships. Bristol said, "Drac-Vin."

Seeing it, the magnitude of what Ot-Mul had amassed filled Jason with an overwhelming feeling of dread. Dread he'd have to keep to himself. "So ... it looks like they will be converging about here," Jason said, pointing to a location in front of where the two symbols would intersect—moving along their relative vector angles. "How long before they converge?"

"Eight hours," Bristol said.

"And our ETA?"

"Four hours."

"So we have four hours to reach *Dreathlor*, get on board, rescue Ricket and Gaddy, and take control of the vessel's helm," Jason said.

"Yes, and get that thing over to the loop wormhole. In essence, we have to get in front of Ot-Mul's forces and beat them to the wormhole."

"Is that even possible? Is that old barge capable of that kind of speed?" Jason asked, realizing implementation of his plan might not be feasible.

"No."

"So how?"

"The prison barge isn't traveling alone. There's an armada of old Craing heavy cruisers ... her protection detail ... a detail that goes wherever she goes. I count ten ships encircling *Dreathlor*."

"Is that supposed to be encouraging?" Jason asked.

For the first time Bristol smiled. "In time, you'll be glad those big cruisers are there."

Jason still didn't get it. Sure, the *Starlight*, with her Caldurian technological advancements, could probably put up a good fight against those heavy cruisers. But he didn't see ... "Wait ... added propulsion?" he asked, seeing now what Bristol realized sooner.

"Each of those heavy cruisers has multiple high-yield drives. Land those big pigs at just the right location, secure them to the outer hull, and we've got ourselves a hot rod."

Jason continued to stare at the display as Bristol brought up an even wider perspective.

"Here is the loop wormhole, our ultimate destination."

Jason took it all in—the Drac-Vin forces, the prison barge, and the loop wormhole. "So exactly where does that wormhole exit, come out?"

Bristol tapped at the console until the display changed again. Two wormholes appeared—one showed the location into it, and the other showed its exit location, at the farthest sides of the display. He manipulated the display and like bending space when folding over a piece of paper, the two points were now virtually on top of one another. Bristol zoomed into the right-hand point and a grouping of several distinct star systems came into view.

"What am I looking at here, Bristol?"

"The beginnings of Allied space. Earth would be somewhere around here ... obviously not in view; too many light-years away from this perspective."

Jason now recognized the section of space Bristol was

zooming in on. He stared at one point of light in particular: Jhardon. Her sister planets were now gone. Destroyed earlier by Ot-Mul's Vanguard fleet. He continued to stare at the small, flickering point in space and thought of Dira. His mind filled with that last image of her standing in her majestic gown … looking so lovely … and the futility of their situation continued to permeate his thoughts. *God* … How she'd looked at him, the sadness in her eyes.

"They'll plow through this corridor of space like—"

Jason cut Bristol off. "That's not going to happen. That wormhole's got to be destroyed. That's all there is to it." He looked over to Lieutenant Grimes, who'd remained quiet for the last few minutes. She turned her face toward him, her expression hard to read.

"What is it?" Jason coaxed.

She let out a long breath. "This is what it's all come down to, isn't it, Captain? Years spent fighting the Craing for the survival of our Allied worlds; for our own existence … Earth's existence. It all comes down to this—what we can, or cannot, accomplish over the next few hours. I guess, I'm just sad that humanity … our history … might be coming to an end."

Jason wanted to tell her to keep the faith, take stock in the fact they always seemed to find a way to pull another rabbit out of the hat. But there were no more rabbits. She was right. This was it. Everything hinged on the next few hours. *Dreathlor* was their last hope.

★ ★ ★

"Captain, we're coming within phase-shift distance," Grimes said.

Jason, seated next to Traveler, got to his feet and approached the cockpit. "Are we visible to them?"

Bristol said, "No. We could be right on top of them and

we'd still be invisible. *Dreathlor's* got ancient technology. The tech on those heavy cruisers is just as archaic. We're safe, in that regard."

"Life signs?"

Grimes checked her console readouts. "Each heavy cruiser has a minimum of three hundred crewmembers. As for the prison barge, I'm having difficulty getting an accurate true reading."

May as well get the show on the road, Jason thought. "Go ahead, phase-shift two hundred miles behind the prison barge armada, Lieutenant."

The bright white flash came and went. Grimes adjusted the primary virtual display, manipulating it with her fingertips to hover high enough above the console for Jason to see the *Dreathlor* prison barge in all its glory.

"What a piece of shit," Bristol said, glancing up at the ass-end of the biggest ship any of them had ever seen. Virtually every inch of the vessel was coated with streaks of what seemed to be orange and brown rust—something not possible in the vacuum of space.

"What's with the rust?" Billy asked, now standing at Jason's side.

"Rust is the conversion of a passive-eating ferrous oxide layer on iron," Bristol said. "This ship isn't made of iron. What you're seeing is Galitamide mineral deposits. Similar to diamond crystals forming on the outside of the hull. One more example of why this prison barge has never been breached. Hull's coated with an impregnable layer that only gets stronger over time."

"Yeah, well, I'm not interested in blowing a hole in it," Jason said. "How come I'm not viewing any of the heavy cruisers?"

"That's because at this view they're too small. Depending on where you're looking, the barge spans up to eight hundred miles," Grimes said. She manipulated the display again, bringing into play the zoom factor. Sure enough, one of the cruisers appeared, its bright blue thrusters on two aft drives.

Seeing Jason's expression, Bristol said, "I know the cruisers look insignificant compared to the barge in size. Just remember, there's no resistance here in space; their combined thrust will do the job."

Jason nodded. "Can you bring up an internal layout of the prison barge?"

Grimes pulled one of the smaller displays forward and expanded it out. It looked like an intricate maze of both small and large compartments, with intersecting corridors. But the bulk of the internal space, Jason determined, was holding cells. The closest thing he could compare it to was the thousands of small indentations found on the surface of a golf ball. Somewhere in the vastness of that internal space were Gaddy and Ricket.

"Captain ... we're being scanned."

CHAPTER 19

idn't you say there was no way these older vessels would be able to detect the *Starlight*?"

Bristol was looking at the console; his fingers moved in a blur over the input device. "I didn't say the scan was generated by any of these ships." He scratched at a row of fresh pimples on his chin—one was beginning to ooze. "It doesn't make any sense." He continued to stare at the lines of code on his display.

Grimes and Jason exchanged a quick glance. Grimes said, "Sometimes it helps to talk things through ... even if we don't fully understand what you're saying to us."

Bristol looked up at Grimes with a furrowed brow. "No, I was wrong."

"We're not being scanned?"

"Yes, we are being scanned, but not by any ship in this vicinity. That's what threw me. The scan has all the markers of a local nature, originating close by. Ingenious really ... one of the heavy cruisers is being used as a proxy to retransmit the scan."

Jason shook his head. "I'm not following."

"It's got to be coming from the Drac-Vin forces. Looks like there's a vessel back there that has some kick-ass tech on board."

"You're telling me Ot-Mul knows we're here?"

"Definitely," he said, turning back to his display.

"I doubt the detection of one tiny, fairly insubstantial ship will divert the course of the Drac-Vin forces," Jason said.

"There's no need for conjecture, Captain. Thirty heavy cruisers and two destroyers just broke away from the fleet," Grimes said. "They're on a direct intercept course for *Dreathlor* prison barge."

"How much time do we have before they get to us?"

"An hour, maybe an hour and a half. But if we can halt the forward progress of the prison ship, we can dramatically extend that timeframe ... make it more like two or three hours."

"The problem will be phase two. We need time to get the prison barge configured with those heavy cruisers ... to build our hot rod. Adding thirty more heavy cruisers to the mix and the potential for a battle in space—"

"Maybe we can cross that bridge in several hours, Cap?"

"You're right, Lieutenant. We need to get our ass over to the barge," Jason said.

"Bring up the prison diagram again."

Grimes did as he asked.

Jason scanned the thousands of lines. "I looked for a central bridge location before. It's an unconventional configuration."

"I suspect it's like that for a reason," Bristol said. "There's probably an AI that pretty much controls every aspect of the ship, including all navigation. Another reason this ship has never been hijacked, they've removed the personal ... organic ... element. *Dreathlor's* AI takes its orders from high command; everyone on the ship is only along for the ride. There is no ship's bridge, per se."

"There is this," Grimes said, pointing to a compartment larger than any around it. "There's significantly more conduits ... cabling, coming out of there."

"Maybe a warden's office," Jason said. "Can you separate

the life form readings in the prisoner holding cells from the rest?"

Bristol turned back to his console. "Yeah … I was looking at this before. With the exception of about fifty organic life forms, the holding cells are empty." Bristol brought up a new layer to the ship's diagram. Yellow icons came to life at various points within the vessel. "I'm assuming these are prisoners, since they're situated within these indentations, the holding cells. Exactly fifty. These others, I guess, are prison personnel … administrators, maintenance workers, and guards. All in all, about one hundred."

"Can we pinpoint Ricket and Gaddy's location?"

"Not through that massive hull. The materials it's made of, its thickness … there's just no way. The good news is it looks like all the prisoners are clustered together, here in one section."

"What about those blue icons moving about here?" Jason asked.

Bristol smiled, "Oh, come on, Captain … guess what a Craing prison ship would have wandering the halls … in spades?"

"Serapins."

"That would be my guess … a shitload of Serapins."

"Forward everything you have to our HUDs, Lieutenant. Keep us apprised of anything happening with those ten cruisers. You may be playing hide-and-seek for a while. Do your best not to engage. Remember, we'll need a ride home." Jason gave Grimes a pat on the shoulder and turned toward the rear of the *Starlight*. All eyes were fixed on him.

"It's *go* time."

★ ★ ★

With the exception of Lieutenant Grimes, who was remaining at the controls of the *Starlight*, the assault team phase-shifted to a mid-ship location on the barge, one large enough to accommodate all nine, and not in proximity to other life forms.

Jason's first impression of the vessel's interior was its decrepitude. Being a naval officer, he'd had opportunities to visit multiple ship graveyards in the past. This old vessel had the same feel as those ships, which had long past been put to rest—where the salt in ocean seas had turned metal surfaces to rust; where years of wear and tear, and inevitable obsolescence, had taken its toll. But this vessel was far and above the dreariest he'd ever seen. The rust had been replaced by streaks of dirt and grime. Chipped layers of varying shades of gray paint covered the bulkheads. What lighting there was filtered down through yellowed fixtures, hanging down from high overhead cables. Dark shadows made every corner, every nook and cranny, a potential hiding place for danger.

"This is one creepy place," Billy said.

Jason agreed. Even the unflappable Traveler seemed to be on edge. "I guess we're in some kind of head ... bathroom." He scanned the ten or twelve protruding fixtures on the deck. They could be toilets—really *big* toilets. His HUD indicated the breathable air was at near-toxic levels.

Rizzo brought up his multi-gun. "Company's coming."

Jason, too, saw the blue icons on his HUD moving in their direction. "Either deal with them now or later ... so let's just take them out now and be on our way."

With their latest multi-gun and battle suit advancements, going up against Serapins was far less of a concern than it had been in past months. But Jason was also well aware that overconfidence could have dire consequences. Billy and Rizzo took point and moved out from the head into a wide corridor. Virtually every inch of the bulkheads held suspended black pipes and conduits. A klaxon began to screech—the repetitive *beewooo beewooo beewooo* blared forth from all directions. Jason hadn't been prepared for this—for them to be discovered this quickly. An ominous sign that things were already moving in a bad direction.

They moved forward, staying left and right of each bulk-head. The first of the Serapins was rounding a corner up ahead. Then Jason's HUD refreshed. No, whatever approached them weren't Serapins.

Their multi-guns came alive in unison. Jason moved into the middle of the corridor and fired. So far, not one of the approaching ... *creatures* ... went down. Even without Bristol telling him, he knew why. What had Bristol called it? *Galita-mide?* These creatures were wearing battle armor. Armor that looked pretty much like the same stuff on the outside hull of *Dreathlor*—its rust-colored, armored, mineral deposits—diamond crystals forming on the outside hull.

The aliens' weapons were of the plasma variety and they weren't having any more of an effect on Jason's and his team's battle suits than Jason's assault team was having against their Galitamide armor. As the two groups moved toward each other, pausing periodically to fire off a new volley of plasma fire, Jason was able to get a better look at what the creatures looked like. They were shorter than a Serapin, maybe five feet tall. Their heads were snakelike and, where the body's armor plates didn't fully cover them, their skin was black—black and wet looking. From what he could see, these creatures would give Serapins a run for their money. Especially since they seemed to be armor wearing, intelligent, and capable of using weapons.

"Looks like we're going to have to handle them old-school," Billy said, slinging his multi-gun over his shoulder and pulling a Ka-Bar knife from a sheath on his upper thigh. Before Billy and Rizzo could meet the approaching throng of snake creatures, Traveler, in three long bounds, moved in front of the team. Jason let a smile form on his lips. This was what the big guy lived for. "Go get 'em, *killer*," Jason said with a chuckle.

Traveler's four-hundred-pound heavy hammer was already three-quarters of the way through its overhead, clockwise swing before the first of the snake creatures tried to dodge out of the way. It was too late. The business end of the hammer found its mark upon the creature's triangular head. The head was torn away from the creature's neck with little resistance. It landed twenty feet further down the corridor. Traveler used his foot to kick over its still-upright body. Billy was next to engage a creature, which used the butt of its weapon and rammed it towards Billy's head. It glanced off the side of his helmet, and Billy was quick to respond by slipping the blade of his knife between the plates of armor on the creature's neck. One downward thrust and it went down like a sack of potatoes.

By the time Jason met his own attacking creature, he'd seen four others go down. He too pulled his Ka-Bar. The creature surprised him by spinning left, then right. It was just enough for the creature to slip in behind Jason and jump onto his back. Within a second, Jason felt the creature's weapon being pulled by its two hands up against his throat. Jason's HUD immediately registered the external pressure on his suit and an alarm tone chimed. He swung his body back and forth trying to dislodge the creature. The suit's external pressure rose to two, then three, then five thousand pounds per square inch. Jason wasn't sure what the suit's tolerance level was for the thinner, more flexible area below his chin. He didn't want to find out. Bending his legs, he thrust himself backward with all his strength. He smashed the creature hard against the bulkhead—actually, one of the thick horizontal pipes that ran along the corridor. Jason heard a decisive *crack* and felt the slackening of pressure around his neck. He let the creature fall free to the deck. With a quick glance he saw the thing was dead, undoubtedly from a broken back.

Jason looked up to see all the creatures were lying about the deck—all were still. But also one of their own was felled. His HUD indicated it was Powell. Billy and Rizzo were kneeling over his body. By the time Jason reached them, the SEAL's life icon became transparent. He was dead.

"Pigmy Mollmols."

Jason turned his attention to Bristol. "What are you talking about?"

"This alien breed, according to my rare species database, is called Pigmy Mollmols; it's a sub-genome species of the Mollmols. There's one of them on board here, too. We should really try to avoid that one."

CHAPTER 20

Jason brought up *Dreathlor*'s internal layout on his HUD. They weren't that far from where he wanted to go—to the large compartment with its various conduit feeds. "This way," Jason said, moving out at a fast jog.

Ten minutes later, what had seemed a relatively nearby destination, in reality, wasn't close at all. The size of the vessel was deceiving. His HUD came alive with activity. Now there were three more groupings of Pigmy Mollmols on the move—coming from both sides and from behind them. In front of them were no less than one hundred Craing combatants. Jason slowed and came to a stop. Until now, he'd been reluctant to phase-shift within the ship. He had noticed, following their last phase-shift maneuver, that Sergeant Jackson had phase-shifted within inches of a major, two-foot-thick bulkhead. Getting accurate readings within this environment was problematic—the consequences could be devastating. Nevertheless, they'd have to chance it.

"We have to phase-shift. Rizzo, Billy, and Bristol, you're with me. The rest of you phase-shift into the adjacent corridor … there should be plenty of room."

Jason took several moments to configure the master control phase-shift parameters via his HUD. "Stand ready!" Jason initiated the phase-shift.

★ ★ ★

Several minutes had passed since the klaxon first started to blare. Ricket heard it but was only remotely able to consider its significance. He was somewhere between consciousness and unconsciousness—between reality and what his mind fabricated.

Above and beyond the fact that his pain threshold was frayed—his injuries were slowly getting to the point he knew he would not be able to survive much longer. Ricket felt himself returning to consciousness. It didn't take much ... even the tormentor's hot breath upon his skin was bringing about renewed shudders of agonizing pain. No longer could his internal nanites keep pace with what was being inflicted on his physiology. He was certain the damage to his body was no longer merely psychological.

Ricket's mind—slow and muddy—went to Gaddy. Was she even alive? He tried to open his eyes, look toward the other, visually distorted, holding cell, and go beyond the confines of his own torment. What he saw instead was the monster he'd come to know as Trancus. Through Ricket's teary eyes, the creature's blurry, dark shape moved toward him. Its foul scent filled Ricket's nostrils. Once again, Ricket tried to contact Gaddy via his NanoCom. No response to his hail. She was there ... though. She was alive ... that much he knew. And then he finally heard her voice.

"I'm so sorry, Ricket. I told him ... I told him everything."

He heard her sobs and the connection went dead. The dark shape grew closer—becoming the entirety of Ricket's world. The smell was more pungent now. Trancus's face was now inches from his own—close enough for Ricket to reach out and touch it. That is, if he had been able to move his hands. He tried, then remembered his arms were extended outward, ninety degrees from his body, like the letter T. Both arms were strapped at the wrist to something cold and hard.

"Ah, you're awake now, Ricket. We have much to discuss. You need to focus on my voice, Ricket."

He was no longer Nelmon Lim. *It's okay, Gaddy. You held out as long as you could.* Now it was up to him ... would he have the will to keep his own secrets from this creature? Assuredly, there was nothing left now of his ravaged body. Trancus had moved on, past just Ricket's feet, and with practiced efficiency, utilized his flesh-scorching device elsewhere. In Ricket's mind's eye, every inch of his epidermis was blackened, charred to a hideous crust.

"Talk to me about this ship you've become so fond of, Ricket ... *The Lilly.*"

Then it became all too clear ... he had already given up his own secrets. *I'm sorry, Captain Reynolds ... I tried.*

★ ★ ★

In a flash, Jason, Billy and Rizzo phase-shifted into the expansive compartment. Immediately, Jason knew he'd guessed right. This was an officer's quarters, perhaps a captain's or, more likely, a warden's. Bulkheads were hidden behind fabric—long, draping curtains hung from high above. The deck plates were concealed beneath ornate throw rugs underneath their feet. The dreary confines of *Dreathlor* had been transformed into an almost cozy ambiance.

Movement came from their right. The threesome turned toward a grouping of furniture. A human male was sitting upright in a chair behind a desk; stunned, his mouth opened but no sound escaped from his lips.

Jason strode over to him and pointed the muzzle of his multi-gun at his head. The man raised his hands. "Don't shoot. I will not resist."

He looked to be middle-aged. His hair was gray at the temples and he wore a neatly trimmed goatee. "How did you get in here ... what is it you want?"

"Never mind how we got in here. I think you know who we've come for. The real question is ... will you stay alive long enough to be of any use to us?"

"I am Superintendent Gettling. I can help you."

"Three things: You're going to tell your security forces, including all those snake-headed fuckers running about the corridors, to stand down. You'll call off any aggression toward our ship. And you'll take us to our two friends being held here, Nelmon Lim and Gaddy Lom. Do it now!"

The expression on the superintendent's face faltered. Where before, uneasy tension was reflected in his forced smile, there was now fear flickering in his eyes.

"I have no control over the squadron of Craing warships. As for the two individuals you speak of ... I am sorry to tell you they were both scheduled for execution this morning."

Jason's fist was up, tightening around Gettling's neck, before he gave it conscious thought. He lifted the prison supervisor off the deck and pulled him forward, dragging him over the top of his desk. As he drew the smaller man in closer, Jason watched as Gettling's eyes began to bulge—his face turning crimson. "Let ... me ... check ... there ... may ... still ... be ... time."

Jason released him. Gettling fell to his knees and gasped for air. Jason pointed his multi-gun at his head. "Stop the execution."

Gettling staggered to his feet and made his way over to his desk. He pressed a button on an antiquated-looking intercom. "AI ... route me to 11140 through 11143 hub management station."

"There currently is no one occupying that management station, Supervisor Gettling. Be advised, you are not to assist the insurgent forces. You do not have authorization—"

Inches from Gettling's face, Jason put a plasma bolt into the small intercom box. Jason brought out his virtual notebook, quickly finding the *Dreathlor* diagram, and projected it in front of the supervisor. "Show me exactly where they are being held."

"Like I said, they were sched—"

Jason moved toward him again. Gettling put his hands up in mock-surrender and said, "Right here. They're located in these two cells," pointing to a specific area on the display. "I can take you there, but it'll take some time."

"Just shut up." Jason reconfigured the phase-shift coordinates for his team. Grabbing Gettling by the upper arm, he said, "Hang on."

They phase-shifted to an area directly above holding cells 11140 through 11143. The elevated regions above the holding cells had decking, which was nothing more than a confluence of sectioned-off tracks and movable metal plates. Traveler was the first one to stumble and fall. A tram plate beneath him rose several inches and transported him forward. Immediately, all the other nearby tram plates, individually, began to activate and rise. Within seconds, the entire team was transported off in multiple directions.

The amount of profanity coming into Jason's open channel only added to the total mayhem of the situation. As an empty tram plate whizzed by Jason's left side, he reached over and grabbed ahold of what looked like the vertical support of a handrail. He pulled himself up and quickly stepped onto another tram-plate, one moving in the opposite direction. He was getting a rough idea how these things worked. Glancing up, he saw the others making their way back to their original phase-shift location. All but Traveler, who was taking out his frustration with the tram plate by using his heavy hammer on it. Jason then saw him phase-shift back to the others.

"Everyone okay?" Jason asked, taking a quick headcount.

"Um … everyone but him," Sergeant Jackson replied, gesturing toward a section of upturned tram plates off to the right.

Jason now saw it. A protruding leg. He gingerly stepped on the now-exposed track's rails and made his way over to the body. Buried beneath two dislodged tram plates was the supervisor, Gettling. Lying on his back, his eyes were open and fixed. Jason left him where he lay and returned to the others.

Jason was being hailed. At first, figuring it was Grimes, he was instantly caught off guard:

"Ricket!"

"Captain. Trancus … he's coming up."

CHAPTER 21

The dark, solitary form stepped into view and held steady at the top of what looked like the landing of a stairwell. Taller than Traveler by at least a foot, the beast was so imposing Jason wondered if he should change the settings on his multi-gun.

"I've got this," came a familiar deep voice to Jason's right. Traveler was already on the move.

From virtually every direction plasma fire suddenly erupted.

"Pigmies and Craing all around us, Cap," Rizzo said over the open channel.

"Find cover!" Jason yelled, diving to a section of the deck Traveler had just used his heavy hammer on to punish several tram plates. A series of plasma bolts pounded into his shoulders and head. Even though there was some minimal cover under the upended metal plates, Jason realized he was a sitting duck if he remained there.

Jason noted Billy was equally in a precarious spot. "Billy, Rizzo ... you're going to need to get on the offensive. Phase-shift to an area behind them. Jackson and Hansen, do your best to hold your positions. Damn it, Bristol, start shooting at something!"

Jason heard a resounding *clang* and spun toward the stairs. Apparently Traveler missed striking the Mollmol—his heavy hammer hit a metal railing instead. The two opponents, quickly upon each other, were magnificent creatures of remarkable strength. In some ways they were evenly matched; both had thighs the size of tree trunks; biceps like watermelons. What Trancus possessed that Traveler didn't was a long, powerful, tail—a tail the snake-headed monster was using to its full advantage. The long black appendage was wrapped tightly around Traveler's midsection. Fists the size of hubcaps flew from both beasts, but as Traveler was held to one place, unable to dodge and weave, he looked to be getting the worse of it.

Jason flinched as a barrage of plasma fire clattered all around him. Two more bolts hit the back of his helmet. A flashing message on his HUD warned of the impending loss of battle-suit integrity. He got to his feet and ran toward the fighting beasts, raising his multi-gun.

"Do not shoot him, Captain. I told you, I have this."

"He's all yours. I'm getting Ricket and Gaddy." Jason moved past the two towering combatants and scurried down the spiral stairway three steps at a time. When he reached the last step, he figured he was thirty or forty feet below the mayhem going on above. The compartment he found himself in was nearly square, and all windows—like being in a large, perfectly clear, ice cube. Each window looked into a separate circular black pit—the four holding cells. Two were empty. The other two held his friends. He heard Ricket's weak voice over the open channel: "Check on Gaddy ... Captain ... check on Gaddy first."

"Will do. Hang in there, Ricket." Jason looked for a way into Gaddy's cell. He paced back and forth, looking for a doorway—a seam in the glass he could pry open. Nothing. He returned to the console in the center of the room and stared blankly at a myriad of levers, dials and antiquated meters. *Shit. This could take all day.* He stepped back to the glass partition. Gaddy's still form lay in a heap at the far side of the second pit. Jason angled the muzzle of his multi-gun away from where she lay and fired. The glass partition held. Quickly calling up his HUD armaments menu he reviewed the settings and selected something called Thermal Charge. Jason stepped back and fired. The explosion knocked him off his feet, throwing him back and into the opposite glass partition. Again, his HUD warned of an impending loss of suit integrity.

Jason got to his feet and through a thick layer of smoke approached Gaddy's holding cell. The partition was gone. He stepped into the pit, hearing fragments of glass crunch beneath his boots. Plasma fire coming from above indicated the battle was still raging on. Jason rushed to Gaddy's side and knelt next to her still body. She faced away from him and he carefully resettled her body onto her back. She looked to be sleeping but he knew she wasn't. Before he'd come down the stairs, her life icon had gone transparent, close to four minutes ago.

"Help her, Captain ... you have to help her," Ricket said over his NanoCom.

"She's gone ... there's nothing I can—"

"You'll need to shock her."

"What do you mean?"

"... I'm taking control of your HUD, Captain. Do not interfere."

Jason froze—and a cascade of overlapping HUD menus appeared, one after another, eventually stopping at a menu setting called:

Defibrillation: Pulseless Ventricular Tachycardia

"Captain, open Gaddy's garment. Expose her chest ... hurry."

Grabbing two fistfuls of material, Jason tore open Gaddy's dingy spacer's jumpsuit.

"Place your fingertips onto her skin."

Jason did as instructed. He saw the HUD menu setting *select* and immediately felt a current pulsate through the gloves of his battle suit. He looked at Gaddy's face. There was no change. Her head still slumped lifelessly to the side.

"Keep your fingers where they are. I'm increasing the charge level."

Again, Jason felt a strong current emanate from his finger-tips; this time, Gaddy's body contracted, going rigid in shock.

"What the flying fuck are you doing to me?" Gaddy's head rose several inches—her eyes were open and looking up at him.

"And why are you copping a feel—"

Jason, at first, didn't realize the emotional impact Gaddy's dire situation had had on him. He pulled her into his arms and held her tightly to his chest. Tears falling freely now, he opened his visor and kissed the top of her head. Eventually, he released her and saw she too was crying. The smile on her lips told him she would live. She would live!

"Stay here ... I need to free Ricket."

Gaddy nodded and pulled her torn jumpsuit back around her body. Jason got to his feet and returned to the center hub compartment. This time he used the center console as a shield before firing at the glass partition of Ricket's holding cell.

The explosion was no less intense than the previous one. Jason wasted no time hurrying into the pit. Ricket was laid out on a metal table, his arms perpendicular to his body, like Christ on the cross. He was completely naked, his arms and legs bound by thick straps, at wrists and ankles. Jason took in the damage to Ricket's flesh and a jagged breath caught in his chest. There were blackened layers of ruined, charred swatch-es covering virtually every inch of skin.

"It looks worse than it actually is ... Captain. What you are seeing is the mind's amazing power to physically manifest. I so believed the Mollmol was inflicting burns to my body's epidermal layer that I actually manifested real burns. But right now my internal nanites are busy, restoring cellular—"

"Just remain still, Ricket. I suspect you're in shock. Let me get you out of here." Jason used his Ka-Bar to slice through Ricket's restraining straps. Using care, he slid both hands un-derneath Ricket, one under his back, the other under his knees, then lifted him into his arms. "Keep still, my friend.

We're going to take care of you."

Ricket's eyes met his. Jason gave him a reassuring smile while inside his mind raged. He wanted to kill the Mollmol—the one called Trancus. Anger flashed and he wanted to scream for Traveler to stop ... to keep the beast alive long enough so he could inflict his own brand of torment—in reciprocity for Ricket's torturous ordeal.

Gaddy stood at the stairway. At the sight of Ricket her hands flew up and covered her mouth. "Oh, Ricket ... I'm so, so sorry."

But her words went unheard. Ricket, although alive, was now unconscious. Internal nanites or not, Jason was well aware he had little time left to phase-shift Ricket to the *Starlight* and into a medical bay. Gaddy, unable to move along with any sense of urgency, did her best to climb the stairs. Tempted to phase-shift them all to the landing above, Jason decided it was too dangerous, not knowing the full situation up there.

"Hold up here, Gaddy," Jason said, when they reached the top steps. He'd been following much of the battle waging above them via his HUD and Billy's mirrored helmet cam feed. They hadn't taken on more losses—in fact, both the Pigmy Mollmols and the Craing combatants, those not already killed, had all run off. Only the battle between Traveler and Trancus continued on. They were still going at it.

Jason watched as the two exhausted opponents moved around, far slower now, yet they continued to inflict harsh damage on each other. Traveler was covered in blood. Jason wasn't sure if the blood was his or belonged to the Mollmol. The one thing in Trancus's favor earlier was no longer an issue. The Mollmol's long black tail was conspicuously absent from its backside. Somehow Traveler had ripped it off the beast. Jason's eyes located the tail, fifteen feet from the two fighters held in one another's grasp. The tail continued to flop and slither, as if in a desperate attempt to find its way to its owner. "Nice touch, Traveler," Jason said aloud.

The team joined Jason. Billy gathered up Gaddy into his arms and, though she protested at first, she eventually relaxed and looked grateful. Now, watching Traveler, it became clear to Jason who'd be victor of the brutal contest. Trancus was now on his knees and struggling for life itself. Then, in one final surge, Traveler brought a hammer-like fist down on the top of the Mollmol's snake-like head. With a definitive *crack*, Trancus was dead. His lifeless body fell over backward.

Jason was just fine with Traveler achieving that righteous honor. The whole thing, pulling the shithead's tail off, was a nice touch, too.

There was still much to do. Jason handed Ricket's unconscious body to Jackson. "Sergeant, take Ricket and Gaddy to the *Starlight*. Get Ricket into the medical bay first thing."

Billy set Gaddy down. She put a hand around Jackson's arm and, seconds later, the three flashed away.

"You're up, Bristol ... it's time you earned your keep."

CHAPTER 22

Jason checked the mission timer on his HUD. "We need to move it along, Bristol ... what's it going to take to bring the AI under our control?"

Two minutes earlier, they'd phase-shifted back into the supervisor's quarters. Bristol now sat at Gettling's desk—accessing his terminal.

"It's already under my control. No real sophistication here ... no elegance. A five-year-old could have written this code."

"Good. We need to get this vessel to a stop, ASAP," Jason said, starting to pace.

"Working on it," Bristol said, eyes intent upon the terminal.

Jason turned to greet Jackson, who'd phase-shifted back in a flash of light.

"Maybe we should bring in a five-year-old," Billy interjected.

Bristol's fingers stopped moving and his eyes looked up. "You want to do this, Billy? I'd be happy to let you try."

"Just finish up, Bristol. Billy was only kidding around." Jason threw Billy a cautionary expression.

"It's already done," Bristol replied, sitting back in his chair. "A few things, though. There's no simple way to breach the hardwire connection that's here." Bristol pointed to a large metal conduit overhead. "We'll have to provide directives via audio commands. Since the AI is programmed to only take orders from the Craing fleet's high command, you'll need to take on that role. I've got the audio feed muted in here … let me know when you're ready to go."

Jason nodded, "Go ahead."

Bristol entered something, sat back, and gestured a thumbs up.

"Awaiting executive directives." The female voice reminded Jason of his fifth grade vice- principle. He never liked the old battle-axe and he instinctively didn't like this AI, either.

"Bring this vessel to a full stop," Jason said.

"Improper protocol; rephrase the command, in accordance with necessary speech conventions."

Jason glared at Bristol, who sat forward and muted the AI. "You'll need to be more specific with your commands."

"Okay, let me try it again."

Bristol unmuted the audio.

"AI, this is Craing fleet high command … bring Dreathlor prison barge to a full stop."

The AI seemed to be considering the command. "Matching voice harmonics … Confirmed. Bringing Dreathlor prison barge to a full stop. Awaiting next executive directive."

Bristol muted the audio input again. "Looks like we're already getting inquiries from those other ships."

"Will they be able to countermand my orders?"

"No … the way I have it configured, your voice print is the only thing the AI now answers to."

"I don't suppose those individual ship commanders will take orders from this AI?"

"No way," Bristol said.

"Fine. Then we'll personally convince them what to do." Jason brought up his virtual notebook, displaying the prison barge, and zoomed in on one of the heavy cruisers. "Bristol … you'll be with me. You can manage our teams' phase-shifts … connecting each to the necessary coordinate. Two teams— Billy, Rizzo and Jackson, you'll take five cruisers, and Traveler, Bristol, Hansen, and I will take the other five. Bristol, you need to put us on the bridge of each of those cruisers, so start figuring out now how to do that."

Jason saw Bristol in the midst of doing something on his HUD, his eyes darting from one location to another. Although he didn't appear to be listening, Jason knew he was. "One more thing, Bristol," he waited for Bristol to make eye contact again, "we're going to instruct all the ship commanders just where to land their cruisers. Do you have optimal locations for them already calculated?"

"Do you also want me to wipe your—"

"Bristol … just answer the question," Jason said.

"I'll have it by the time you need it." Bristol's eyes were darting around his HUD again.

Jason waited several more seconds and was about to say something when Bristol held up a finger, indicating he still needed time. Five seconds later, he said, "Done. Both teams can phase-shift whenever you're ready."

"Remember, everyone, we have zero time for delays. We'll do what we have to … understood?" Jason nodded toward Bristol. The two teams phase-shifted away simultaneously.

★ ★ ★

Jason, Traveler, Hansen, and Bristol arrived on the bridge of the first heavy cruiser. Traveler's form materialized in the middle of a console that Jason hoped wasn't important to her navigation. Startled *yelps* erupted from the Craing around them. Only half-occupied, the bridge looked identical to all other Craing heavy-cruiser bridges he'd seen in the past. Once Traveler disengaged himself, the three wasted no time striding over to the raised platform where the three commanding officers sat, their mouths agape. The fourth command chair was empty. Jason caught Traveler's eye and nodded toward the chair. The rhino-warrior swung his heavy hammer over his head and let it come down on the empty seat. It flattened down to the size of a tortilla. More screams erupted, this time from the three officers. As they clambered to their feet, their hands came up in the universal gesture of surrender.

★ ★ ★

Jason and his team next phase-shifted, one after another, onto the other four cruisers' bridges. All but one of the incursions was a complete success. The third phase-shift had been met with much heavier resistance. Hansen, who had phase-shifted in closest to six armed Craing soldiers, took plasma fire directly to his helmet and visor. Considering the protective nature of their battle suits, it was an unfortunate fluke—an unfortunate outcome for Hansen.

Updates over comms from Billy indicated his team's visits to the other set of five Craing cruisers were even better—with no injuries. Apparently, Sergeant Jackson was almost as impressive as Traveler when it came to demonstrating potential pain and violence. One unexpected outcome to their surprise visits was the officers' requests to be taken prisoner. Over the proceeding weeks, word had widely spread about the tyrannical nature of fleet commander Ot-Mul ... Ot-Mul and his indestructible four battle droids. Jason knew first hand how only one of those mechanical beasts could evoke terror; four would be a nightmare. One more obstacle he'd have to overcome in the upcoming days.

Bristol, good to his word, had all landing positions figured out. One by one, the cruiser commanders were directed just where to attach their big warships onto the hull of *Dreathlor* prison barge. With a bit of maneuvering, Bristol had them situate each vessel so its big drives were pointing in the precise orientation, allowing for maximum rear thrust. The individual ship commanders knew how to clamp on to the prison barge's hull, so their vessels wouldn't fly off into space when their drives were energized. All in all, the entire maneuver, with the ten warships, took close to two hours. They had less than a half an hour before they'd have company.

Bristol set up communication linkage with each ship commander. He was adamant their timing needed to be perfect and, since Jason's crew hadn't arrived with the necessary equipment to take control of the ships remotely, they'd have to do so in a far cruder manner.

Jason was the last one to phase-shift back onto the *Starlight*. Beforehand, they worked out a process where each man would phase-shift into a specific location at the back section of the vessel. No one was to dillydally, once there, or he'd find himself getting violently knocked out of the way by the next team member phase-shifting in. One apparent built-in safeguard though: It didn't permit a phase-shift of organic matter *into* other organic matter. But the resulting *shove* from the same could result in broken bones, or worse.

Jason arrived on the *Starlight* to see Ricket standing in the narrow corridor before him. Seeing him alive and, with the exception of several large scabs on his face and arms, looking almost normal, was a great relief.

"Captain, I'd like to talk to you about Bristol's calculations."

"Well, hello to you too, Ricket," Jason said with a smile.

Jason saw Bristol at the bow of the *Starlight* seated next to Grimes.

"Bristol, get those commanders firing up their drives. Let's get this show on the road!"

On his way up the aisle, Jason passed by the medical bay. He slowed and saw Gaddy being attended to. Another ten paces and he stood between Grimes and Bristol. Out the front observation window Jason saw one of the heavy cruisers firing up its drives. Lieutenant Grimes changed the view perspective to include another three of the cruisers. These and seven more were all throttling up. Jason turned and saw Ricket by his side. "Is this going to work?"

"I do not believe so, Captain. As I was trying to tell you, their combined thrust, along with that of *Dreathlor*'s own large ion engines, still won't be sufficient to arrive at the wormhole in time. The calculations were incorrect."

"Well, not everyone has a computer for a brain, Ricket," Bristol said irritably, without turning around.

Grimes changed the display again. *Dreathlor* prison barge now took up the entire view. Bristol, using his NanoCom to communicate with each of the commanding officers, was talking fast, his squeaky voice spewing off directives. He'd earlier designated each ship a number, from one to ten. He now ordered ship nine to throttle back ten percent, and ship two to kick it up twenty percent.

"He's got the prison barge going in the right direction, Captain," Grimes volunteered. "But Ricket's right; although we're somewhat ahead of the thirty break-off ships, we're not achieving the speed necessary to reach the wormhole before Ot-Mul." She changed the display perspective again to show the prison ship's location in relation to the pursuing thirty Craing warship armada and then changed it again to show the correlation between *Dreathlor* prison barge and Ot-Mul's massive Drac-Vin forces.

CHAPTER 23

Captain, sorry I didn't see this before. It's pretty small. Hard to detect, but it makes perfect sense that he'd do it—"

"What is it, Lieutenant?" Jason asked.

"According to my long-range scans, Ot-Mul has dispatched one of his four battle droids, along with those thirty breakaway vessels now in pursuit. As I said, it makes sense ... you know, since he's having a problem keeping his forces together. He's sending along a watchdog."

Jason continued to stare at Lieutenant Grimes.

"What is it ... do I have something on my face?" She wiped at her cheeks, mystified.

Jason slapped his forehead with the palm of his hand. "That's it ... you're a genius, Grimes! We're going about this all wrong."

Both Ricket and Bristol turned their attention toward Jason.

"We've seen it time and time again ... Ot-Mul's forces, as enormous as they are, are only bound together by concern and fear of Ot-Mul's reprisals ... in part by that advanced ship of his, but more so by those battle droids. It's certainly not from a sense of loyalty, or to honor his cause. And that just doesn't hold up in the long run. Why? Because the minute their fear of reprisal disappears, his Drac-Vin forces will scatter like cockroaches in the light."

"So how do we take away their fear of reprisal?" Grimes asked.

"That's the million dollar question." Jason, rubbing at the

three-day-old stubble on his chin, turned to face those seated behind him. In one unanimous voice they all said together:

"Set a trap!"

★ ★ ★

It took fifteen minutes to get an open channel through to Allied space, specifically to the admiral on board the *Minian*.

"Look, I'm ecstatic you've rescued Ricket and Gaddy ... that's wonderful news, Jason. But this half-baked idea of yours, it's too damn risky."

Jason, standing at the stern of the *Starlight*, was using his virtual notebook to display before him his father's holographic image.

"You need to stick to your plan, son ... get that prison ship into that wormhole and close it down ... whatever that takes."

"And then what, Dad? Do you think Ot-Mul will just pick up his marbles and go away? You don't think he'll travel an extra month or two, or whatever's necessary, to reach another loop wormhole, and eventually find his way back to Allied space? Then what? You going to come up with a few hundred thousand more warships to fight him by then?"

"What you're talking about is an all-or-nothing gamble. Putting everything on the line ... billions of lives at risk, in one roll of the dice," the admiral said.

"What you're not getting, Dad, is that an attack is coming anyway; it's inevitable. Either now, or two months from now, it'll be over for Allied space ... Earth included. We're dealing with a powerful, but deranged, leader. We should use that to our advantage and take him out. I assure you, Dad, when we take out Ot-Mul, his Drac-Vin forces will surrender; or, worst case scenario, scatter to the far reaches of space."

The admiral was quiet for several moments while he considered Jason's words. "If—and this is a big *if*, right now—I approve just what you're planning … what would you need from me?"

"A call to battle."

"So you're talking about a last stand?"

"Yes, and it will require every asset you can get your hands on. You'll need to reenlist the Allied worlds … including any that broke away, preferring to go it alone months ago. You'll also need the *Minian* and *The Lilly*."

"What's the plan?"

"Ot-Mul is no fool. He's bringing his forces through that wormhole, but he won't come through it himself, or send his battle droids through it all at once. We have to convince him he has no other choice than to come through it from the get-go, along with his droids."

The admiral was slowly nodding his head. "You see us picking them off as they come through the wormhole … pigs to the slaughter. He'll have no choice but to rush through it himself to defend his massacred Drac-Vin. I like it."

"The second he does that, we drive *Dreathlor* into the wormhole and blow it up … closing the wormhole down … cutting Ot-Mul off from the rest of his forces.

"There's another big risk here," Jason quickly added. "Initially, many warships will come through that wormhole. Maybe thousands. And we will still have to deal with the battle droids and Ot-Mul's advanced destroyer. It could be close … we could still lose everything."

Jason knew he'd said all he could. The decision was out of his hands. He'd follow his father's command.

"You've made your case, Jason. But it's not completely up to me. This call to battle you're talking about … I'm not sure there'll be enough of a positive consensus from the Allied worlds. Some have cut all ties with my command … it could take days—"

"This is happening now. Right now. Within the next hour

the first of Ot-Mul's warships will start funneling into Allied space. At the very least, the *Minian* and *The Lilly* need to be there, ready to fire off everything they've got. I suggest you open up an interchange wormhole and get those three recon-ditioned Craing fleets moved over. Five thousand warships will go a long way toward slowing down the Drac-Vin. It will also leave Ot-Mul little choice but to join in the fight."

"Okay, son. We'll do this your way. You can count on the majority of assets under my control to arrive there within the next forty minutes. I won't leave Earth completely unpro-tected, though. As for the others who were once part of the Alliance, I'll reach out to them. That's all I can do. Realize an undertaking like this … this call to battle is a massive logistical nightmare. I have a lot to do. I'll contact you when we're in position."

Jason said, "Just so you know … the war will be lost or won, one way or another, as a result of what transpires here." Jason cut the connection.

★ ★ ★

Word spread quickly throughout what remained of the Allied worlds. Dira was called away from her mother's bed-side when she learned of the imminent battle—a battle due to take place closer to Jhardon than to any of the other Allied star systems. More destruction, more strife, looked to be on the horizon. As if her people hadn't suffered enough.

She found her father sitting at his desk, three aides stand-ing around him. He stood when he saw Dira enter the room.

"Leave us."

Looking frustrated, the three aides protested. Viceroy Rhonn said, "We need to make our stance clear, Your Maj-esty."

"And we will, I assure you, Viceroy Rhonn. The princess,

your future queen, must be brought up to speed. Leave us now."

Reluctantly, the three aides left the king's side, hurrying to leave the antechamber. Viceroy Rhonn made no attempt to hide his disdain for Dira as he brushed past her.

"Rhonn's an ass. Why do you keep him so close? You know he hates me."

"He hates everybody, Dira. Especially those he can't control. He balances out, though, others who are more concerned with kissing my backside. You'll need to learn this, Daughter: you must rule from a position of knowledge ... informed decisions. Surrounding oneself only with 'yes men' is a sure way to run astray."

"What is happening, Father? I've been told there will be another battle. A battle to end all battles. And here, close to Jhardon space."

King Caparri placed an arm around Dira's shoulder and together they moved toward the door. "It is true. Earth's high command has requested our participation, as well as that of the other Allied planetary systems. We have been asked to join forces—to come together one more time."

Two doors down from the king's antechamber they entered his map room. Dira had been in the room many times before, had played there as a child. Before coming to an understanding of the virtual technology behind the room's facade, to her it was simply a magical place—the heavens above literally within reach. Here, she first dreamt of exploring the far outer reaches of space ... she loved this chamber. It had been, at least partially, one reason she'd left home to crew on board *The Lilly*. That, and to get away from her oppressive parents.

As if walking into space itself, they stood together in the middle of the large, totally dark, room. Then, in a blaze of color and light above and all around them, Jhardon's star system came alive.

Her father, his face full of wonder as he took in the virtual planetary system glowing all around them, spoke softly. "Jhardon space … our home. What's left of our home …" Like God Himself, the king used his outstretched hands to reposition the virtual planets around them. Jhardon was closest now, taking up much of the heavenly scene. As the beautiful emerald planet rotated on its axis, soon the blackened scorched side of the planet came into view. Dira felt the familiar dread, the squeezing of her heart.

"This is what awaits the other planets, Dira."

"Perhaps it's time to let others—"

"Is that how you'll rule, Daughter? Letting others fight for you? Letting other nations defend our planet?"

"I'm not capable of making those kinds of decisions! That's your job," Dira snapped back.

"My place is with your mother … you know our ways. The choice I've made."

"Let me heal her! Let me bring the technology here to make her well again, Father. She needs a MediPod. You can continue to rule together, as you have, and I can …"

"That is not our way, Dira. Genetic alterations, nanite-infused physiologies … the Queen of Jhardon cannot undergo such abominations."

"Well, guess what, Father? The queen-to-be has had all of that done. I'm packed with nanites and have had multiple alterations to my genome. I thought you knew that!" Looking at her father's face, she realized he did not. He looked deeply troubled.

"I cannot undo the damage you have done to your own body … the dishonor you bring upon our honorable lineage. What I can do is preserve what we do have … what the Queen symbolizes to her people. So you will stop with any more talk of immorality … things that are contrary to the Jhardon way of life. Is that understood?"

Dira opened her mouth to refute her father's narrow-mindedness, but stopped. This was not the time. She left the map room without saying another word.

CHAPTER 24

Jason had taken over Bristol's seat in the cockpit and was now reviewing their plan as it appeared on his virtual notepad. Much of Jason's strategy hinged on Ot-Mul staying in touch with his forces as they exited the near end of the wormhole and into Allied space. Jason was fairly confident he also would be sending through the wormhole one of his four battle droids in that first batch of ships. The droid's advanced Caldurian technology would be Ot-Mul's eyes and ears, back in his command ship, and would also stymie thoughts of desertion from his warship commanders. The irony of the situation demanded the Allied forces keep that droid in one piece—at least long enough for it to communicate back to Ot-Mul that his Drac-Vin forces were being annihilated.

Gaddy, who'd made a full recovery after her stint in the medical bay, now assumed the popular position of standing between the two cockpit seats. Jason was only half listening to what they were saying.

Grimes switched to a logistical view on her display to show Allied space. "You see, Gaddy, the loop wormhole is approximately one light-year away from the nearest star system … which is here … the Jhardonian system."

Jason looked up from his virtual notepad to see what Grimes was referring to.

"Although technically a part of what's called the Alliance, Earth is approximately thirty light-years from Jhardon and about that same distance away from most other Allied systems, as well."

"So how far away are Ot-Mul's Drac-Vin right now?" Gaddy asked.

"They are still back here, at Alnitak, which is a triple star system; it's within a zone people on Earth refer to as Orion's Belt. It's about seven hundred and sixty light-years away." Grimes changed the display again, showing the Drac-Vin forces on a direct vector toward the loop wormhole; the *Starlight* and *Dreathlor* prison barge were on a thirty degree angle secondary vector—one that put them slightly farther away from the loop wormhole than Ot-Mul's ships; and then the thirty or so warships in close pursuit behind *Dreathlor*.

"So we're going to reach the wormhole after Ot-Mul?" Gaddy asked, looking confused. "I thought the plan was to get there beforehand, so we can close it down."

This time Jason answered, "That's no longer the plan. We're still going to shut down the wormhole, but the idea is to coax Ot-Mul into going through it early on—separate him from the rest of his forces. Even the odds."

"And, again, how are we shutting down this wormhole? I didn't know that was even possible," Gaddy added.

The answer came from Ricket, who was seated in the first row, directly behind the cockpit. "We'll have to bring *Dreathlor*'s ion engines into an unstable state. Right before things go critical, we'll put her at the opening of the wormhole."

Gaddy turned toward the display, then back to Ricket. "I'm confused. With all Ot-Mul's warships in a bottleneck at the wormhole, how do you plan on getting the prison barge into it too?"

Jason said, "We're still working that out. As of right now, we're hoping every ship just moves out of *Dreathlor*'s way. Undoubtedly, she'll eventually come under fire. We'll have an opportunity then to see just how impregnable that hull of hers really is." Jason stood. "Here, take my seat, Gaddy. It's time I checked in with the admiral."

Jason stepped out of the way as Gaddy took his seat. "Ricket, let's take a walk."

Together, they made their way down the aisle. Most of the team was asleep. *Good, they're going to need their rest*, Jason thought. He had been able to catnap a little over the past few hours, but definitely felt a twinge of jealousy as he passed Traveler, sitting off by himself, snoring loudly enough to wake the dead.

Jason moved toward the same location on the *Starlight's* stern as before, and brought out his virtual notebook. About forty minutes had passed—time to reconnect with the admiral. Jason began going through communication protocols to obtain an interstellar channel when Ricket put up a hand to stop him.

"I've made the connection for you, Captain." He tapped at a virtual icon on the notepad and Admiral Reynolds's head and upper torso appeared before them.

"Ricket … you're a sight for sore eyes, my friend."

"Thank you, Admiral. It is good to see you, too."

"Where are we at, Dad?" Jason asked.

"Not as far along as I planned to be. Our three Craing fleets are moving much slower than I hoped. We're using both the *Minian* and *The Lilly* to generate interchange wormholes for them. Less than half, about twenty-five hundred ships, have arrived so far in Allied space."

"So you're there now?" Jason asked.

"Correct … As for bringing together our Allied friends … that's not going so well, either. In fact, there's more than a little hostility from them that we're planning on battling Ot-Mul's forces in their backyard. They feel they should have been part of our conversation, which they absolutely should have been."

"So what's your feeling? They going to help us or not?"

"I don't know … I can't force them to. All indications are they're going to batten down the hatches and try to weather the attack without bringing undue attention to themselves."

"This won't work without their ships, Dad. We'll need ten … hell, twenty thousand warships, minimum."

"We still have some time. I haven't given up yet. But what it gets down to is this: they'll listen to one of their own worlds far more than they will an old admiral from Earth. Bringing Jhardon on board would go a long way toward influencing the other systems. I can reach—"

"No, I'll do that. Just keep doing what you're doing, Dad."

Jason cut the connection and answered a hail from Grimes.

"Go ahead, Lieutenant."

"Captain, the first of Ot-Mul's fleet is closing in on the wormhole."

"We still have time … he'll need to stage his assets. He's got some major work ahead of him before sending forth those warships. What's our ETA?"

"Twenty minutes."

"Keep me up to date." He disconnected and turned to Ricket. "Can you get me an interstellar connection to Jhardon?"

Ricket, who'd taken over Jason's virtual notebook midway through his conversation with the admiral, was currently busy doing something with it. Jason waited for him to finish. It always amazed Jason to watch Ricket at work. Even with the reversal from the *transformation of eternity* process changing him back from a cyborg into his natural Craing state of being, he was still chockfull of technology. More than once he'd added new internal nano-devices into his physiology. Perhaps he missed certain abilities he'd possessed as a cyborg? Or, more likely, he wanted the best of both worlds.

"Captain, I have made the connection. A representative is holding for you. I must prepare for my return to *Dreathlor* prison barge." Ricket handed over Jason's virtual notebook and headed off toward the bow of the ship.

Jason made the connection. While he formulated in his

mind what he was going to say to Jhardon's high command, Dira's image appeared, bringing all thoughts of diplomacy and strategic angling to an abrupt stop.

Dira smiled briefly but quickly resumed her role as Princess Caparri. "What is it, Captain Reynolds? This is not a ... good time. There are matters of state I'm attending to."

"Sorry. I know you're busy." Jason let out a breath and did his best to ignore the fact that Dira looked spectacular. Even this digitized, holographic representation of her was having a profound effect on him. "By now you've learned of the imminent attack. Ot-Mul will be bringing his forces ... all of them, through a loop wormhole, which is closer to Jhardon than to other Allied systems."

"I've been briefed," she said, her expression stern. "My people have suffered. That is, what's left of them from the last time Ot-Mul attacked us. We're a defeated, suffering society; what more could you possibly want from us at this point?"

She was right. Who was he to ask more from her people? Then reality set in.

"Dira—Princess Caparri, when close to two hundred thousand Drac-Vin warships start funneling through that wormhole, those forces will have one directive: To be the arrow—create a swath of destruction from Jhardon through all of your neighboring star systems. And then aim further, all the way to Earth, thirty light-years away. What once composed the Allied Worlds will exist no more. Understand this ... none of us can hide from that reality. What Ot-Mul started months ago, he's come back to finish ... and your planet will be the first one ceasing to exist."

Dira stared back, looking shocked, while her violet eyes continued to meet Jason's stare in silence. She was clearly unsettled. She looked on the verge of tears. "How can you ask this? Ask for my people, who have lost so much, to be thrust into the middle of things again? It's too much!"

"All I'm asking for is for you to reach out to the neighboring Allied worlds."

"Me?"

"Yes, you, Dira. They'll listen to you … you're one of them. Tell them it's now or never—to get every one of their space-faring ships headed toward that wormhole immediately. They need to move fast … right now!"

She nodded, her eyes losing focus as she contemplated what was needed of her. She nodded again quickly, regaining her composure. "I'll do this for you, Jason." There was no smile—no kindness in her tone. She turned, walked away quickly and then she was gone—the connection cut.

CHAPTER 25

Jason made his way to the front of the ship and found Ricket and Bristol sitting together, reviewing the prison barge schematics. Billy and Sergeant Jackson stood behind their seats, looking over their shoulders. Before joining their impromptu meeting, Jason looked into the cockpit. Grimes looked tired. She'd need to be relieved soon.

"Want me to relieve you for a while?"

"Maybe in a few ... I'm tracking some new movement behind us."

Jason moved into the cockpit and sat next to her. "Show me."

He hadn't expected to see the armada of thirty ships so near. "They've closed in on us."

"I've had my eye on them. But it's only been in the last minute or two that they've really kicked into high gear. They're outpacing us now ... nearly twice our speed."

"How long?"

"They'll be upon us within four minutes."

Jason turned back toward the crew compartment. "Guys, anything we can do to get the prison barge moving faster?"

Both Ricket and Bristol looked up. Ricket said, "No, Captain ... if anything, she's slowing down."

"Why's that?"

"We've been pushing her ion engines at near maximum for over two hours. I'd guess it's an internal safety function, caused by overheating. Although we'll need to capitalize on that same function later on, right now it's a problem."

What was also a problem was the *Starlight*, sitting in open space with thirty warships poised to overtake her. Not to mention that battle droid—the icon for which, at that moment, Jason had lost sight of on the display.

"This is crazy! It's time we phase-shift into the prison barge. Ricket, find us a suitable location there and forward the coordinates to Lieutenant Grimes."

The words had no sooner left his lips when a series of intensely bright energy bolts struck the *Starlight*. A cacophony of thunderously loud sounds filled the interior of the small ship. *Boom Boom Boom* poundings, as one plasma strike after another relentlessly struck her.

Jason reached for something to hold on to, while Billy and Jackson, standing behind him, were thrown to the deck. An alarm blared from the console and Grimes, teeth clenched, spewed a series of curse words Jason never would have guessed were in her vocabulary.

"It's the damn droid!" Grimes yelled over the noise.

Jason got a glimpse of it through the forward observation window—and then it was gone.

"It's coming around to take out our propulsion. Shields are failing!"

"Can you get a lock on it?"

Grimes was busy maneuvering the little ship—not taking her eyes off the console for even a second. She steered the ship through a rapid series of maneuvers that threw Jason from side to side, then forward and backward, to the point he wondered if he would throw up from space sickness.

The *Starlight* began returning fire and the concussive pounding to her shields lessened somewhat.

"Ricket, can you get us out of here?"

"Working on it …"

Jason looked up to see the battle droid sitting less than seventy-five yards away—directly in front of them. "What's it doing?"

"My sensors tell me the thing's switching to micro-missiles," Ricket replied, standing now to Jason's left.

"Incoming!" Grimes yelled.

The bright white flash was the last thing Jason saw before everything changed.

Several long moments passed before he realized he was still in one piece; that it had only been the ship phase-shifting to *somewhere* else and not the life-ending strike of a micro missile. They were now within *Dreathlor prison barge*. Collectively, he heard the rest of the team around him let out their breaths. Slowly, one by one, the *Starlight's* console and cabin lights came back online. Grimes was still gripping her controls and looking intently forward, through the observation window. Jason placed a hand on her shoulder and gave it a light squeeze. "Hey ... you okay?"

"Yeah. That was intense." She pointed out the window. "Where are we?"

Jason followed her gaze and smiled, "That's right, you weren't with us. What you're looking at are thousands of holding cells."

"They call them *pits*," Gaddy added, from farther back in the cabin.

They were positioned up high, maybe two hundred feet above the dimpled black landscape below. Jason leaned forward and tried to make heads or tails out of where they'd ended up.

"Cap, you might want to come take a look at this," Billy said.

Jason got to his feet and headed aft. Billy was standing about mid-way back and looking out a side window. From this perspective, things made more sense. The *Starlight* wasn't parked on top of anything—it was precariously embedded into a structural support beam.

The ship began to shift forward. Jason looked up to see

Traveler standing up near his seat. "Nobody move. Stay perfectly still. We need to phase-shift down to the deck." Carefully, Jason looked for Ricket. He was still forward, near the cockpit.

"Phase-shift systems, as well as most others, are down, Captain."

"Without this ship and its ability to phase-shift, everything comes unhinged," Jason said.

Traveler sat back down and the *Starlight* wavered, then slowly eased back to a level position again. Jason was about to say something but held his tongue.

"Ricket … see what you can do to bring vital systems back online. Bristol, you're coming with me."

"What happened to nobody move?"

"We need to concoct some way for this prison ship to blow up. Will you be able to do that?"

Bristol, back to chewing the inside of his cheek, shrugged. "Shouldn't be a problem."

"You don't sound overly confident. Ricket, be prepared to phase-shift us to wherever we need to be."

"I don't need Ricket's help to blow up this old pig."

"Fine. Listen, Bristol, this is what I want you to do. As slowly and carefully as possible, walk forward toward me."

While Bristol did as he was told, Jason did the same until they met roughly in the middle of the aisle. The *Starlight* began to tilt backward. Both Bristol and Jason took a half step toward the cockpit. The ship leveled out and momentarily teetered there, before coming to rest. "My guess is we're at the pivot point. Our sudden departure should have minimal impact on the ship's levelness."

Another shrug from Bristol as Jason pulled up the ship's schematics and mirrored them to Bristol's HUD. He zoomed in on what he was fairly certain was the old barge's engineering section. "Here?" Jason asked.

"That's it, but I'm not so sure our combat suits are sufficient protection from the radiation that's emitted in there. Not to mention its over-the-top magnetic fields. Robots and droids go in there, not organics with a functioning brain."

"Well, we're going to have to chance it. We're just about out of time."

"Captain, I would be happy to go, my physiology is better—"

"No, Ricket, that's not an option. Especially after what you've been through over the last few days. Just get this ship operational."

Jason took one more look at the schematic, checked to see if Bristol was ready, and phase-shifted into the middle of engineering.

★ ★ ★

Their phase-shift into engineering wasn't a smooth one. Jason had the impression his body was rushing—being propelled for an instant—before he was slammed face first into a bulkhead. Gravity. He tried to push himself away from the bulkhead but found it impossible to move.

Bristol, who was less than three feet away, pushed away from the bulkhead and looked back at Jason. He smiled and shook his head. "Captain ... I could let you think I'm a lot stronger than I look, but I know time is ticking. You need to go into your HUD suit environ settings and readjust the suit's gravity compensators. Put it somewhere around eighty percent."

Jason did as he was told and immediately felt things return to normal. He pushed off from the bulkhead and joined Bristol in the middle of the large compartment.

"What a shithole," Bristol said, turning around on his heels to take in the dark dingy space. Jason agreed. How this ship still functioned at all was a mystery. Everything looked old and rusted, as if it belonged in his junkyard back home. The compartment was egg-shaped and clearly not intended for human, or other organic, life forms. There were no flat decks to walk on, and virtually every surface had sharp angles and protruding pipes. It was only by sheer good luck they weren't killed when they phase-shifted in here. Bristol was on the move again, and heading for a long console by the opposite bulkhead.

"Terrific."

"What is it?"

"There's no human way—or Craing way, for that matter—to interface with this equipment." He pointed to a row of slim connector interfaces on the console.

Jason was being hailed.

"Captain!"

"What is it, Lieutenant?"

"The battle droid … it's attempting to breach the prison barge's hull."

"Is that even possible?"

"I have no idea … But Ricket seems to think the droid may have advanced drilling capabilities. He says we should hurry up."

Jason had to chuckle at that. "Well, we'll just stop having our tea party and get back to work, then. Keep me updated on Ricket's progress." Jason cut the connection and returned to his open channel with Bristol.

Bristol stood, his hands on his narrow hips, and looked overhead. "Our only option is to go after the fusion cooling coils. Anything else we do will immediately shut down the engines. We also have to disable all the temperature sensors."

"How do we do that? Is that something you and I can do in a hurry?" Jason asked.

"Hold on … I'm reviewing the schematics."

For the first time, Jason heard something other than the loud drone of ion engines. It sounded like heavy power equipment. It sounded like … drilling.

CHAPTER 26

We need Ricket," Bristol told Jason.

"Are you sure?"

"Yes. I wouldn't know what to do with any of this old crap."

"Fine," Jason said, annoyed they'd just wasted five precious minutes. He hailed Ricket and described their current situation. In less than a minute, Ricket phase-shifted into the engineering compartment. He was immediately thrown against the side bulkhead.

Jason had forgotten to mention he'd need to change his suit settings. Fortunately, Ricket seemed unhurt. He was also far quicker making the necessary adjustments to his suit's gravitational compensation settings.

"Captain ... the battle droid is attempting to breach the outer hull. I'm not sure how much time we have before it succeeds."

"Then you need to hurry, Ricket," Jason said, gesturing towards the old console.

Ricket, who carried a small satchel over one shoulder, did a quick look around the compartment and stepped over to the console.

"Hey ... where'd you get the tools?" Bristol asked, gesturing toward the satchel.

"Aft storage compartment," Ricket replied. Several small hand-held devices were placed on the console and what looked like a spool of thin optical cable. He also had a toothpaste-sized tube of some kind of transparent gel. Bristol moved to Ricket's side and the two proceeded to squirt ample amounts of the gooey stuff into several open connectors, then inserted the cables between the connectors, as well as into one of Ricket's hand-held devices.

"Captain, not having any viable way to connect to the ion engine's circuitry, I've attempted to make a gel-interface."

"Using that stuff in the tube?"

"Yes. It's not perfect. But we've now established basic system protocols and can direct the mechanism to ignore the temperature sensors."

"That sounds like a good thing," Jason said, encouraged.

"Well, yes. But we still have the problem of shutting down the cooling coils."

"What does the ship use for cooling?" Jason asked.

"Water. It's a closed system."

"Can we break the pipes feeding the …"

"No, Captain … the pipes and conduits on this ship are made of the same exotic materials as on the hull. We wouldn't have enough time."

"Does the cooling system share the water with the rest of the ship, or is it a separate, independent system?"

"No … it's a shared system," Ricket replied.

"Good. I have an idea. But I'll need Traveler and his hammer."

Bristol gave Jason a sideways glance and smiled. "The toilets?"

Jason nodded and hailed Traveler.

"Yes, Captain."

"Are you able to phase-shift off the *Starlight* without it becoming overly unsteady?"

"I will try to do that."

"Get the others to help … you'll need a few to counterbalance you—then meet them at the pivotal point, just like Bristol and I did."

"I will try."

"Grab up your heavy hammer and stand by for a diagram showing all of the ship's heads locations. They'll be similar to the one we entered before rescuing Ricket."

"I remember that place. It was foul."

"Well, you're probably not going to love what comes next, either. Destroy the toilets and flood the bathrooms. Destroy every toilet on the ship. It's important that every water seal is broken. Sorry, shitty job ... one that has to be completed very quickly. Come to think of it, go ahead and enlist Jackson's help ... bring him with you." Jason cut the connection and turned back to Ricket and Bristol. "Hope that does the trick."

Jason answered an incoming hail from Grimes. "Go ahead, Lieutenant."

"All indications suggest the battle droid is having trouble breaching the hull. It moves from one position to another ... I think it's looking for a weakened point of entry."

Jason realized he was no longer hearing a drilling noise. "That's good news, Lieutenant."

"Captain, can you send either Bristol or Ricket back here? We still don't have our phase-shift function restored."

"Hang on, I think we're almost done here," Jason replied, clicking off. His HUD showed a rise in external temperatures. Traveler and Jackson must have already been making good progress.

"Captain, the cooling coils are shutting down from a lack of circulating water. Normally, the engines, or other parallel systems, would initiate the shutdown process."

"It's becoming unstable?"

Ricket checked one, and then the other, hand-held device and looked up. "No ... it's already moving toward critical."

Jason wasted no time. "Listen, when you phase-shift back to the *Starlight*, enlist the help of the others to counterbalance the weight you add to the ship. Just like when you phase-shifted off the ship, you'll need to reverse the process.

Bristol, you're first."

★ ★ ★

It took a full four minutes to get the three back on board, followed by Jackson and Traveler. The *Starlight* became off-balanced multiple times, swaying up and down like a tee-ter-totter. Even the slightest movement by any of the crew caused a problem.

Both Ricket and Bristol were steadily working on the *Starlight's* phase-shift problem and her other vital systems.

"Captain, external heating temps are reaching four hundred degrees and rising fast," Grimes reported.

Jason, standing mid-ship alongside Billy, said, "Understood. Just be ready to phase-shift us into open space. You hear Ricket's go-ahead, make the shift. Don't wait for my command."

Another thought crossed Jason's mind. Were his ten heavy cruisers still affixed to *Dreathlor's* outer hull? He posed the question to Grimes.

Jason heard Ricket over the open channel: "Go! Phase-shift systems operational."

In a flash, they were back into open space. Jason quickly ran down the aisle toward the cockpit. As he reached the co-pilot seat, Grimes was bringing the *Starlight's* drive up to full throttle. She looked over to Jason. "Five of the ten cruisers are still there."

"Give them the go-ahead to head for the loop wormhole. Tell them to bring their drives up to maximum."

Only then, as Jason watched *Dreathlor* prison barge slowly move toward the distant loop wormhole, the now-crowded staging area less than a light-year away, did he realize he was sending the crew on those five heavy cruisers to their certain death. No matter how he tried to justify the fate of that old barge in his head, he was having difficulty coming to terms with the fatal outcome for those crewmembers.

"Battle droid's back and making its way toward us, Captain," Grimes said.

Jason was still watching the progress of the prison barge. It would reach the outskirts of Ot-Mul's Drac-Vin armada within minutes. "Let me know when the prison barge is poised to enter the wormhole ... if it makes it that far. Keep an eye on that droid, and also on the other three, which undoubtedly will be close to Ot-Mul's command ship. Phase-shift us away to safety as you deem necessary."

"Where are you going?"

"To make sure our reception party is ready."

By the time Jason reached the stern, he was finalizing his interstellar connection back to the *Minian*.

★ ★ ★

His father was waiting for Jason's hail. His holographic form abruptly appeared—the admiral looking less than happy. "Where the hell have you been?"

"You mean besides averting a battle droid, and trying to figure out how to make the engines of an impregnable prison barge go critical ... while steering the damn thing into a wormhole?"

"A lot is riding on you. Until now, nobody was sure you were even alive. Anyway ... moving on, I don't know what you said to Dira, but it seemed to work. Warships are coming in from every corner of Allied space. Nothing compared to Drac-Vin, mind you ... but Jason, Ot-Mul's forces will have a real fight on their hands. Like nothing the Alliance has ever assembled before."

"That's good. Excellent news, Dad. We're doing everything we can on this side. Expect the first wave of Ot-Mul's warships to start entering your end of the wormhole anytime now. He'll send through a battle droid … unless I've totally misread him. That will be key."

"Well, we're as ready as we'll ever be. More assets are arriving all the time, but we've got a multi-fleet barricade established. We've got close to fifteen thousand ships ready to unload everything they've got at anything sticking its head out of that wormhole."

"Good. Now I just need to give Ot-Mul a little incentive. Be ready. Everything is hinging on me coaxing Ot-Mul to enter that wormhole earlier rather than later."

As the admiral's feed faded away, Jason was formulating exactly what he was going to say to the supreme commander of the Drac-Vin forces. He was as ready as he'd ever be. He was concerned Ot-Mul had yet to send any ship through the loop wormhole. *What the hell is he waiting for?* He used his NanoCom to hail Ricket.

"Go for Ricket."

"I need to establish a visual comms connection to Ot-Mul."

"I'm on my way."

Jason saw Ricket emerge from the forward end of the ship and hurry down the aisle. He took Jason's virtual notebook from him and got to work. As was evident by the two white flashes, the *Starlight* phase-shifted twice within the last few minutes—Grimes doing her best to evade the thirty Craing cruisers and the battle droid. Ricket handed the virtual notebook back to Jason.

"I have directed an incoming hail to the command ship. Ot-Mul will know it's coming specifically from Captain Jason Reynolds."

CHAPTER 27

With the exception of the psychopathic Captain Stalls, Jason could not remember ever having such a strong visceral response to another individual. But now, seeing Ot-Mul's visual representation hovering in front of him, it was enough to make his clenched knuckles turn white with sudden rage. He did his best to keep his expression passive, even bored-looking.

Jason wanted to be the first one to speak—to set the stage for their ensuing conversation. "Can you feel it?"

Ot-Mul, who had been poised to say something, stopped to consider Jason's strange question.

"It's all coming to an end, Ot-Mul. How many defeats have you suffered now? Let's count them off ... The Craing worlds have embraced independence, leaving you basically homeless. You're now space hobos. Also, those three fleets—Fleet 9, Fleet 173, and Fleet 25, the fleets you sent to secure Earth's solar system—have willingly joined the Alliance. And now you're about to lose that big prison barge as well." Jason chuckled out loud. "It's no wonder you can't hold on to your people ... are they still deserting at every opportunity?"

Jason's words were starting to have the intended effect. Ot-Mul, surely not used to this level of verbal disrespect, at least not to his face, turned ice cold. "And you, Captain Reynolds? What of your own world? Has your populace enjoyed the little playthings I've introduced into your home world's environment? Nothing like a few million molt weevils to stir things up, huh? And how many Allied worlds has my Vanguard fleet destroyed at last count? Is it in the hundreds or in the thousands?" A smile washed over the Craing commander's face as he looked aside, as if relishing the memory of something horribly pleasant. His eyes came back to Jason. "It's really quite spectacular ... invigorating, really ... you see, to watch that kind of utter destruction, knowing all stems from my directives. There's a word for that kind of command ... influence ... that extinguishes billions of lives, just like that." Ot-Mul clicked his little fingers—holding his hand up high enough for Jason to see it. "The word is God, Captain. I am a God ... and I am your God."

It was then Jason realized just how delusional the small Craing bastard was ... how drunk with his own power he'd become.

Ot-Mul's brow elevated, as if a new thought was crossing his mind. "Wasn't one of those planets only partially destroyed? Jhardon? A lovely planet ... it will be my first stop, on my way back to Allied space. Within the hour it will be nothing more than space dust. Must finish what I start, eh? Tidy things up." The smile remained on Ot-Mul's thin lips as he stared back at Jason.

Jason's mind's eye flashed to Dira and he felt his inner rage escalate.

"As for the loss of an old, antiquated prison barge," Ot-Mul continued, "well, that has little effect on the inevitable, Captain Reynolds. You want it ... take it ... it's my gift to you."

"Thank you. I accept your gift. Unfortunately, its longevity will be short lived."

Ot-Mul's smile slightly wavered but quickly returned—looking forced. "And why is that, Captain?"

Jason saw a message waiting for him on his HUD, and Grimes was signaling from the front of the ship.

"Let's just say that any influence you've yielded over Allied space has come to an end. Take a look around, Ot-Mul … because this is where you and your fleet will remain, in this sector of space, for years to come … if not indefinitely."

Silence followed as realization slowly set in. Ot-Mul was looking away now—most likely at a logistical screen, which showed the progression of *Dreathlor* prison barge toward the loop wormhole. He looked back at Jason. "Foolish. Your fatal mistake was telling me your intentions. That prison barge will be destroyed long before it reaches that wormhole. After that, you will live long enough to watch the destruction, annihilation, of everything you care about. Then I will, mercifully, let you die." The comms feed evaporated, leaving Jason staring at a bulkhead.

"Captain!"

He was halfway back to the cockpit. "One second." He slid into the open seat next to Grimes. "What's happening?"

"That's happening," Grimes replied, exasperated.

One look at *Dreathlor* prison barge and Jason knew. It had slowed down to a crawl.

"They've been picking off the heavy cruisers affixed to the hull. There's only two left and they're both on the starboard side of the barge … it's completely off kilter."

Jason nodded, letting it all sink in. He needed Ricket. He turned and found him standing at his side. Of course he was! "Ricket, if we were to set the *Starlight* down on the port side of the prison barge could it compensate enough—"

"Yes … just might, Captain. The Caldurian antimatter drive technology provides for an impressive thrust to weight ratio."

Suddenly all getting to their feet, the rest of the team picked up on the fact that soon they'd be getting off the ship. Billy, his visor up and soggy stogie protruding from the corner of his mouth, interjected, "So we'll be target practice for a while?"

"The *Starlight*'s shields are far more robust than those on any of the Craing ships. Is that enough defense against, potentially, thousands of warships? Probably not. But, Captain … there's a far bigger issue at hand."

"*Dreathlor* is going critical," Jason said.

Ricket didn't say anything. Like Ricket, Jason knew the odds of survival for any of the *Starlight*'s crew was practically zero. He tried to push the bleakness of the situation out of his mind.

"How close is the prison barge to the wormhole now?"

Grimes glanced at her readings. "Up till now, the remaining affixed heavy cruisers have been propelling the barge to come in from the side … skirting the Drac-Vin forces, for the most part. But as you can see, that's all changed. I'd say no less than one thousand ships are flocking, poised to surround *Dreathlor*. To answer your question, if the cruisers were unimpeded and had the *Starlight*'s added thrust … I'd say five minutes out from the mouth of the wormhole."

Jason turned back to Ricket. "Do we have that long before those ion engines go?"

"Maybe … we'd have to move now, Captain. I've provided the *Starlight* with the necessary coordinates."

Jason nodded toward Grimes. "Do it."

Immediately, there came the familiar white flash. Grimes positioned them several hundred feet above the hull of the *Dreathlor* prison barge. As she brought the little ship down, Jason's eyes held fast to the logistical display. Ot-Mul's fleet had slowed. Those that were virtually on top of them had moved away.

"Incoming, Captain. Five, ten, thirty … one hundred thousand fusion-tipped missiles inbound and locked on to us," Grimes said. She looked back to Jason, immediately confused by his smile. "What? Not even *Dreathlor* will survive that kind of nuclear barrage."

It was Billy who enlightened her. Pointing to the display,

he said, "Looks like the Drac-Vin forces are making a beeline for the wormhole."

Grimes shook her head; she still wasn't getting it.

Billy leaned in closer and squinted his eyes. "Look, there … Ot-Mul, and three of his four battle droids, they are getting the hell out of Dodge. Don't you see … the plan worked … Ot-Mul's entering the wormhole."

The *Starlight* rocked as Grimes put her down onto the prison barge. She wasted no time grappling onto the hull surface and bringing the drive up to full throttle. Jason spotted Bristol earlier, seated mid-ship—still on his comms. He'd continued to maintain contact with each of the two remaining heavy cruisers; his work was cut out for him—coordinating the thrust of the mismatched four ships for optimum speed, as well as steering the lumbering prison barge toward the wormhole. All in all, no small feat.

Jason noticed Ricket was getting jittery, moving from foot to foot.

"What is it, Ricket?"

"The prison barge … *Dreathlor* … it's going to blow up within the next two minutes."

"How do you know—"

Ricket cut him off, "I don't know, Captain, how I know … but somehow I do."

And Jason knew enough not to doubt anything Ricket said. His expression, alone, put a chill down Jason's back. Ricket was scared. "Close your visor, Billy. Grimes, initialize your SuitPac." Currently, she was the only one who hadn't activated her battle suit. Both did as told and Jason used his HUD to phase-shift the team, as a whole unit, into open space.

CHAPTER 28

He didn't phase-shift away with the others. Quickly, Jason took over the now-vacated pilot's seat. First, he ensured each of his team's life icons were still active and accounted for. Fortunately, he'd phase-shifted them to a section of open space some distance from the prison barge, as well as from any Drac-Vin warships. If Ricket was correct, he now had less than two minutes to do what needed to be done. He took a quick glance at logistics and saw incoming Craing missiles rapidly approaching—like an ominous dense cloud. External temperature readings on the *Starlight* were now spiking … beyond a doubt, *Dreathlor* was going to blow up anytime now. He brought the little Caldurian ship's drive up to maximum and pushed it past its red line. Jason felt its G-forces increase slightly and heard the drive pitch whirling higher. Warning tones sounded around the cockpit. Earlier, Jason realized after talking to Ricket and Grimes that the moon-sized prison barge wouldn't make it into the mouth of the wormhole before the missiles hit. His decision to phase-shift everyone off the *Starlight* had been impulsive … but one he was still glad he'd made. What he was now planning was as close to committing suicide as he'd ever come. The approaching missile cloud was still poised to overtake the prison barge but at least he'd prolonged the inevitable.

Jason was being hailed.

"Go for Captain."

"I would have preferred to stay on board with you, Captain," Ricket said.

"I appreciate that, Ricket. I didn't see the need for us all to die. Listen … I need something … anything I can do to increase the propulsion on the *Starlight* … even if it's only for several seconds."

There was silence for several agonizingly long moments. Then an abstract thought occurred to Jason. "Ricket, what would happen if I requested an interchange wormhole … while still affixed to the prison barge?"

"I don't know, Captain … it may be too late—"

Jason cut Ricket off and quickly went about initiating the necessary steps to request and bring about a short-distance interchange wormhole. Ricket's two-minute window of survival was coming to an end. Jason was resigned to the fact that if the exploding ion engines on *Dreathlor* didn't kill him, those incoming missiles surely would.

He waited in silence—he wondered which of the three possibilities would come first. While he watched, Jason saw more and more Drac-Vin forces move into the mouth of the wormhole. That was at least something positive. He only wished he'd witnessed Ot-Mul's expression upon confronting the Allied welcoming party on the wormhole's other end.

Warning messages were now popping up on multiple console displays in rapid succession. Apparently the temperature on *Dreathlor's* outer hull was so hot that the *Starlight's* landing struts were beginning to soften … *soon they'll melt.* The first of the approaching missiles was nearly upon him. He contemplated targeting them with the *Starlight's* plasma cannon … but with so many inbound, what was the point? And then it happened—the interchange wormhole request was granted. Space began to distort around him and a new wormhole formed right in front of the prison barge. This was the largest interchange wormhole Jason had ever seen. Everything was happening in the blink of an eye and before he knew it, the two ships were crossing the threshold. There was no time lag—the *Dreathlor* prison barge, with the attached *Starlight* going along for the ride, was catapulted across thousands of miles of open space.

When Jason realized what had just happened, he let out a slow breath and waited for his heart to start beating again. A quick check of the console told him the missiles were no longer an immediate threat. Instead, looming before him through the observation window was the gaping mouth of the loop wormhole. Huge and black, it completely filled his field of view. There were also hundreds of Drac-Vin warships surrounding them—all moving toward the blackness ahead.

A smile crossed Jason's lips. Willing his hands to move, he triggered the little *Starlight* to disengage its grappling hold on the prison barge's hull. He brought the ship's propulsion system back into the black safe range and steered the *Starlight* away from the prison barge and the fast-approaching wormhole. He pinpointed the location of the assault team, then phase-shifted to their position, where they still were—several thousand miles back the way he'd come.

The team had formed into a V-formation, using their battle suits' integrated propulsion thrusters to navigate them forward. But with the closure of the loop wormhole, and limited phase-shift capability, they surely would die soon. Jason brought the *Starlight* in close and waved to the team from the observation window. No one waved back.

It didn't take long before, one by one, they phase-shifted on board—using the same procedure to enter the stern of the ship they'd used before—then each quickly getting out of the way to make room for the next. Jason stayed in the pilot's seat and Grimes took the seat next to him. Billy and Ricket, the rest of the team behind them, stood at the entrance to the cockpit. Grimes said, "Good thing that worked out okay, Captain … because I was most definitely ready to kill you."

But Jason wasn't really listening. His eyes were focused

on the display. All eyes moved to the display. The prison barge was entering the wormhole. It was difficult to make out, as hundreds of thousands of warships, in the process of also funneling in, were close around it.

The explosion was magnificent! A brilliant display of white, and blue, and many colors—amazing colors—some colors Jason had never seen before. A collective cheer filled the confines of the *Starlight*. Whoops and high-fives continued for several minutes before Jason stood, gesturing for Grimes to swap seats.

"Can we verify that the wormhole has indeed been shut down?"

"It's no more, Captain … gravitational readings are completely gone; the spatial anomaly has disappeared," Ricket replied.

"Good," Jason said. "We've got to return to Allied space, Lieutenant."

She slid into her seat and immediately went to work. "Captain, hmm … I think that last interchange wormhole stunt, which was amazing by the way, jumbled the *Starlight's* interstellar comms. I'm not getting anything back from the interchange. Phase-shifting's not an option right now either."

"We have another problem," Jason said.

"I see it," Grimes said, now taking evasive action.

It was the last remaining battle droid. At least Jason hoped it was the last one. "Can you phase-shift us out of here?"

"Working on it," she said.

The droid was closing in on their position and firing its energy weapon. The *Streamline* began to shake violently.

"Shields are quickly becoming overwhelmed. We're in deep trouble, Captain," Grimes said.

The battle droid had come to a halt thirty miles off the *Starlight's* bow. "I've got a lock on it, firing plasma—"

The last words never left her lips.

The *Starlight's* primary weapon was no longer functioning. Grimes turned toward Jason, "Shields are failing and we have no way to defend ourselves. We definitely can't out-maneuver that thing …"

"We've defeated those things before, Cap," Billy said. "I'd rather go out fighting than wait in here for it to turn us into space dust."

Such a thought never crossed Jason's mind. *Why not?* "Grimes, Ricket and Bristol, keep trying to get something back online … in the meantime, we're stepping out for a few."

Jason was the first to phase-shift to open space, approximately thirty yards in front of the battle droid. Next came Billy, then Rizzo, and then Traveler and Jackson. Gaddy was the last one to appear. They formed a semi-circle around the Caldurian droid. It had stopped firing on the *Starlight* and seemed to be assessing a new, unorthodox, situation. At such close range, Jason could see the droid's spinning, churning, reflective blades. Its small turret-like head was turning, from one combatant to another.

Jason used an open comms channel to instruct the others to set their multi-guns to an option called *Expansion Gum*. He'd had good luck with this HUD armament setting before—and getting those razor-sharp blades disabled was an absolute necessity. In the past, he'd seen battle droids slice through battle-suit armor like butter.

"Ensure your phase-shields are set on max, as well."

The battle droid slowly but steadily moved foreword, directly toward Jason. The droid began firing its plasma weapon—its turret head continually spinning this way and that, targeting all six of them at once. Jason's shields were becoming depleted, almost immediately.

The crew returned fire, but this time there was no multi-gun recoil or kickback. Just as he remembered, the weapon acted more like a high-tech squirt gun. A viscous stream of brown sludge spewed forth from each multi-gun muzzle. The battle droid's spinning razor-sharp blades, now full of viscous brown goop, suddenly seized up.

Jason's shields were down to twenty percent and he guessed the others were in a similar position. "Let's take this droid asshole out," he yelled.

They switched back to their multi-guns' highest-level plasma setting and fired nonstop until their muzzles turned red hot from the scorching heat.

"When your shields are cooked, get back to the ship and let them regenerate."

Gaddy was the first to phase-shift away. Billy soon followed. Jason next phase-shifted back into the ship. He needed five minutes. He hurried to the cockpit and watched through the observation window. What he saw surprised him. Apparently Traveler had brought his heavy hammer to open space. He was using it now to beat the living daylights out of the battle droid.

CHAPTER 29

Traveler had a history with battle droids. He'd just barely survived his last encounter a few months back on a space platform above Terplin, and if there was one thing Jason knew about rhino-warriors, they don't easily forget getting their ass handed back to them. The team continued to watch Traveler through the *Starlight*'s observation window.

"Should we … I don't know … do something?" Grimes asked.

"Nah … he's just venting a little pent-up steam. Probably best not to get in the middle of that, anyway," Billy said with a wry grin.

Traveler's grip on his heavy hammer was held high up on the handle, allowing him to reduce the arc of his swing. Like interstellar gladiators, the two combatants were both dishing out, and receiving, a horrific beating. There's no audible sound in outer space, but if there were, Jason was sure he'd be cringing with each devastating blow cast.

The battle droid connected with Traveler's jaw—spinning the rhino-beast around—and striking him on the opposite side of the head. Jason tensed and wondered if Traveler had finally met his match—was he finished? The battle droid moved in closer, proceeding to pummel Traveler's mid-section with another ten driving blows. Again, the droid moved around Traveler until it was positioned behind him, facing his back.

Traveler spun around with unimaginable speed. With his right arm fully extended outward, the heavy hammer connected across the droid's turret head. Stunned, the droid stood motionless. It had taken Jason a good year to read all of Traveler's various expressions—a subtle combination of muscular movements beneath his hide, around his eyes, beneath his horns, and along his strong jaw. Jason's rhino-warrior friend was definitely smiling now, and thoroughly enjoying himself.

All fight had left the battered droid. Now, it was just a matter of finishing the battle. Traveler hammered away at the battle droid's turret head, like driving the head of a nail home, and delivered the fatal blow. With nothing left of the droid's turret head, Traveler stopped. He gave the lifeless droid a decisive kick—sending it end-over-end into deep space.

★ ★ ★

Jason kept a wary eye on what remained of Ot-Mul's warships. Like a swarm of hiveless bees they continued to circle, as if hoping the loop wormhole would somehow miraculously reappear. For the most part, they left the *Starlight* alone. With the exception of several too-close flybys, the *Starlight* still remained in her current position—pretty much dead in space.

Both Ricket and Bristol were hard at work. Bristol's legs protruded from an access panel at the stern of the ship, while Ricket, nowhere to be seen, had crawled through the panel opening and lay cramped beneath the deck, alongside the ship's drive unit.

Lieutenant Grimes was asleep in the copilot seat. Jason too tried to grab a few minutes of sleep, but he couldn't turn off his reeling mind: *How many of Ot-Mul's Drac-Vin warships made it through the wormhole before it was demolished? Fifty thousand? One hundred thousand?* And what about the planet most near to their relative proximity ... Jhardon? What about Dira? Was she alive?

Jason got up and moved into the rear cabin. He found Billy there, sitting across from the small medical bay. Jason took the open seat next to him.

He gestured toward the right. "Traveler still in there?"

"Yeah, he's taken quite a thrashing. Too many broken bones to count. Must've hurt like a son of a bitch. Not that he'd ever show it." Jason assessed the closed sliding door to the medical bay. The bay had nowhere near the ultra-superior capabilities provided to one in a MediPod, but with its multiple articulating arms and advanced technology—including the ability to perform most surgical procedures on any number of various species—it was another example of Caldurian *other-worldly* sophistication.

"So what do you think we'll find back in Allied space?" Billy asked.

"Right now? The battle of all battles! We should be there."

"It's all come down to that—one final decisive fight—hasn't it? Winner takes all ... grabs all the marbles." Billy stared at Jason.

Jason nodded. "The odds are not in our favor ... you know that, right?"

"I know. With that said, Cap ... one can only hope. Speaking of hope, what would you do? I mean, if the Alliance prevails?"

Jason contemplated on that for a moment.

"I know what I'd do," Billy continued. "I'd return to Earth ... at least for a while."

"What would you do there?" Jason asked, surprised by Billy's admission.

"Hunt zombies ... or whatever those things are called."

"Weevil people; the kids coined the term *peovils*."

"Dira said a good number of them can be brought back ... made human again. Well, the president needs qualified leaders," Billy said, "so I'd get a team together and hunt peovils. Maybe even Orion would join me. Be nice, too, to be on solid ground again."

Jason could see Billy immediately regretted mentioning Dira's name. "Sorry, buddy ... I know that's—"

Jason smiled and held up a palm. "Hey, no worries, Billy. And since we're talking rainbows and unicorns and what ifs ... first, I'd give each of my kids a bone-crushing hug and a kiss. Then, I'd figure out how to get Dira back into my life. Hell ... maybe Jhardon needs a royal jester, or someone to prune her majesty's royal shrubbery."

Billy and Jason burst out laughing at the multiple connotations that duty might entail. But soon, the tightness around Jason's heart returned. Once again, he found himself putting up a wall—shutting down his emotions. *Is Dira still alive?*

Bristol and Ricket made their way down the aisle. They stopped at Jason's side, both looking very tired. Ricket was covered from head to toe in dark dirty grime.

"Status?"

"Things are pretty fried," Bristol said. "We had to make some choices."

"What kind of choices?"

"Like either shields, or the ability to phase-shift."

"You chose phase-shifting?"

Both Bristol and Ricket nodded.

"Interstellar comms?" Jason asked.

"Comms should be operational. We won't know if calling up an interchange wormhole is in the cards, though, until we try it."

Jason felt encouraged. "You're awful quiet back there, Ricket ... you have anything to add?"

"One of the other choices we had to make is where our limited power resources are to be allocated."

Jason raised his eyebrows and waited.

"The primary plasma weapon had to be disabled."

Jason let that sink in. He noticed Grimes had joined their impromptu meeting and was rubbing the sleep from her eyes. "So we're unsure if we can call up an interchange wormhole ... but if we can, we'll be exiting it totally defenseless. Is that the gist of it?" Grimes asked, looking irritated.

"No shields, no weapons," Bristol said flatly.

"That's terrific. Good job, boys. Remind me never to let you work on my car," Grimes huffed.

"They had some tough choices to make. I can't say I'd make different ones. We'll just have to think things through very thoroughly before we return to Allied space," Jason told her.

Grimes crossed her arms over her chest and continued to stare at Bristol and Ricket. She was clearly fuming. The stress of the whole situation was taking its toll on her.

"The good news," Billy said, "is we probably won't need shields or weapons … we'll show up in Allied space to a blaze of plasma fire, rail munitions, and exploding nuclear missiles. We'll never know what hit us first."

All eyes were on Billy and no one said anything. Bristol was the first to laugh. After that, laughter filled the cabin. Grimes, her arms now unfolded, stood with her hands on hips, looking at them with contempt. But, eventually, a smile found its way onto her lips and she just shook her head.

The door opened to the medical bay and Traveler emerged. He stretched out his gargantuan arms and breathed in a monumental breath, then exhaled. "I am ready for battle. I am ready for the battle of a lifetime." He looked at his fellow combatants, holding each of their eyes, one at a time. "We are warriors and I am honored to fight at your side."

Jason held Grimes' stare and shrugged, "In for a dollar …"

She smiled and put a hand on Traveler's arm. "We're honored to be at your side, too, Traveler. If this is going to be the end … there's no one I'd rather have fighting next to me than you … than all of you."

CHAPTER 30

The request for an interchange wormhole was granted and it was time to return to Allied space. Their main problem lay in setting up the outpoint coordinates. The last thing they could afford to do was show up in the middle of an interstellar battle without the benefit of functioning shields or weapons. Unfortunately, exactly where that battle would occur was not something they could accurately pinpoint on their own. In the end, Jason contacted *The Lilly* and determined that yes, an immense space battle was indeed going on, and received from them a set of coordinates that would put the *Starlight* close enough, yet not too close, to the action.

One added piece of news Jason got from his brief conversation with Seaman Gordon on *The Lilly* was that there were approximately forty thousand Drac-Vin warships now engaging the newly-formed Allied fleet. But, Jason expected, it was those three remaining battle droids that were causing most of the Allied forces' devastating losses.

With the exception of Lieutenant Grimes, sitting at the controls, everyone was on their feet. "Go ahead, Lieutenant … we're as ready as we'll ever be."

With that, Grimes entered the *Starlight* into the mouth of the interchange wormhole.

Something substantial must have occurred within the last fifteen minutes since Jason spoke to Seaman Gordon. The battle had moved—assets repositioned. Jason barely had time to grab ahold of the back of Grimes' seat before the *Starlight* was violently struck by some object protruding from a light cruiser's underbelly. The impact tore open the back quarter of their vessel. In an instant, the *Starlight* depressurized. Although they were now weightless, Grimes managed to maintain sufficient propulsion speed, and she still seemed to have at least partial navigation control. With a quick check of his HUD, Jason saw everyone was still on board.

"Everyone okay?"

"What the hell was that?" Billy yelled back.

"Craing light cruiser … one of theirs, not ours," Grimes replied. "We're not so much in the middle of the battle as caught in a thoroughfare of fast-moving Drac-Vin traffic."

Jason had already figured that out for himself. Massive ships, dwarfing the small *Starlight*, were whizzing by on all sides. "Phase-shift us out of here, Grimes!"

"Phase-shift system is down, sir." Grimes brought the little ship up to speed and they were pretty much moving in unison with the other ships.

Jason, once oriented, noted that according to the logistical display on the console they were moving along in the right direction. The nearby vessels were probably the last ships to exit the loop wormhole before it closed down. Where the *really* big battle was being waged was approximately one hundred million miles away—about the same distance as Earth from the sun. Not that far—considering the vastness of stellar space.

His NanoCom was out of range, so Jason used his battle suit's comms to hail *The Lilly*. He again reached Seaman Gordon.

"We need an extraction."

"All vessels, including the shuttles, are currently in use, Captain."

Frustrated, Jason barely held back from screaming at the clueless communications officer. "Just connect me to the XO."

"Captain, the XO is not in command of *The Lilly* … it's

your brother, Brian."

"I know who my brother is, Seaman ... connect me."

A moment passed before Gordon came back on: "Captain Reynolds, the other Captain Reynolds says he's too busy to speak to you right now. He says there's a war going on and you'll just have to cool your jets for a while. His words, not mine, Captain."

"We're losing propulsion, Captain," Grimes said. "I'm doing my best to get us out of the way ... off to the side of the road, so to speak."

Terrific, Jason thought. Next, he tried the *Minian*. Seaman Chase answered his hail.

"I need to speak to the admiral."

Jason expected to be connected with one of the admiral's sub-commanders. Without a doubt, the admiral was the most important man in the sector. Everything revolved around the decision-making rulings of his father.

"Good, you made it back."

"Dad?"

"Who else would it be?"

"I don't know ... listen, we're back but behind enemy lines. The *Starlight*'s been heavily damaged. We need an extraction."

"There's only so many vessels with phase-shift technology, Captain." There was a brief moment of silence. "We've got your position coordinates. Hang tight." The connection terminated.

"Captain!"

Now what? "Yes ... what is it, Lieutenant?"

"There's a ..."

Jason waited for her to finish the sentence but instead saw what she was alluding to on the display in front of her. It was a dreadnaught—scratch that—a meganaught. It was approaching from behind and moving at an incredible speed.

"I take it we're still not far enough off the road?"

"Um, no … not even close. We'll be a squashed bug on the front grill of an eighteen-wheeler, Captain."

"ETA?"

"About a minute and a half."

Jason resigned himself to the fact they would, once again, have to singly phase-shift into open space. About to turn his attention to the team, he saw a bright white flash, which had emanated off their bow. Jason had never been happier to see an inanimate thing … it was *The Lilly*!

★ ★ ★

They phase-shifted as a group directly into the corridor of Deck 4 on board *The Lilly*. Jason wanted them to be as close to the bridge as possible. He hurried into the bridge and heard the familiar announcement from the AI, "Captain Jason Reynolds on deck."

Brian was seated in the command chair. He watched Jason approach. He didn't stand or make any movement, other than to look over to McBride. "Put us back in the battle, Helm."

Maybe it was the course of events over the past twelve hours; maybe, it was nearly getting atomized by an approaching meganaught, but right now, Jason was in no mood for his brother's bullshit. Jason strode over to Brian and stood peering down at him.

McBride phase-shifted *The Lilly* out of the path of the meganaught.

"You will stand when a superior officer enters the bridge. You will transfer command, in accordance to fleet mandates." Jason took a step closer to his brother, feeling his anger peak. "What the hell's wrong with you?"

The sound of a familiar, distinctive hiss came from the back of the bridge. It was the hopper—Brian's seven-foot-tall lizard protector. Its teeth were bared and every muscle of its tense green body was poised, ready for action. Jason had seen in the past what the creature was capable of. It was a killer—could rip the beating heart from its quarry in the fraction of a second.

Brian casually looked back to the hopper and held up his hand. The gesture had little effect on the beast, which continued to stare at Jason. "You can relieve me only when I say you can relieve me. I am the captain of this vessel. More important, we're in the midst of a battle here, if you haven't noticed, and the world doesn't stop turning just because you've decided to drop in for a visit."

Jason couldn't believe what he was hearing. *What the hell has come over my brother?* But Jason knew full well what had happened: He'd become accustomed to captaining the most powerful warship, with the exception of the *Minian*, in the known universe. Jason knew from firsthand experience how intoxicating wielding such power could be. He also knew Brian was not the man to be positioned anywhere near that kind of controlling power. His actions, right then, demonstrated that Brian hadn't changed from the two-sided person he'd been back on Halimar, when he played as go-between between the Craing and the Alliance. He was an opportunist, at best, and most likely a traitor.

"Get up and leave the bridge!" Jason's hands were moving fast—ready to physically extricate Brian from the command chair. The movement of something fast … something green … caught Jason's attention. The hopper was already in the air, ready to kill—dive on top of Jason and end his life—all in the blink of an eye. That is, if Traveler hadn't first grabbed the beast around the neck. Now, elevating the hopper eight feet off the deck, Traveler continued to hold it in his viselike grip. Legs flailed, while its arms and razor-sharp claws swiped frantically in the air. Then the hopper was ripping, tearing, at Traveler's outstretched arm. Blood flowed crimson onto the deck of the bridge. And then came a decisive loud snap. The hopper, limp in Traveler's grip, was dead. Traveler released his grip, letting the green beast fall in a heap at his feet.

CHAPTER 31

Brian knelt at the hopper's side while yelling profanities at Traveler. Traveler ignored him. Incensed, Brian spun and addressed Jason directly. "What right did you have to kill it? Who the hell do you think you are?"

"Brian ... that lizard, whatever the hell it was, was a ticking time bomb. You saw it ... it was on the verge of attacking ... me ... your own brother. Truth is, it never should have been allowed on the bridge—or on *The Lilly*, either, for that matter."

"You'll pay for this, Jason. I promise you that."

"Well, talk like that isn't going to help." Jason made eye contact with Billy, who was standing alongside Orion, watching the show.

"Escort my brother off the bridge. If he gives you any trouble, let him cool off in the brig."

Perkins, entering the bridge, had his head down—concentrating on his virtual notebook. He glanced up just in time to avoid walking into Traveler, and noticed the rhino-warrior's arm, covered in blood, and the dead hopper, lying in a heap on the deck. "Good God, what happened?"

"Never mind that now ... bring me up to speed, XO. Fast!"

★ ★ ★

Ot-Mul had been played. Again, Captain Reynolds had

gotten the best of him. Two thirds of his fleet—one hundred and fifty thousand plus warships—were marooned ninety-three thousand light-years back, with no easy access to a loop wormhole. It would be a year before they could travel the distance necessary to reach him.

The truth was, his forces still outnumbered the mismatched Allied fleets by nearly two-to-one. With his three remaining battle droids, and his assault-class destroyer, the *Assailant*, Ot-Mul felt he would easily come away from this battle victorious.

He continued to ponder the strategic aspects of the day ahead. There'd been a few skirmishes so far, but for the most part, vessels both large and small on either side were jockeying for prime positioning—moving assets from one spatial location to another.

"My Lor—Admiral. The small Allied vessel from the Orion system, used to commandeer *Dreathlor* ... well, it is indeed here now. At least, what's left of that ship. She was destroyed by the *Craing-Pri*, one of our newer meganaughts."

"When was this?" Ot-Mul snapped at his second. "And was Reynolds ... was he still on board?"

"No organic material was detected. Apparently, they had abandoned ship. There is something else ..."

"Well? Spit it out, Captain."

"It has been confirmed, although undetected by any of our sensors, that *The Lilly's* been visually observed nearby. It is assumed Captain Reynolds, and his crew, have reunited with the ship."

Ot-Mul's first reaction was a flash of anger—a strong desire to lash out at the fat little captain. Beat him down into his seat cushions. But as the seconds ticked by he calmed himself. *Of course Reynolds is back on* The Lilly! The war about to rage in space would be more decisive than any in all known history. It deserved to have qualified combatants. When Ot-Mul achieved victory, defeating a worthy opponent like Reynolds would make his victory that much sweeter.

"Captain Gee, I want to know the relative positions of *The Lilly* and the *Minian* at all times."

"With their phase-shift capabilities, Admiral ... that will be impossible."

"No, it's not, you imbecilic turd. We have fifty thousand warships ... fifty thousand eyes, visual points of detection, throughout this small sector of space. If visual contact is all we can count on, then have each and every crewmember keep on the lookout. I want constant updates. Is that understood?"

"Yes, understood, Admiral."

The captain scurried off and left Ot-Mul free to return to his own thoughts. Soon the most important battle of the century would begin in earnest. He continued to stare at the constantly updating spatial representation displayed on one of the monitors. The closest planetary system was Jhardon. Ot-Mul's expression turned sour. Turning to his third in command, sitting on the raised platform just past Captain Gee's vacated seat, he said, "Fleet Captain Shine."

"Yes, Admiral."

"I have an important project for you."

"Now ... while we're still mobilizing, sir?"

Ot-Mul continued to stare at Shine, expressionless.

"Of course, Admiral. What is your command?"

Ot-Mul stood and approached the bank of monitors integrated into the far bulkhead. "Show me Jhardon."

The largest of the displays changed to a full-screen, live, visual feed of Jhardon in mid-orbit revolution, and showed her half-scorched, blackened side, inflicted during the attack by his Vanguard ships. As the planet turned, her bright emerald-green side began to come into view. Spectacularly beautiful, he thought, looked at from this perspective. Ot-Mul let a smile intrude on his sour face.

"Captain Shine ... bring me the princess. Princess Dira Caparri."

"Dead or alive, my Lord?"

Ot-Mul contemplated the question for several moments. "You will address me as Admiral. I want her alive. Send a convoy of warships ... they are not to return without the princess. Is that understood?"

"Yes, Admiral. She will be brought to you by the end of the day."

★ ★ ★

Dira was encouraged by her father's recent appearance in front of the emergency-held Allied planets' assembly of magistrates. Fear of the impending battle, one that sealed the fate of virtually every world in their sector, was running rampant. So the king opted to make a personal appearance, instead of a virtual one ... another good sign. She was at his side there, clearly fortifying her current role as princess, and her future one, Queen of Jhardon. They'd made the trip to Wormly together, on board the king's private schooner. It was a barren and ugly planet, three light-years' distance from Jhardon. Wormly's capital was host to close to one thousand planetary leaders. King Caparri was the de facto guest of honor—the elder statesman who, more often than not, swayed general consensus to that of his own disposition.

In the end, the trip was one of politics more than anything else. The decision for the Allied worlds to join together, once more, only really ever had one option—there would be no lying low, no hiding from the impending Drac-Vin invasion. It was to be a unified Allied force, led by a commander from Earth—Admiral Reynolds. By the end of the conference, it had been decided ... the Alliance would provide him whatever military support they were capable of delivering.

On return, the royal schooner was less than an hour out from Jhardon. Dira sat across from the king, watching him peruse a stack of reports—all demanding the king's scrupulous attention. Too soon, such matters would be her responsibility. *Do I have what the position demands?* She couldn't imagine she'd ever possess anywhere near the kind of prestige her father held among the other Allied leaders—what's more, she didn't want to. She didn't want any of this life. He was making a terrible mistake, placing such responsibility in her young, inexperienced hands.

Dira's thoughts turned to her mother. The queen was still gravely ill, lying at death's door. What would she want for her daughter? And would she want the king to follow through with his plans for *Kharmlish*—the ancient practice of committing suicide, where king and queen journeyed together into the heavenly worlds? Knowing her mother as well as she did, she couldn't imagine she'd want that to happen … she was far too practical.

She noticed her father looking at her, and smiled. "Why don't you put those reports aside for a while. Rest, father."

"No … there'll be twice as many added to these tomorrow." Wearily, he returned her smile. "There's something else I wanted to speak with you about." The king placed the stack of reports on the seat next to him. "Jhardon has suffered a terrible fate … its innocence is forever gone. Our planet is no longer the same world and it is time for the monarchy to end. It would be different if you wanted it to continue, but I know you do not. I have been studying the governments of other worlds, including Oricon, Aldermore, and Earth, with their more democratic institutions. Moving forward, I would like your help scripting a new constitution for our people. Will you help me, help Jhardon, with that?"

Dira was momentarily speechless. *How … what had changed?*

"You are no more suited to govern a planet than I am to being a medical doctor. Come, daughter, sit next to me. We have much to discuss."

CHAPTER 32

Jason sipped at his coffee and put it back down on the ready room conference table. The overhead lights were dimmed and he waited for his father to appear on the display. His mind kept returning to Ot-Mul. He was capable of terrible things. Atrocities. If things went sideways, he wondered how that would play out for the ones he truly cared about ... his own family.

"Captain, am I disturbing you?"

"No ... come on in, Ricket."

"I'd like to speak with you about the battle droids."

It took a few seconds for Jason to mentally change gears. "They are a problem. A problem we don't have a ready answer for."

"I may have something that will, at least partially, help."

The display across the table came alive with a live feed of Admiral Reynolds, looking frazzled.

"Hold on, Ricket," Jason said.

"What's this I hear about your brother? You threw him off the bridge?" the admiral asked, his expression hard to read.

"I dealt with it," Jason said.

"Indeed. Not your finest hour ... and you killed the hopper?"

"Actually, Traveler did. But the damn thing was on the verge of attacking ... attacking me!"

The admiral seemed to be weighing his words. "Truth is, the thing scared the shit out of me," he said. "Why the creature had such a hard-on for your brother, I never figured out. But throwing your brother off the bridge in the middle of a battle was irresponsible. You owe him an apology."

"I know. I'm not so sure he'll want to speak to me any time soon."

"Anyway … we have far more important things to discuss," the admiral said.

"Ricket was just about to tell me something he's come up with concerning the battle droids."

"Any help you can provide, Ricket, would be greatly appreciated," the admiral said.

"I was reviewing the *Minian*'s phase-synthesizer database. I've found the manufacturing specifications for the battle droids. I thought they'd been lost, but I was able to recover them."

"So, we can make our own … fight fire with fire?"

"Yes and no, Admiral. The battle droids are highly technical, complicated Caldurian wonders. To build and manufacture a battle droid, turnout time will take us days, if not a full week. And that's for one."

"We'll be lucky if we have hours before Ot-Mul attacks. He's got his fleets strategically positioned in such a way that the Alliance will be forced to fend off incursions from multiple flanks. That's what happens when you face an opponent who literally has twice the number of military assets at his disposal."

"What I had in mind was something called a MagBot," Ricket said.

"What is that?" Jason asked.

"It's a battle droid of sorts … only it's half the size and has one-tenth the complexity of the full-sized battle droids. It utilizes a cocktail of unique minerals, which are all synthesized within the manufacturing process. The little droids produce incredible magnetic properties. Enough to alter gravitational fields, and bend local spatial properties to the point they're nearly untouchable. If we can produce enough of these Mag-Bots, we'll be able to keep Ot-Mul's battle droids fairly busy."

"Can they destroy them?" the admiral asked.

"I doubt it. Maybe. But they'd definitely slow them down, while inflicting their own unique hardship on Ot-Mul's warships. They may be our best short-term solution."

"How soon can we have them?"

"I have a batch cooking now. I should have thirty of them ready in an hour."

"That's excellent, Ricket. Keep me abreast of your progress. But now I need to speak to the captain."

Ricket nodded at the admiral and Jason and left the ready room.

"That's somewhat encouraging," Jason said.

The admiral didn't answer. He looked as if he were trying to figure out how to say something difficult.

"Just spit it out, Dad. What is it?"

His father looked pained. His eyes had softened and he was clearly wrestling with something. "Jason, there's really no easy way to say this, so I'll just say it."

Jason had no idea what was coming, but with the day he'd already been having, he wasn't looking forward to it.

"Dira's ..."

Surprised, Jason cut him off, "She's dead, isn't she? Ot-Mul kept his promise ... going after the ones who matter most to me."

"I honestly don't know, Jason. She was with her father, on the king's private schooner. They had time to get off a distress call. Apparently, a small convoy of Craing light cruisers intercepted their ship. Their schooner was no more than ten minutes out from Jhardon's orbit when they were attacked."

"What happened to the schooner? Were there bodies ... any survivors?"

"The schooner was still in one piece. Drives had been taken out. There was a breach. Thirty-seven dead ... no survivors." The admiral lifted a palm to hold off the next question. "No, Dira and the king were not on board. They were not among the dead."

Jason's mind reeled. Ot-Mul would keep her alive—killing her would rob him of the full impact he wanted to impart. He would wait and kill her in front of Jason ... that he knew, and that was Jason's only glimmer of hope: he could possibly save her.

"Son ... I'm sorry. I love Dira like a daughter. I was the one who first brought her on board *The Lilly*. But I need to know you're going to stay on post ... fighting the Drac-Vin is your primary objective. Too many lives are at stake ... hell, everything is at stake and none of us can lose sight of that."

Jason inwardly conceded his father was right. As hard as it would be, he needed to keep his head in the game. Saving Dira meant everything to him, but not at the risk of them losing the war. Something else occurred to him. "Dad, he's going to do everything in his power to grab the kids ... hell, he'd go after Nan if she were in this sector."

Jason didn't like the way his father's facial expression suddenly altered. He looked as white as a ghost.

"What the hell is happening? Dad?"

"She insisted. She's the goddamn president of the United States! You know her better than anyone; you've tried telling her no."

"Insisted on what? You're not making any damn sense."

"Right before I contacted you ... I ... I obliged ... I ... opened an interchange wormhole for a small convoy. Nan's come for the kids, Jason ... she wants them away from the action. That, and get one-on-one updates on the impending battle situation. Understand, she was never going to be anywhere close to the front line ... in and out fast. She's easily a light-year away—"

"Damn it! When's the last time you spoke to her? To her convoy?"

The admiral didn't answer for several beats. "I sent Mollie and Boomer to her convoy via a shuttle. I needed to be back here. I haven't heard that anything's gone astray. I'm sure everyone's fine."

Jason wasn't going to underestimate Ot-Mul. He was a sick fuck and revenge meant everything to him. Jason used his NanoCom to hail Orion.

"Gunny, I need you to check on the disposition of a small convoy from Earth. They recently arrived through an interchange wormhole requested by the *Minian*. Also, there's a shuttle ..."

Jason glanced over to his father.

"The *Perilous*," the admiral said.

"The shuttle should have intersected the president's convoy by now." The admiral looked worried.

"Give me a few seconds, Cap. Things are heating up on multiple fronts. Looks like the Drac-Vin forces are about to make their move."

"It's the kids, Gunny. And Nan. If Ot-Mul detected their whereabouts, he's coming for them. He's already got Dira."

"Oh my God, Captain ... I see them. There's fifteen cruisers and one destroyer closing in on the convoy."

CHAPTER 33

Boomer sat in between Mollie and Petty Officer Priscilla Miller. Across the aisle from them was Secretary of Defense Ben Walker. Boomer liked the old, somewhat gruff, government man. He was funny and didn't treat her like a nine-, almost ten-year-old.

She was excited she'd soon see her mother again, but didn't like the idea of leaving her dad up here in space. She felt it was her responsibility to watch over him. Sure, she was just a young kid, but she was resourceful—something her father once remarked was a most important factor when placed in a dangerous situation. She was more resourceful than anyone knew. She'd continued her close combat training. There was never a shortage of SEALs or other highly trained military people around on the *Minian* and *The Lilly*. Sometimes she'd had to tell a fib, here and there, to get them to work with her—saying the request came from her father, or her grandfather.

Boomer always knew she would make outer space her home. She loved the uncertainty space traveling provided, the mysteries of alien worlds, and the simple fact that space life was always a bit unsafe. But now more than usual she felt a little too vulnerable. Why had she agreed to leave Teardrop and Dewdrop behind? The two droids were rarely not at her and Mollie's sides. But they'd both begun to have issues—technical problems. Ricket said it was a software thing … they'd be fine after he had a chance to work on them. So there they remained up on *The Lilly's* Deck 4B in Ricket's little workshop.

Boomer looked over to her sister. How could they possibly share the same DNA? Mollie couldn't be more different. Sure, they were best friends, and constantly getting into trouble together—which was fun. But in the end, Mollie was much more like their mom. She even wore her hair in the same style—had similar mannerisms. Boomer took after her dad and wanted to grow up to captain her own ship someday—hopefully, *The Lilly.* She loved *The Lilly* ... the ship was her home for close to two years and she couldn't imagine living anywhere else. She knew her dad felt the same way, although he'd probably never admit it.

"Get your stuff together, girls. We're almost there," Priscilla said.

Boomer looked out the side observation window toward a distant cluster of white, bug-like, vessels. That would be her mother's small armada of converted Craing warships. Excitement at seeing her mother again made her smile.

"I can't wait to see Mom again," Mollie said, grabbing up her backpack between her feet.

"How long will we stay on Earth?" Boomer asked, directing her question to Ben Walker.

"That's not up to me, Boomer. At the very least, till things settle down up here and Ot-Mul and his forces are firmly dealt with."

Boomer was well aware of the Allied worlds' desperate situation with the Drac-Vin. The latter were probably going to win ... that was the feeling most grown-ups held. She'd picked up on private, soft-spoken conversations and overheard meetings taking place in the adjoining ready room on the *Minian.* She felt she should be allowed to stay in space, be with her father and grandfather. Heck, Earth was no picnic ground either, with all those gross, zombie *peovils* running about everywhere.

"I'm staying with Mom. That's all I know," Mollie said

to Secretary Walker and then directed her familiar, *know-it-all* smirk back at Boomer.

"Good!" Boomer replied.

Light poured in from the side observation windows as the *Perilous* entered the cruiser's voluminous flight deck area. The shuttle settled softly onto the deck and immediately the rear hatch opened. The four passengers stood then—as did the three SEALs, their armed protection detail, seated at the back of the *Perilous*. They headed for the extended gangway.

Boomer was in the middle of the pack and tried to see around the adults. *Something's not right.* She wasn't exactly sure what—it was more a feeling than anything she could put her finger on. There was a lot of commotion below, on the deck, but from her limited perspective, all she saw were Craing. That by itself was not unusual. With all the merging of Craing and U.S. forces over the last few months, she'd seen many of the little aliens. But not exclusively Craing, like now … where were the humans? Where were the military personnel her mother had waiting for them? *Where's my mother?*

"This isn't right!" Boomer yelled. "It's a trap!"

Petty Officer Miller was already moving, doing her best to corral Boomer and Mollie down the gangway. Their security detail, two in front and one behind, were bringing their multi-guns to bear, taking defensive stances. Secretary of Defense Ben Walker was in the process of crouching down when the first plasma blast hit his left eye. He was dead before his body tumbled off the gangway.

Instinctively, Boomer activated her SuitPac on her belt, then reached over and activated Mollie's as well. Plasma fire was coming from virtually every direction. Snipers! They'd been in hiding, at key vantage points, all around the flight deck, just waiting to pick them off. One by one the three SEALs were targeted. Although they wore battle suits, the suits' protective shielding couldn't compensate, withstand the assault of the overwhelming barrage of hundreds of incoming plasma strikes simultaneously striking. All three toppled off the gangway. Petty Officer Miller, who still hadn't activated her battle suit, was lying atop Mollie, covering her with her own body. She frantically looked for Boomer, desperate to protect her as well.

But Boomer was already on the move. Her last words to Mollie, via her NanoCom, were: "Activate Priscilla's SuitPac. Reach behind you and—"

Her words caught in her throat. A swarm of armed Craing soldiers had surged around Petty Officer Miller and Mollie. A singular plasma blast, striking between the petty officer's shoulders, ended her life.

Boomer, already sixty-five feet away, literally began running for her life. Up ahead was a small, somewhat hidden, stairwell. She knew the layout of the Craing light cruiser fairly well; she'd explored much of it before. Granted, she didn't know it like she knew *The Lilly* or the *Minian*, but she'd easily been on a half-dozen or more of these disgusting, greasy ships over the past year. They always smelled of charred flesh—most surfaces coated with a thin layer of gunk. Her HUD clearly showed a small army of Craing in pursuit. Two other teams were approaching from outside the flight deck—one team from the deck above, the crew quarters area, and the other, from below. She tried to remember what was down there, but it wasn't coming to her. She reached the stairwell, bypassing the hatchway, and ducked into a small dark alcove. This was one of the smaller, hidden secret areas she'd discovered in the past. The alcove turned into a dark and narrow passageway. Turning her helmet light on enabled her to pick up her pace. With a glance, she saw that Mollie's life icon was still active; she was being moved to another area of the ship.

Boomer had hoped, prayed, Mollie would not be killed. She'd counted on that when she'd made her escape. *Ot-Mul would want us as hostages.* Well, Boomer wasn't going to let that happen. This wasn't her first rodeo. She'd get away from them and rescue her sister … *is she my sister?*

She reached the end of the passageway and found the metal rung ladder. She stopped to catch her breath. Looking up, she saw that the ladder reached high above her—intersecting multiple decks along the way. The light from her helmet cast illumination only part of the way up. The shaft reminded Boomer of a chimney—dark and cramped and scary. She noticed another set of life icons coming into view on her HUD. She'd changed the settings for those she was in contact with. The three-letter designation—one of the newer icons—simply read Mom.

Boomer started up the ladder and hoped she wouldn't lose hold of the slippery rungs.

★ ★ ★

This wasn't the first time Nan had occupied one of their small, eight-by-eight-foot holding cells. Here too sat a bucket in the corner, metal bars, and the gagging smell of charred flesh. Years of smoke rising up from the Grand Sacellum—from the grilling caldrons below—permeated the air around her. She seemed to recall making a promise to herself to never ever be placed in this position again. She pictured Jason's face and then his admonishment … *How could you come here? How could you take such a risk?*

Her hand reflexively went to her belly and the tiny life growing inside.

"Are you okay, Nan? Are you experiencing any pain?"

Nan shook her head and looked over at her neighbor in the cell adjacent. Dira was looking at her, concern in her eyes. Nan always considered her striking—beautiful—but seeing her now, in her formal attire, her shimmering robes and exotic makeup, she really was breathtaking. She didn't blame Jason one iota for falling in love with this Jhardonian princess. Hell, she too could fall in love with her … and she didn't think of women in that way.

"I'm fine. Just aggravated at myself. I shouldn't have come. I just …"

"You don't have to explain," Dira said.

"You should sit … do not exert yourself," came the deep voice of King Caparri. He'd been so quiet; Nan had forgotten he was being held in the holding cell next to hers to the right.

Nan leaned against the bars, which actually helped. She smiled at the king and brought her attention back to Dira on her left. "I just felt so isolated. I needed to see the kids."

"And Jason," Dira added.

This was still uneven territory for the two women. Another complication: she was pregnant with Jason's baby. But she wasn't going to make light of it. "Dira … I will always love Jason. He will always be a part of my life … even if that's solely because we'll share three kids. He's made it clear to me where his heart lies, what he wants. He wants you. I pushed him away so many times in the past. It was never fair. And then, when this pregnancy occurred, well, it just happened. You two still hadn't taken your relationship to the next level … it just happened. But I don't regret it and I'm hoping you can get over it." Nan looked over to Dira and saw that she was smiling.

"I'm glad to hear you say that, Nan. What Jason and I have is special. But you'd be surprised at how … what's the best word—innocent—it still is. We haven't actually …"

Nan held up her palms in mock surrender and laughed, "I don't need to know the details. But I'm happy for you and Jason. It will be so wonderful if you, if we survive long enough …" Nan's voice broke and her eyes welled up with tears. Everything was such a mess. Such a damnable mess. Before she could say another word, she heard the mechanical sound of the lift ascending, followed by a clanging as the gate lifted. Four Craing were dragging someone. In the dark, it was hard to tell.

"Mollie? Oh my God … is that you, Mollie?"

CHAPTER 34

Boomer waited for a grouping of eight Craing soldiers to move past her, then continued down the corridor. *For goodness sakes, how many of the little buggers are there?* Once she'd climbed free of the chimney-like shaft and onto the current deck, she began keeping her eyes open for new places to hide. At least she had a clear destination. She'd been watching her HUD and Mollie's life icon joined her mother's and Dira's. She knew exactly where they were; they'd been taken to the holding cells. Minutes earlier, she'd contacted her father and told him what had transpired—their abduction, and that both Secretary Ben Walker and Petty Officer Miller had been shot and killed. He said he was on his way, telling her to stay put, hidden, until he got there; he made her promise not to try anything foolish on her own.

Boomer actually considered doing as he'd instructed, but then reason set in—the *what ifs* took over. What if her mother, sister, and Dira were tortured … or worse, killed, before her father could get there? What if her father never arrived … No, Boomer was here, now, and her father wasn't. She couldn't just hide; she had to do something.

In the past, Mollie and Boomer weren't allowed to use their SuitPacs unless there was an emergency. That was stupid, because now she was unfamiliar with all its functionality. It wasn't something she'd been able to sneak in trying out, either—the second she'd initiated the suit, it was detected by *The Lilly's* or the *Minian's* AI. So here she was, clueless on how to phase-shift. She'd forgotten what HUD menu or sub-menu to access. But Boomer wasn't about to give up—she'd ... *what did they call it?* Oh yeah, she'd multitask. She'd walk, run, hide ... and, along the way, figure out the stupid HUD menu system.

★ ★ ★

"Oh my God, Mollie, are you okay?"

"I'm okay—" Mollie answered groggily, just coming around. "Boomer ... she's ..."

Two of the four Craing soldiers held Mollie securely in their grasp. The third soldier gestured for Nan to step backward as he unlocked the cell door.

"She's okay, Mollie. She contacted me via NanoCom." At least, she had been ten minutes ago, Nan thought. She'd told Boomer to stay hidden. Not to try to rescue them. Apparently, Jason told her the same thing. The good news was he was en route—he and his team would get them out of here.

They threw Mollie into the cell and she staggered into her mother's arms. Angered, Nan rushed the closing door, directing a kick at the closest Craing. She connected solidly to his stomach, driving him backward onto the catwalk. Startled, the other three jumped back. That was all King Caparri needed to make his move. He reached through the bars, his arms outstretched. Two necks were caught in strangleholds, by thick forearms and strong biceps. Two simultaneous *cracks* indicated both Craing soldiers were now dead. The king let their limp bodies drop down to the catwalk.

Dira yelled as she saw what was about to happen. "No!"

But her screams had no effect on the two remaining Craing. Both soldiers raised their weapons and fired into King Caparri's holding cell. The blasts were sufficient to catapult him backward, into the rear of the cell. He remained standing for several moments, as if suspended, but then slowly slid down to the deck where he lay motionless.

"Father! Oh my god … Father!" Dira continued to scream … pleading for the king to say something … to show her he was still alive.

The Craing soldiers sneered at the captives and headed back toward the lift, dragging the corpses of the two dead soldiers behind them.

Nan, in the cell closest to the fallen king, moved to the bars separating them. "King Caparri!" She reached an arm through the bars and was able, barely, to touch his face. Dira continued to cry out from the cell on the opposite side.

Mollie joined Nan's side and in a soft, almost whispered, voice asked, "King Caparri?"

His eyes opened. "Dira … you need to stop that relentless screeching. I'm not dead, but hearing you howl is making me wish I were." He slowly turned his head in his daughter's direction and gave her a weak smile. He then turned his gaze toward Nan and Mollie. "You must be Mollie? I've heard much about you. You and your sister are brave little girls. Like my own Dira, you don't shy away from a fight."

Mollie smiled at that. "We're not actually sisters, you know. Boomer and me."

"I do know that. But I suspect you are, in most ways … now, let me rest." With that, the king drifted into unconsciousness.

Nan turned back to Dira, who was leaning against the bars of her cell. "He's breathing … I think he was just stunned."

Dira took in a tight breath and nodded. A faint smile crossed her lips. "I thought I'd lost him."

★ ★ ★

Boomer had the distinct feeling they'd figured out how to track her movements. Four separate groups were closing in on her position from four separate directions. She hurried along a corridor while flipping through one wrong HUD menu after another. *Where is it!* Each time she thought she'd figured it out, she discovered it was just another dead end. She cursed her father for keeping her in the dark about the workings of the battle suit. *Wait ... this might be it.* She followed the prompts and a new menu came up ... she found it! Now she needed to figure out the coordinates of where it was she wanted to go. She glanced at the life icons approaching her position and quickly turned down an intersecting corridor.

The plasma blast struck her visor, propelling her backward and onto the deck. Unhurt, she clamored to her feet and saw the approaching army of Craing men rushing toward her. With a fast check of her HUD, she saw there were just as many coming up behind her. She was trapped.

She knew the suits had plasma weapons integrated at both wrists. In fact, she'd passed through the menus for those several times by mistake. She needed to bring the weapons into a ready state ... so they could be accessed from the primary HUD screen at all times. *Now, where was that setting?* More plasma blasts were hitting her battle suit, nearly knocking her off her feet again. As the Craing soldiers converged on her, front and back, she quickly spun around, not wanting them to get close enough to grab her. There were now sixteen Craing soldiers surrounding her. All were armed and yelling for her to stand still and raise her hands. It was only then that she noticed she'd found the weapons menu. She toggled the activation prompt. The integrated plasma weapon's icon was now added to her primary HUD screen. She straightened her arms out and fired. The kickback on her shoulders was enough to spin her body—which was a good thing, because it allowed her to rotate like a top while continuing to fire at the soldiers. One by one they went down. She had no idea what strength setting she'd put on the wrist weapons, but it seemed to be effective. Charred black holes appeared in the chest, arms, and faces of the Craing soldiers. When they fell to the deck they didn't get back up. With a moment's more practice, Boomer felt in control and could use her wrist-mounted weapons with fairly accurate results. The last of the Craing soldiers had given up and were now running down the corridor. She let them go. She wasn't about to shoot them in the back. There'd be nothing sporting about that.

Boomer looked around the deck at the carnage she'd caused. She felt bad for what she'd done. She didn't know how a girl her age was supposed to feel after having done something so ... what was the word ... *cut-throat?* But it was either shoot or be captured. She turned her attention back to her HUD. She was finally getting the hang of it. She easily found the phase-shift menu again and went to work figuring out the coordinates settings. Then she called up the proximity overlay screen. She toggled it on and instantly a faint line diagram of the ship showed her position and, more importantly, where her mother, Mollie and Dira were being held in actual pinpoint reference to everything else. Ten seconds later, there was a bright white flash and she was gone.

CHAPTER 35

Mere seconds before Jason could give the command to phase-shift away, *The Lilly* was struck by repeated plasma fire.

"All hell's breaking out, Captain," Orion said, not taking her eyes from the tactical console. "The battle's on ... they're coming from all flanks. Locally, the *Tigress*, *Rosenthal*, and *Gordita* are under attack by four Craing cruisers and a battle droid."

"On screen!" Jason had been afraid this would happen. Those who meant the most to him were held captive by Ot-Mul, thousands of miles away—but, for now, he couldn't abandon this position. Added to that, the *Gordita*, a heavy cruiser named by Mollie, held a special place in his heart. The old Craing ship and her crew had once saved his bacon and he'd like to return the favor.

"Cap ... the war is on. Virtually every Allied ship ... all our fleets ... are engaged in fighting the Drac-Vin. And more enemy warships are en route to our position."

Of course they are, Jason thought. *Crap!* There'd be no ducking out for a quick rescue mission anytime soon. "Listen up, everyone ... we've learned a lot over the last few years. We know how to defeat the Craing. We're smarter and far more capable. Gunny, synchronize your actions with the Helm. Don't waste time trying to bring down their shields. We're going to conduct four consecutive phase-shifts that will put us right in the middle of each cruiser's bridge compartment. Is that clear?"

Orion and McBride exchanged quick glances. Jason watched as Ricket entered the bridge and moved to his side. He half expected Ricket to object, but no objection came. "Do it! Go!"

McBride was bent over the helm console—still working out the phase-shift coordinates. Gunny was now standing and, Jason guessed, probably beefing up their shielding to key or vulnerable areas around *The Lilly's* hull. She turned toward Jason. "We can do four phase-shifts but we'll need to recharge after that ... don't forget, we also have that droid to contend with."

"You have your orders, Gunny."

"Aye, Captain."

Jason watched the overhead display. The three gleaming white U.S. warships were taking a beating from the four, nearly identical, drab, brownish-gray Craing cruisers ... but not from the droid. *Why is it just sitting there? Why hasn't the droid attacked?*

"Ready!" McBride said.

"Go," Jason repeated.

The first phase-shift took them from open space into darkness. The overhead display showed the inside, the guts, of the first Craing cruiser; off to the side, an exposed portion—open to space—could be seen where the Craing ship's bridge used to be. Atmosphere was already rushing outside from where *The Lilly* breached the vessel's hull. A whirlwind of unsecured equipment pieces, and more than a few bodies, flew towards several gaping fractures. *The Lilly's* hull instantly displaced whatever matter it came into contact with. Then the second flash occurred and, once again, their overhead display showed the inside of another Craing cruiser. This time they seemed to have phase-shifted directly into the middle of the cruiser's bridge—superimposed on top of it. Jason figured the crew's death was instantaneous. After completing two more phase-shifts, two more bright-white flashes, *The Lilly* returned to open space.

"Report," Jason said.

"All four Craing cruisers are down for the count, Captain. The *Tigress, Rosenthal,* and *Gordita* have taken on damage, but they're still in the fight."

Jason brought his attention back to the battle droid, which hadn't veered from its position. And then, with incredible speed, it did move.

"Droid's engaging the *Rosenthal,* Captain," Orion barked.

"Target that droid," Jason commanded. Before further orders could leave his lips, the battle droid flew headlong into the *Rosenthal*'s mid section—breaching her hull and disappearing from view. Not too unlike *The Lilly*'s action against the four Craing warships.

Orion added a new segment onto the overhead display and Jason could see the droid moving inside the ship's structure—like a parasite eating its victim from within.

Jason knew the U.S. warship was already lost. "Nuke that ship, along with the droid."

Orion wasted no time firing four nuclear-tipped missiles. At the close distance of three hundred miles, the *Rosenthal* became a ball afire in less than two seconds. In the vacuum of space, the flames dissipated nearly as quickly as they'd begun.

"Droid's still alive and kicking, Captain," Orion said.

All eyes were on the display. The battle droid, looking no worse for wear, was making for the Tigress. Damn it to hell!

"Captain, perhaps now's a good time to send out the MagBots?" Ricket asked.

Jason at first almost ignored the interruption, then turned toward Ricket. "They're ready? Now?"

"Yes, Captain. I've integrated their dispersal into tactical. They fire from missile tubes four and five."

Gunny didn't wait for Jason's command. "Firing tubes

four and five!" She turned toward Ricket, "Do you fire a Magbot?"

Ricket nodded. "Although you probably didn't need to fire both tubes. I believe you just emptied our entire arsenal."

Jason was only half-listening to their discussion. His eyes were on the above display and the tiny little swarm about to overtake the larger, now slowing, battle droid, which had turned to engage the MagBots.

"Zoom," Jason said.

The feed, now full frame, showed in incredible detail both the battle droid and the close to one thousand smaller, mechanical droids. The latter moved in unison, like a flock of birds, or a swarm of bees. At the last moment, the MagBots split into two, then three, separate groups. The battle droid fired its plasma weapon, its turret head spinning left and right, picking off MagBots one at a time. As the three swarms overtook the battle droid it moved into the black cluster—all becoming one—in an almost fluid-like dance.

"The combined gravitational properties of the MagBots have brought the battle droid under their directional control, Captain."

"I can see that, Ricket. They appear to have distracted it … but the damn thing is still a threat … still lethal."

Ricket gestured toward the display: "They are small and no match for the battle droid on their own, but massed together like this, they are quite powerful."

Then Jason noticed the MagBots were using their magnetic properties, singly, to attach themselves onto the battle droid. Some were still fired on, destroyed by the battle droid's lethal plasma gun, but far less frequently. As if wearing a thick black cloak, the battle droid became totally engulfed. Astonished, Jason continued to watch, as the battle droid became nothing more than a ball.

"What's happening now?" Jason asked.

"The battle droid is expending huge amounts of energy

to free itself. It cannot. It will completely exhaust its power reserves in a matter of minutes."

"That's wonderful, Ricket! You've come up with a way to defeat these things."

"I'm sorry to say that what you've just observed will not, in all likelihood, happen again. That battle droid and the other two remaining droids have been in constant contact. They will not fall prey again to a trap like this one. They will adapt."

"That's unfortunate," Jason said, instantly discouraged.

"But they do have a few other tricks up their sleeves ... is that the correct phrase, Captain?"

Jason didn't answer his question. Instead, he posed one of his own. "Are those MagBots still viable?"

"No, Captain. Like the battle droid, they have exhausted their power reserves."

"You have more cooking?"

"Many more. You'll have another batch here in *The Lilly* in nine minutes."

"Captain ... ten Craing cruisers approaching."

Ricket placed a hand on Jason's sleeve. "Captain, may I have that one?"

"Which one?"

"That battle droid."

"Why? It's dead ... useless."

"Oh, no. Not useless. I may be able to reprogram it. Manufacture a replacement power cell."

"Then yes, Ricket, you most certainty can have it. Have Grimes phase-shift a shuttle there, and Billy or Rizzo can grab it. They'll need to hurry, though. We're about to have company."

CHAPTER 36

Ot-Mul watched with frustration as his second battle droid was incapacitated—neutralized by some kind of droid swarm, and then snatched up by a shuttle deployed from The Lilly. The Assailant stayed undetected while it moved stealthily into position. Temporarily hidden from the ongoing fight on the front line, Ot-Mul couldn't take his eyes off his main objective for any extended timeframe … but he needed to ensure Captain Reynolds continued to suffer for his past actions too.

While his heavily armed ship could not phase-shift like the two Caldurian vessels, the *Assailant* could do something they could not—it could become invisible. The warship's cloaking shields had proven to be a game-changer. You can't shoot what you can't *visibly* see or what you don't detect on sensors. But he was not ready to engage Captain Reynolds directly; not yet. He would, for now, continue to shred the Allied forces and to keep his two remaining battle droids at arms' length from the Caldurian ships.

After checking on the status of the overall battle, Ot-Mul was pleased to see the Allied forces weren't faring well, es-pecially in the skirmishes where his battle droids were ac-tive. And where the Assailant had participated. And added to that, his successful capture of the captain's family and the one called Dira—he knew the captain must be emotionally wrung by now. Good. He let a rare smile cross his small slit of a mouth. This was what he'd aimed for. He had to savor these moments—not rush to end things. That's when mistakes happened. Now, he needed to up the stakes. He knew the Allied forces called his combined fleets, from space comms chatter, Drac-Vin. Ot-Mul said it out loud, "Drac-Vin." It had a nice sound to it.

"Admiral, our cruisers are approaching. Shall we join the fight?"

"No, Captain Gee. For now, I'm satisfied keeping *The Lilly* occupied. Our eight ships are expendable. Let's just hope their captains aren't totally incompetent, as I need a little more time. Bring us back to the front line."

★ ★ ★

Admiral Reynolds split his time between the bridge and the ready room. He was responsible for captaining the *Minian* when engaged in battle, while his high military ranking and experience conferred upon him the top leadership position—supreme commander in charge of the Allied forces' overall strategy. He rushed back to the ready room where three officers—Captain Michaels, Captain Jones, and Lieutenant Commander Richards—sat around the conference table locked in heated discussion.

"They're fucking wiping us out, all along the Montrang system ... look for yourselves," Captain Michaels shouted at the other two. He got to his feet and stood in front of the primary display and pointed to the logistical view of a section of space. Clearly, red enemy icons outnumbered their light blue ones. The disparity was continuing to grow as he stood there. "We just lost two more light cruisers in the time it took me to stand up. We're spread too thin." Michaels looked relieved to see the admiral enter. "Sir ... we need to pick our battles ... not attempt to take them on from every flank."

"Thank you for your input, but put a sock in it, for now.

There is reason behind what seems like obvious madness, Captain. We hold a strong visible presence at each one of our strategic positions. We are losing assets, yes, but our current positioning also provides another critical function … we're keeping the enemy occupied until we can successfully deploy a counter attack."

"What counter attack? When does that happen? Because at this rate, we haven't anything left to go against the enemy with."

"Ricket has the *Minian's* phase-synthesizer churning out a new secret weapon, something called MagBots … lots and lots of the things."

"Excuse my language, Admiral, but where the hell are they? I won't have a fleet to return to in ten minutes."

"Just settle down, Captain; getting your panties in a knot won't accomplish anything." But, the truth was, the admiral was equally frustrated. He brought two fingers to his ear and hailed Ricket.

"Go for Ricket."

"The MagBots?"

"I had to halt their production, Admiral. I've changed the code so the Bots can be more autonomous as well as adaptive—"

The admiral cut him off mid-sentence. "Don't spout that technical bullshit to me right now, Ricket. I need those things now, and I need a hell of a lot of them."

"The first of the MagBots are being phase-shifted into the *Minian's* weapons ordnance depository as we speak, Admiral. Please instruct your bridge crew to be judicious in their deployment. Just a few go a long way with these Bots … where a thousand can do the job well, ten thousand easily overkills."

"I understand. How many do we have to work with?"

"A few million, and counting. These Bots cannot be produced on the fly—phase-synthesized—as most of the *Minian's* other ordnances are. Too complicated. Also, please realize this large quantity of Bots won't go as far as you would think ... not when dealing with tens of thousands of enemy warships ... not to mention, their two remaining battle droids."

"Fine. How are things going on *The Lilly*?"

"No damage; we're engaging four, excuse me, now three, Craing vessels while our phase-shift system recharges."

"I want to know the instant that happens. *The Lilly's* needed elsewhere."

"I'll let the captain know, sir."

"Thank you, Ricket." The admiral cut the connection and turned back to his three commanders. "Looks like we're back in business. At the very least, we should be ready to even things up a little. I need to know the hot spots ... where we're most vulnerable ... not just where your own assets are located. The *Minian* will phase-shift in, deploy MagBots, then move on to the next hot spot. You have three minutes to come up with a deployment strategy and get it off to my helm commander." The admiral didn't wait for a response. He'd been hearing the voice of his bridge tactical officer, Lieutenant Porter, in his NanoCom—there were incoming fighter drones.

★ ★ ★

The admiral entered the bridge, his eyes leveled on the overhead display.

"They really want to bring down the *Minian*, sir. Enough so, they've redeployed close to three thousand warships to our current position. Their combined force of drone fighters alone comes to ten thousand. This is a major assault, Admiral," Porter informed him from tactical.

The admiral appraised his own, significantly smaller, assets on the logistical display: a mix of five hundred cruisers, fifty smaller destroyers, and one dreadnaught. They couldn't stay in their present location, opposing the enemy, and still deploy MagBots at strategic locations throughout the Allied forces.

"We're not staying."

The bridge went quiet—all heads turned toward the admiral. The admiral's temporary XO Captain Craft looked ready to come unhinged. "Hold on, Admiral. Leave now and you're putting a death sentence—"

"Spare me the lecture, Captain," the admiral said. "First things first. Tactical … deploy one hundred thousand Mag-Bots. Direct them evenly into one hundred of the closest-approaching warships. Deploy our own Caldurian fighter drones; they shouldn't have a problem going up against the Craing fighter drones." The admiral addressed the comms station. "Seaman Peralta, contact the others … let them know we're not abandoning them … that we'll be back … just as soon as we make some deliveries."

"Aye, sir."

"Helm, do you have the deployment coordinates from Captain Michaels?"

"Aye, sir. Just in."

The admiral turned back to Porter at Tactical. "MagBots?"

"Deploying now, sir."

He turned his attention upward, toward the wraparound display, and watched on a zoomed-in feed as several heavy cruisers came into contact with what looked like a swarm of bees. Thousands of bees. The display segment again zoomed in. The little MagBots were moving in tight unison—swirling—funneling around several of the big Craing warships.

"What the fu—" Seaman Peralta caught himself mid-swear and shut his mouth.

The admiral was equally astonished. The grouped together MagBots traveled at incredible speeds, exerting magnetic pulses and creating powerfully disruptive fields. And then it happened: One of the Drac-Vin heavy cruisers began to waver—then slowly spin lengthwise, stubby wingtip over wingtip. One by one, five other nearby cruisers started to exhibit the same phenomenon.

"The centrifugal force ... G-forces ... alone will kill everyone on board," Peralta said.

Now, twenty heavy cruisers were spinning, and the Mag-Bots moved out, exiting the now- disabled vessels—moving toward other Craing ships within the fleet.

"Drac-Vin have their hands full here. Let's hope our drone fighters fare as well. Helm, phase-shift us to the first of our drop-in coordinates."

"Aye, sir. Phase-shifting now."

In a bright white flash, the *Minian* disappeared.

CHAPTER 37

Bristol didn't like having his sleep disrupted. He tried covering his head with his pillow, but the persistent *ding ding ding* tones continued. He sat up and glared at the cabin hatch.

"Who the hell is it?"

The AI said, "You have a visitor, Seaman Bristol. Jack is waiting for you."

"What the hell does he want? Tell him to get lost."

The persistent dinging tone ceased and the AI became quiet. Bristol fell back and closed his eyes.

"Jack would like me to deliver you a message, Bristol."

"Uhhg! I … am … trying … to … sleep!"

"He says it has to do with your brother."

Bristol sat up in bed and looked over to the hatch. "Open it."

The AI did as asked and the closed hatch disappeared. Jack, the Zoo's caretaker, dressed in familiar green coveralls, peered inside.

"Come in!" Bristol ordered.

Tentatively, Jack took two steps in and looked about the small, dark crew cabin. As his eyes adjusted in the dimness, he found Bristol lying in bed. "It's about your brother."

"Yeah, I heard. AI … secure the hatch."

The hatch reappeared, again solid, and the cabin lights came on.

"What about my brother?"

"I was doing my rounds this morning. Same rounds I do every morning—"

"Old man ... just get to the point. I don't give a rat's ass about your rounds."

"Your brother ... Stalls ... was standing ... looking in from the portal window from HAB 12."

"What did he say?"

"I don't know."

"What do you mean you don't know? Were you there or not?"

"I can't hear what's going on within any of the habitats ... you do know they're not actually here, on *The Lilly*, don't you? It's a portal, not a direct window."

"Of course I know that! Just tell me what he was doing."

"He was banging on the portal window, trying to get someone's attention. He was mouthing your name, Bristol, over and over again. That's why I'm here."

Bristol nodded and began chewing on the inside of his lip. He wondered what his brother wanted. Probably to get out of there. Well, he couldn't blame him for that. "Okay, I'll be down in a minute."

★ ★ ★

Bristol had Ricket's long string of Caldurian alphanumeric digits on his virtual notepad. Bristol wasn't stupid. He knew his brother and how conniving he could be. Escape would not be an option. He gestured for him to get back ... far back away from the portal window. He waited while Stalls walked twenty paces back. Stalls did as he was told, clearly annoyed. Bristol indicated for him to get even farther back. He moved over to the HAB 12 portal access panel and started entering the code. It irritated him that Ricket could recite the code from memory. He entered in the final ten digits. His brother, still back within the alien environment, looked nervously over his shoulder every so often.

Beep beep beep. The portal opened.

Bristol walked to the now open portal.

"Hey, little brother, it's good to see another friendly face," Stalls yelled.

"I'm surprised you're still alive ... thought you'd be a Serapin's lunch or dinner by now," Bristol said, happy to see Stalls still among the living. His brother looked a mess—his jump suit was grimy, spotted with several rust-colored splotches. Bristol surmised the stains were dried blood. He also looked tired ... and something else. Happy. "What do you want? You know I can't let you out of there. The captain would throw me out an airlock, or worse, put me in there with you."

"No, little brother, I don't want out of here," Stalls said, with his typical cocky smile. "I'm finding this place quite interesting. I've discovered a few ... surprising aspects ... things I can work with. But I do need a few things from you."

"Um ... I don't know. Like I said, the captain—"

"Just a few things. I am your brother, Bristol. Are you going to deny your own flesh and blood a few necessities ... things that can keep him alive? Come on ... you know what this place is like."

"What is it you want?"

"I need a way to recharge my weapon power packs, for one. Some kind of recharger unit. I also need one of those larger weapons you have on board ... I think you call them multi-guns?"

"Is that it?" Bristol asked.

"More jump suits. I found water, but I need a few changes of clothes, for between washings. And one more thing ... I'd like a way to communicate with you. It gets lonely in here."

Bristol was not used to seeing this more vulnerable side to his brother. He thought about his last request. He knew NanoCom worked within habitats to a certain extent, but Stalls didn't have any internal nano-devices. Bristol needed to come up with something he could wear—something rugged that wouldn't need recharging. "Give me a few hours. I'll see what I can come up with."

"I knew I could count on you, little brother. I'll be in your debt."

"Uh huh … okay, whatever."

At that moment, the portal window timed out and closed between the two brothers.

"You can't give him that stuff. You know that, right?"

Bristol turned around to see Jack standing nearby, sweeping the corridor, a broom handle gripped in both hands. Bristol shrugged, as if he didn't care one way or another. He'd just have to return when the old fart was asleep, or shoveling elephant shit in HAB 4.

Bristol returned to his quarters and sat down at his small desk, which looked like a narrow countertop. Over the last few months, he'd transformed the small desk into a fairly adequate work area. He scanned the row upon row of small, stacked component containers containing a diverse range of technologies: Craing, human, Caldurian and numerous others. He began opening little drawers and pulling out the components he'd need to build suitable communication gear for his brother. He checked the time and saw he had about an hour before his shift started on the bridge. Everyone now did doubles: battle station time. Fine … he could sleep when he was dead.

★ ★ ★

Bristol had everything ready to go. He'd run out of time and had to give up the idea of building a communication device from scratch. He checked the time again and saw he had ten minutes before he was expected on the bridge. He had to move fast. He looked at the long duffle bag lying on his bed. He was taking a risk here. Going against the direct orders of the captain. He hadn't a doubt Captain Reynolds would throw his ass into HAB 12 to join his brother if what he was about to do was discovered. That would only happen if Jack caught him.

Bristol pinched the two recess sensors on the SuitPac to initialize his battle suit. As the helmet enveloped his head and the HUD came alive, Bristol went to work, isolating the coordinates of the Zoo. Jack's life icon was not there. Now or never ... he snatched the duffle off the bed and phase-shifted back to the Zoo.

He stood within the Zoo's main corridor; to his left was the first habitat, where several bored-looking saber-toothed tigers gazed back at him. Across the way was the aqua-blue marine habitat where the Drapple sometimes made an appearance. Bristol continued toward HAB 12. One more check to see if there were any nearby life icons. All was clear. He saw it was now dusk within HAB 12, and his brother had erected his RCM about one hundred feet from the portal window. A soft amber light emitted through the tent-like fabric.

Bristol brought out his virtual notepad and began entering the code on the access panel. Three quarters of the way through the process he saw movement on his HUD. A new life icon appeared, moving in his direction; Jack entered the Zoo. Shit! Bristol continued entering the last few digits. *Beep beep beep.*

"What are you doing there?" came Jack's craggy voice from the other end of the Zoo corridor.

Bristol ignored him and hastened to the portal window. His brother, barefoot, was standing off in the distance.

"I said stop!"

Bristol turned to face the angered, red-faced caretaker. Jack's eyes widened when he saw Bristol's face behind the visor.

"I warned you. There's no way you're going to give that pirate any of the things he wanted."

Bristol pulled the strap of the duffle bag from around his shoulder and hefted the bag onto the ground within HAB 12. Stalls slowly started to walk toward the portal. Bristol held up a hand for his brother to stay back. Stalls stopped, but looked concerned. Bristol indecisively looked at his brother and then Jack. Then, having estimated the portal's timeout period was about to elapse, Bristol turned, grabbed Jack by the shoulders and physically manhandled him ten steps into HAB 12, throwing the old caretaker to the ground. Bristol ran back into the Zoo, just as Jack got back to his feet. "He's all yours," Bristol yelled across to his brother.

Stalls rushed forward, grabbed on to the fabric at the nape of the older man's coveralls, and held him in place. Bristol deactivated his battle suit and waited for it to withdraw back into the small SuitPac device on the belt of his spacer's jumpsuit.

Bristol took another look up and down the corridor to ensure no one else was around. He knew the AI was well aware of his actions … he'd have to worry about that later. He unclipped the SuitPac from his belt and tossed the device to his brother. "Between this battle suit and what's inside that duffle, you're good to go."

"Thanks, Bristol … I mean that. What do you want me to do with him?"

Bristol avoided making eye contact with Jack.

"No! You can't leave me here. Not here … not HAB 12."

"Feed him to the Serapins."

Bristol took a step back, turned, and hurried away toward the bridge. Jack's screams continued to echo within the confines of the Zoo for several more seconds—then suddenly ceased. Bristol surmised the portal window had reinitialized.

CHAPTER 38

Another dozen or two Craing warships moved into their small corner of space. *The Lilly*'s available plasma and rail cannons were firing non-stop. No sooner were the first eight heavy cruisers destroyed or disabled than another ten or twenty ships arrived on the scene. It became clear—it was all part of the Drac-Vin's strategy to keep *The Lilly* fully engaged. The very last thing Jason wanted was for his actions to become predictable to the Craing. Unfortunately, that seemed to be the case. By now, the enemy could calculate ahead; know when *The Lilly* needed to recharge its phase-shift systems. It was no accident the Drac-Vin ships were pushing back hard at the present moment, just when *The Lilly* had finalized its last phase-shift of four.

"Shields are down to forty percent, Captain," Gunny said.

Jason acknowledged Orion with a curt nod, while keeping his attention focused ahead on the wrap-around display. Forty was the shields' lowest percent level yet—the enemy, most definitely, had smartened up.

"Incoming. Fighter drones … three hundred. Our shields are showing several hot spots, too. If repeated firings continue at us, we'll start losing our nanites' protective coating."

"How long before we can phase-shift out of here, Helm?"

"Regeneration times are getting longer and longer, sir. At least five more minutes," McBride replied.

"Gunny, get all available fighters into space. Let Lieutenant Grimes know we need a buffer between incoming fire, and the vulnerable areas showing on our hull."

"Shields down to thirty-five percent and dropping, Captain."

It had been a long time since Jason held doubts of *The Lilly's* capacity to hold its own in a battle. But right now, things were not looking good. Long-range logistics showed a near endless parade of Craing warships heading their way. What he needed to do was get *The Lilly* the hell away from this area of space, but without the capacity to phase-shift they were stranded here.

"Incoming hail, Captain," Seaman Gordon said. "It's from a newly arrived Drac-Vin vessel ... oh ... it's the *Assailant*, Captain."

"Where'd they come from?" Orion asked, her face showing concern.

"Put it on the wrap-around," Jason said.

Jason would know that face anywhere. The cold, beady eyes, the small tuft of black hair at the top of his Craing head, and that little smirking mouth. "Ot-Mul. Nice of you to join the party."

"Thank you, Captain Reynolds. It is so nice to see you again, too. We have much catching up to do. Unfortunately, I am somewhat busy right now ... so many battles ... so little time."

"Don't let me keep you, Ot-Mul. Maybe later, then—"

"Before I go, I'd like to share something with you. Think of it as a special gift from me to you."

With that, the camera feed within the *Assailant's* bridge area changed to a different site. The new location seemed dark and ... eerily familiar. Jason turned toward Gunny. "Can you get a fix on the *Assailant*?"

"No, sir ... it's like she's close, but there again ... not really *there*. I'm working on it."

There was movement on the display. Jason saw metal bars, a familiar-looking metal railing, and the decking of a narrow catwalk. This was a Craing cruiser's prison ... where hundreds of small holding cells were stacked above the ship's Grand Sacellum. They were watching the current feed from, Jason guessed, a weapon-mounted camera. Three Craing soldiers were walking in front of the moving camera. What Jason saw up ahead, in the dim light of the holding cells, captivated his attention. Nan was in one, several holding cells away ... and Dira, too, in another, farther holding cell. Their faces looked tight and tense as the Craing soldiers approached them.

"Gunny, get a team dispatched to those coordinates. Billy, Rizzo, Traveler, and whoever else we can spare. I want them in a shuttle and en route in—"

"All shuttles are currently in use. We've been using them to phase-shift into enemy ships."

"Find one! Do it now!"

"Aye, sir," Gunny said, turning her attention back to her board.

Jason continued to watch the feed. The Craing soldiers were now standing in front of Nan's holding cell. He now realized a second person was in her cell, too. Mollie! Jason's heart was ready to pound out of his chest. Was he about to see a systematic execution of everyone he loved? Was this kind of vengeance Ot-Mul's strategy all along? To rip Jason's personal world apart before his Drac-Vin fleets decimated what remained of the Alliance?

Where was Boomer? Jason watched the feed, wishing he could manipulate the camera ... see into the other adjoining cells. *Damn!* He never felt so helpless. Then he remembered, of course ... Boomer had escaped; she was hiding elsewhere on that ship. Would she try to rescue them ... should he even suggest such a thing? She wasn't even ten yet ... but then again, she was a little girl who could kick the ass of most full-grown men.

A loud metal *clang* brought Jason's attention back to the here and now. Un-oiled hinges screamed as a cell door swung open. *The Lilly's* bridge became deadly quiet. Everyone knew what was about to happen.

"Gordon, get Boomer ... hail her NanoCom ... wait ... she's hailing me."

Jason heard her childlike voice. "Dad?"

"Where are you, sweetie?"

"Um ... I think I'm ... let me see—"

"Can you phase-shift to the upper decks, into the holding cell area?"

"I just tried to do that. I ended up in the Grand Sacellum."

"That's good! You're very close ... you need to get up to the ..." Jason stared at the feed. Something was happening. He didn't quite understand. The soldier with the gun-mounted camera let the muzzle of his weapon drop—all Jason could see were legs—a scuffle was taking place. Now there was angry shouting. All three—Nan, Mollie and Dira—were screaming, "Stop! God ... Stop ... Oh no ... please don't—"

Jason's eyes blurred as tears welled in his eyes. Suddenly, the Craing soldier's weapon pointed higher up again. Jason's breath caught in his chest as that same weapon fired—bright flashes, once, twice, three times.

King Caparri's face looked distorted from agonizing pain. His upper torso showed three charred, smoldering plasma strikes. His eyes, glazing over, fluttered, and shut. His body crumpled and fell out of view. Dira's screams continued—the camera found the now-prone body of the dead king, lying on the grimy deck. Dira's screams had turned into desperate sobbing.

The soldier's attached camera pointed toward Dira's cell. She sat huddled on the deck, her face in her hands. Another sound. One of pain. Jason recognized Nan's voice.

"Oh God ... Oh my God."

The camera jerked around and found Nan. She looked scared—her face white—eyes wide and full of fear. "He's coming!"

Both Mollie and Dira began talking to her, asking her

what was wrong. Dira was back on her feet and reaching through the bars. "Nan … you need to sit. Get down on the deck and listen to me."

Nan screamed, "I'm having the baby … I'm having the baby—"

The video feed disappeared. On the overhead display was only Ot-Mul's contemptuous face.

"Put it back! I need to see it! You fuck … put it back!" Jason screamed toward the overhead display. "I am going to kill you. Know that … I'm going to rip your ugly Craing head from your neck and—"

"Now now, Captain Reynolds. Please. Let's maintain some level of professionalism." Ot-Mul took a sip of something from a cup, licked his lips, and set the cup back down, out of view. "I must say … that was about the most exciting bit of … what do you humans call it? TV? I, for one, was riveted. Weren't you?"

"I'm going to kill you." Jason was having a hard time staying on his feet. He was well aware he was about to come completely unglued.

"I know you want to get back to the show. Truth is, I do, too." Ot-Mul smiled with excitement. "Who will be next? Huh … perhaps your pretty ex-wife and her little infant cub. They can join the recently departed King Caparri … or maybe it will be Dira? A beautiful specimen … I must say, I've had certain … thoughts … about her myself. Or should it be your child, Mollie? That is her name, yes? Well, stay tuned … we'll talk again in a few minutes."

The feed went black.

CHAPTER 39

Boomer's next attempt to phase-shift to a higher deck was more successful this time. She'd accomplished a phase-shift—but it was only as high as deck two, and she was now standing within a holding cell there. There was screaming coming from above. She heard her mother's voice. *Something is coming.* What was coming? Whatever it was, Boomer knew she needed to get up there—fast. She had a pretty good idea now how to move—how to set her phase-shift coordinates to a higher access plane via the virtual representation of the ship on her HUD. She needed to avoid phase-shifting right on top of someone; her shift coordinates would need to be some distance away from where she saw the life icons were—where they were all bunched together. She double-checked to see where, exactly, she needed to go—it was deck eight. The screams from above had dissipated somewhat. The Craing soldiers there had moved away, were now descending on the lift. Good. Boomer phase-shifted.

Again, Boomer found she'd phase-shifted into a holding cell. She was directly across from the four-sided, expansive open space, just opposite her mother and Mollie. *But why's Mom lying on the deck with her clothes off?* She squinted her eyes, then used the HUD's zoom capability. *Oh my God!*

"That is the most disgusting thing I've ever seen!" Boomer wasn't aware she'd spoken the words out loud. Both Mollie and Dira looked across the open quad-space in her direction.

"Boomer?" they said in unison.

"I'm coming," she replied. She picked a location direct-ly across the catwalk, just outside their holding cells, and phase-shifted.

She appeared on the catwalk in a flash and looked down into the holding cell. Sure enough, a small head protruded between her mother's legs. Boomer involuntarily cringed.

"She's having a baby ... don't make that face!" Mollie said, reprimanding her.

Her mother screamed.

"Keep breathing ... in and out ... in and out," Dira said.

Boomer knew what having a baby was all about. She also knew Dira was a doctor and needed to be in there, next to her mother. She set her sights on the far side of Dira's cell and phase-shifted inside. Dira quickly glanced at her but another scream from her mother pulled her attention away. Boomer rushed forward, put both arms around Dira's shoulders, and phase-shifted again.

They were now within the same cell as Mollie and her mother. Dira rushed to Nan's side and began to help support the emerging baby from her mother's body. Boomer looked at Mollie. "That's so gross."

"I think it's cool," Mollie said.

The little body was out and now in Dira's arms. "It's a boy!" she said, but her excitement was short-lived. The baby wasn't making any sounds. Nan was crying. She said, "He's too young ... he's too young to be born ... oh my god ..."

Tears were running down Dira's face. Using two fingers, she started gentle chest compressions on the baby's tiny upper torso. She shook her head.

"I have an idea," Boomer said. She immediately initiat-ed the steps necessary to retract her battle suit. As the last of the suit segments compressed back into the little SuitPac, she moved over to Dira's side. "Can we put the baby in the suit?"

Dira looked at Boomer, her brow furrowed; then, as re-alization took hold, a smile spread across her lips. "Give it to me!" She took the small SuitPac device and placed it on the infant's chest. Carefully, she placed the baby on the pile of Nan's discarded clothing. She compressed the two activation sensors, quickly taking her hand away.

The SuitPac quickly began to transform. A tiny version of the battle suit took shape around the infant's little body. Within seconds, Boomer was looking into the tiny helmet's visor. The baby still wasn't moving. His eyes were closed.

Nan said, "Give him to me." She held the suit-clad baby in her arms and stared into the small visor. "Breathe ... oh god ... please breathe, little one."

The baby made a noise. Not exactly a cry, more like a gulp or gasp. Boomer looked to Dira with a hopeful expression. "Will he be okay?"

Dira moved to Nan's side and stared at the baby's face. "I think so. I think you've just created a preemie's incubator, Boomer. The battle suits have all kinds of life support functions ... even limited MediPod capabilities. You saved the baby's life, Boomer."

Nan reached for Boomer with her free arm and pulled her close. Her tears fell and splashed onto the baby's small visor.

Mollie giggled, "Look, his little fingers are grabbing my fingers."

Boomer watched as the tiny fingers wrapped around Mollie's pinkie. She turned to see Dira looking toward the adjacent cell. The body of a large man, dressed in fancy clothes, lay inside. It was the king ... Dira's father.

Boomer moved closer to Dira and put her arms around her, holding her tight.

"I'm sorry, Dira. I wish I had two SuitPacs with me."

Dira placed a comforting hand on top of Boomer's arm. "It wouldn't have helped ... he was beyond saving. He died bravely, though. He was a brave and wonderful father. A magnificent leader ... the people's king."

The sound of lift motors engaging eight decks below brought them back to the reality of their situation.

Dira looked around the small cell. "Nan, you need to get your clothes back on … we need to hide the baby. Damn! I'm not supposed to be in this cell." She looked at Boomer and shook her head. "You're not even supposed to be here."

The sound of the lift's rise within the open shaft spurred them to move quickly. Nan handed the baby to Dira and pulled on her dressy slacks. She swayed on her feet and looked as if she was going to topple over. While Nan finished buttoning her blouse, Dira looked about the cramped holding cell for a place to hide the baby. "There, in the corner." Dira placed the small shape in the SuitPac down on the deck. "Boomer, sit here, right in front of him, and try not to move. Block their view of him, okay?"

Boomer nodded and did as she was told. She watched her mother finger-brush her hair, so as not to look like she'd just delivered a baby. Mollie stood in front of her mother, while Dira stepped back, close to her own cell, and leaned against the bars.

The lift reached deck eight. As the metal gate clanged open, Boomer closed her eyes and settled her breathing—willing her pounding heart to slow down. A sense of calmness returned to her entire being, just as Chief Petty Officer Woodrow had taught her months earlier. She'd need to be a warrior now … not a helpless girl. She closed her eyes and listened. There were four of them. Short steps … all were Craing. She waited for them to come into view down the catwalk.

Three soldiers were in front, the fourth following behind them. All were armed with energy weapons—the one in the rear had his weapon held high—something mounted atop the muzzle. Boomer guessed it was a camera. The Craing soldier was videoing this … recording them being killed?

The four soldiers halt in front of their holding cells and become uneasy. They look back and forth in the cell Dira occupied before. They yammer between themselves. Boomer listened, her internal nano-devices translating their Terplin. They're certain the one with violet skin had occupied a different cell. What they're not sure of—had another soldier moved her into this other cell? Were new orders issued they're not privy to?

The soldier out front seemed to come to a decision and was already unlocking the cell door. The other three had their weapons trained inside. The door hinges screeched loudly as the door swung open. The baby began to cry ... softly at first, and then louder.

The first soldier moved into the cell and roughly pushed Nan and Dira out of the way. Boomer, still seated with her arms around her knees, looked up into the face of the Craing soldier. His head turned side to side, like a confused puppy, as more crying sounds came from behind her. Boomer waited for him to make his move. Then, she'd make her own move.

CHAPTER 40

They were operating with all available hands on the bridge. Like Jason, his XO, Lieutenant Commander Perkins, was well into his third straight duty shift. "Shields down to ten percent," he announced, "and we're about to lose both the starboard and port-side rear plasma cannons. It's the heat … it's affecting them all."

"Phase-shift system up?" Jason asked.

"It should've been back alive two minutes ago," McBride said, turning in his chair, apologetic. "We're completely flanked from all sides … we're literally at the center point of several thousand enemy warships, Captain."

"Seaman Gordon, hail the *Minian* … scratch that … put out a distress call to the *Minian*."

"*Minian*'s waiting for her own phase-shift system to recharge, sir."

No sooner was Jason on his feet than *The Lilly* violently jerked, sending him sprawling across the command chair. "Damage report!"

"Shields down. We're now taking direct hits. Multiple hull breaches reported on decks one and three."

The Lilly shook violently again, and the sounds of plasma fire, bombarding the ship's hull, were loud enough to hurt Jason's ears. "Make an announcement … everyone's to activate their SuitPacs, if they haven't done so already." He hesitated before saying the next words … words he had hoped he'd never have to say: "Be prepared to abandon ship."

The young communications officer looked back at Jason with a shocked expression. Perkins moved over to the comms panel and made the announcement himself. Jason triggered his own SuitPac while registering the dire enormity of their present situation, showing on the logistics segment of the wrap-around display. He wondered whether he was now the last person alive in his family. Thoughts of Mollie and Boomer flooded his emotions with love and sadness. His next thoughts were of Nan and their unborn child. Then, of Dira, and the true love they'd never experience together. Perhaps, it was most fitting, he would soon be joining them.

Jason stared at the numerous individual display segments. Each view revealed a disheartening display of overwhelming Drac-Vin superiority. *There's so many of them.*

"Captain ... we have partial phase-shift capability," McBride said.

"What exactly does that mean, Ensign?"

"The systems never fully recharged. We may be able to get out of the epicenter of this mess, though."

"Give the orders for our fighter pilots to phase-shift back into the flight deck."

It felt like hours but, in reality, was less than two minutes for *The Lilly*'s last fighters to be secured back on board.

"Do it, Ensign! Put us somewhere out of the action ... Go!"

The flash came and went. All sounds of battle vanished and Jason was able to stand straight, without grasping the back of his command chair. "Where the hell are we?"

"Thirty thousand miles out from our previous position," McBride said.

Orion added, "It's a relatively unoccupied section of space. But venting to space ... Drac-Vin sensors will pick us up, eventually."

Jason sat down. "Casualties?"

"Twenty dead. Forty injured. Medical is overwhelmed,"

Perkins said.

"So what's left that's still working?"

"Critical damage throughout the ship," Perkins said. "We still have minimal sub-FTL propulsion; one plasma cannon and one rail cannon are operational; but with the phase-syn-thesizer only partially working … most of our phase-shift ordnances won't be available."

"How about shields? Any chance we can get them par-tially back up?" Jason asked Orion directly.

"No … no way, Captain."

The finality of her statement took the rest of the bridge crew by surprise. Without shields, their fate was sealed. It was only a matter of time.

Ricket entered the bridge, breathing hard. He rushed to the command chair and tried to catch his breath. "Most of the DeckPorts are down."

"Got any good news to share, Ricket?" Jason asked, at-tempting a weak smile.

"Perhaps I do, Captain." Ricket turned back towards the entrance to the bridge.

Jason didn't immediately comprehend what he was look-ing at. The entrance was blocked by something. A battle droid! Jason jumped to his feet and raised his arms, ready to fire on the mechanical beast.

"No, Captain!" Ricket shouted. "This droid's been re-pro-grammed. That's where I've been the last five hours. Revising it into an Allied asset, plus giving it several new capabilities."

"Captain, a ship … the *Assailant* has arrived in our local space," Orion said. "She's obviously fast and has cloaking de-vices. She wasn't anywhere near here several moments ago."

"We're being hailed, Captain," Seaman Gordon said.

This was what Jason had dreaded—Ot-Mul resuming his live-video feeds. Who would be slaughtered before his eyes this time? Were any of them even alive still? He contemplat-ed not answering the hail. Just finish up the battle between them, between warships. But he had to know ... one way or another.

"Captain, no less than a thousand ships are moving into this area of space. They're positioning themselves—flanking us again."

"A new hail, Captain—"

"I'm well aware Ot-Mul wants to resume his—"

"No, Captain ... there's a second hail. It's from ... an Admiral Ti."

Jason then realized all the approaching vessels' icons, as viewed on the logistical display segment, weren't the same bright red color. Some were green, indicating they weren't exactly Allied ships—but more like *possible* friendlies. What he was seeing was the lost fleet of the Mau. Once, close to four hundred warships had abruptly left the sector. Not totally un-expected—especially since the Craing, specifically Ot-Mul, and his Vanguard fleet of dreadnaughts, had destroyed their planetary system ... in essence, making the Mau fleet of four hundred ships homeless. And yet now, here they were.

"Please have Admiral Ti stand by. Put Ot-Mul on screen."

The Drac-Vin commander looked positively ecstatic. He was making no attempt to hide his jubilance. "Ah, Captain ... I was beginning to wonder if you were going to speak with me again. Perhaps your feelings have been hurt. I mean ... look at that ship of yours. It's ruined. Beyond repair. But that is not why we are now speaking, is it? Our TV show is about to resume ... Shall we?"

"One second, Admiral. I have one last command to give my tactical officer first." Jason turned away from the Craing commander. "Gunny ... I need you to do something for me." In the span of sixty seconds, Jason quietly outlined to Orion exactly what he wanted her and a small team to immediately do. She nodded and quickly left the bridge. Jason turned back to the overhead display.

Ot-Mul's smug face was no longer there. Instead, Jason

was again looking at a live feed—panning over one dark holding cell after another within a Craing heavy cruiser. And the same four soldiers, seemingly, were moving down a catwalk. Jason's throat felt dry—constricted. His heart pounded in his chest, realizing what he was about to see would be the end of someone's life ... someone he loved.

The same weapon-mounted camera chronicled the visual story, playing up on the display segment above him. *The Lilly's* bridge had gone quiet. The Craing soldiers reached the metal door and unlocked it. A weapon's muzzle, holding the camera, was leveled on Nan. Her face was devoid of all color—white, and moist with perspiration. She looked sick ... terrible.

There was something odd, though. Why ... how ... had Dira managed to get into the same cell? Following was a commotion—pushing and shoving—Nan and Dira were shoved violently against the cell's bars. Mollie went sprawling in the opposite direction. Jason didn't understand. *What's Boomer doing there, huddled on the deck?* How did that happen? It didn't matter how ... Boomer was about to die. Jason was about to see his little girl shot, from point blank range, and there was nothing he could do about it.

Ot-Mul's face returned to the screen. He held up his palms. "This! This ... is what it's all come down to, Captain. Before I give the order for that little girl to die, I needed to see your face. I wanted to hear you beg for her life. I also wanted to let you know I've already dispatched my battle droid. It will reach your already-decimated ship within minutes. In mere moments, everything, and everyone, important to you, will be ... no more. But first, you will witness your daughter's demise." The feed switched back to the holding cell.

CHAPTER 41

Orion and Sergeant Jackson phase-shifted together onto the Mau vessel within minutes of the captain's directive. No convincing, or haggling, was necessary to bring the Mau officer on board with Jason's plan. Ti, a Mau admiral, had lost everything to the Craing—to Ot-Mul—and her need for revenge was as strong today as it had been months earlier, when she watched her home planet atomized by the Vanguard fleet of dreadnaughts. Ti made it clear—she alone would confront the Drac-Vin leader ... in person ... in her own way.

Orion was instructed where on the Mau vessel to phase-shift to and that only two could go. The given phase-shift coordinates put Orion and Jackson into a large holding area. They arrived in a white flash and immediately Orion checked her HUD. Although they weren't visible to her yet, on her HUD she saw they were surrounded by no less than twenty armed Mau icons.

"I hope you're right about them being friendly, Gunny," Jackson remarked over their open comms channel.

"I'm right. And I'll remind you again ... this race of people is highly empathic and telepathic. Watch your thoughts and emotions carefully."

"Copy that."

Orion watched as the Mau moved in closer around them. She was well aware of the emotional impact these people were capable of inflicting ... something the captain had reminded her of prior to them phase-shifting onto the Mau ship. The second they set foot on the vessel, the Mau's collective feelings of hopelessness and despair began to infiltrate her mind. She wondered if Captain Ti's call to *The Lilly* was only a ruse to get them on board—but then again, what would be the point? Two Allied crewmembers held on board a Mau ship would hardly represent a strategic coup. No, what she was feeling was nothing more than the negative charge these people were projecting. She now understood why no more than two people were allowed to phase-shift here. It was for her and Jackson's own good, as well as for that of the Mau.

The Mau admiral, evident by her dark purple-blue robe, approached closer to them. What Orion felt was extreme uneasiness. She caught herself counting the seconds she'd be forced to remain in the Mau officer's presence.

"I am Ti, admiral of the Mau fleet. I thank you for agreeing to our terms and for your presence here. The Mau fleet has withdrawn, as I discussed with your captain. Admiral Ot-Mul should have little concern about our ship's presence in this sector. Only when I give the command will my warships return and engage the enemy."

Orion watched as the Mau officer communicated with her, finding it fascinating. Ti's wide, gaping mouth never actually moved, and her face was truly one of the more frightening things Orion had ever seen. She was certain she'd have nightmares about her for a long while to come … but, given the current state of affairs, nightmares were surely the least of her problems.

Ti gestured to the Mau circled around them. "These Mau, specially chosen for this mission, have powerful empathic capabilities."

Orion moved as if her skeletal system was devoid of movable joints. Stiff and awkward, she turned to look at Sergeant Jackson.

"Will your phase-shift technology enable us, all together, to transport onto the Craing vessel?" asked Admiral Ti.

Orion did the calculations in her mind and nodded. She

and Jackson, wearing additional rhino-warrior's phase-shift belts, were capable of transporting over a thousand pounds each. The Mau were slight, waif-like people. There would be no over-weight issues here. "It will not be a problem. Time is of the essence ... we are ready now, if you are."

★ ★ ★

Billy Hernandez checked his weapon for the fifth time in ten minutes.

"I'm betting that multi-gun is as ready now as it was two minutes ago," Lieutenant Grimes said from the pilot's seat.

Billy, seated next to her in the cockpit, didn't reply. She was right. It was a nervous reaction to a stressful situation. He didn't like that they were such a small team for this mission. He looked over his shoulder into the cabin behind him and saw the entirety of his team—Rizzo and Traveler.

"What we've pieced together," Grimes continued, "was that the U.S. heavy cruiser was infiltrated by the Drac-Vin. Once on board, the Craing crewmembers were systematically expelled out an airlock. Readings show the remains of some three hundred dead Craing two hundred miles from here."

Billy transferred the stub of his cigar from one corner of his mouth to the other. "They didn't need an army to infiltrate and capture that cruiser."

The stark-white U.S. heavy cruiser was now within view and Grimes made no attempt to slow their progress. "I agree ... all they needed was one battle droid. Looks like there's a security force of approximately fifty Drac-Vin stationed at various key locations around the ship. You sure you'll be able to handle them? I could tag along, in case you need backup," Grimes added.

"No. As long as that battle droid is no longer around, this should be a piece of cake."

"Then what's got you so nervous?"

"Everything important to the captain is locked within that ship. His world stops revolving if something happens to any of them. It's a big responsibility, and I value his friendship. I don't think he'd ever forgive me if this mission failed."

Grimes thought about that for a moment, then shrugged. "Guess you better not fuck it up then."

Billy got to his feet. "Circle around the block a few times. I'll let you know when we're on our way off."

"No worries. I'll be listening on the open channel," Grimes replied, tapping the side of her helmet. She brought the *Perilous* in close to the cruiser—like other Caldurian vessels, there was little chance they'd be picked up on sensors. Grimes reached out and put a hand on Billy's arm. "According to my readings, they're being held in the holding cells ... on one of the top decks. They're not alone. I'd hurry."

★ ★ ★

The three phase-shifted onto deck eight, forty yards away from the cell where the prisoners were held. Billy was instantly aware of distant screaming.

"Don't shoot her! She's just a little girl ... please ..."

It was Nan and she was obviously terrified. Billy opened a joint channel to the four prisoners' NanoCom: "This is Billy ... we're here ... get down ... get on the deck. Do it now!"

After a moment's hesitation, they all complied. Billy, Rizzo and Traveler closed in on the holding cell, and halted twenty feet away. Ahead were four Craing soldiers—two inside the cell and two outside. The four were armed with energy weapons pointed at their prisoners' heads.

"Rizzo, you take out the two on the catwalk ... I've got the other two."

They brought their weapons up and fired simultaneously, without hesitation. Four flashes, four plasma bolts—the

Craing soldiers fell where they stood. Billy checked his HUD to verify the soldiers were indeed dead. Five yellow life-icons remained, which didn't visually match what he was actually seeing: two kids, Nan, and Dira. Billy entered the holding cell first. Nan, sitting on the floor, was holding on to Boomer, while Dira hugged Mollie.

"Whoa ..." Rizzo said, noticing the tiny black battle suit Nan now cradled in her arms.

Billy unslung a small pack from over his shoulder, opened it, and retrieved four water bottles. While the prisoners drank, he clipped a new SuitPac onto each of their belts or waistbands.

Traveler, standing guard on the catwalk, grunted and raised his own multi-gun. "More are coming."

Billy helped Nan to her feet. "Time for each of you to initialize your battle suits." Nan, Mollie, Boomer, and Dira complied. Billy hadn't taken his eyes off the baby's little face behind the visor—he asked, "Got a name for him yet?"

"Not yet. Any suggestions?"

Billy shrugged his shoulders and then smiled. "William's a good name."

"Like in ... Billy is short for William?" she said.

The sound of plasma fire erupted all around them. Drac-Vin soldiers were shooting from across the quad opening. Mollie took two blasts to her chest and was kicked backwards, into the metal bars. Within seconds, Billy was aware soldiers were firing in at them from multiple vantage points. He ensured Mollie was all right and communicated to Grimes that they were on their way out of here. He was about to start phase-shifting them over when Dira rushed from the holding cell.

"We need to get out of here ... Dira," Billy said, catching up to her on the catwalk. She was taking plasma fire to her battle suit as she looked into another cell.

"I need to bring him with us ... bring him home."

Billy now saw what she was looking at. "That won't be a problem, Dira," Billy said. He phase-shifted into the holding cell where the king's body lay motionless. Again, he removed his pack, opened it, and withdrew an extra SuitPac.

CHAPTER 42

Jason watched the action taking place in real-time on the multiple feed segments above him; as the battle raged on around them, two other significant events were also unfolding. Orion and Jackson were with the Mau, and Billy's team was safely on board the captured U.S. cruiser. But it was Billy's helmet cam perspective that currently captured Jason's attention. He watched as both Mollie and Boomer, then Nan and Dira, were rescued. Then he saw the small bundle Nan was holding in her arms—and, with a glimpse into the tiny visor, his infant son's face could be seen. Some part of his tension subsided ... like sun breaking through the clouds after a terrible storm. Jason wanted Billy to stop, just hold there; let him gaze for even a few moments at his baby son's beautiful face. Billy was then following behind Dira. Her formal princess attire—replaced by a battle suit. She stopped on the catwalk and looked in at her deceased father.

"Captain, the battle droid is closing in on us," Perkins said.

Jason's eyes stayed on the display. Billy retrieved an extra SuitPac from his pack and was preparing the king's body for transfer ... Then, Jason was given one more glimpse of Dira's pretty face. He wondered if he would never see her again—hell, if he would see any of them again.

Jason's attention was next drawn to another feed segment on the display.

★ ★ ★

As expected, Ot-Mul was well prepared for their arrival. He was, in fact, waiting for them. Orion was first to phase-shift onto the bridge of the Assailant. She arrived arm-in-arm with ten Mau, including Admiral Ti. Two seconds later, Sergeant Jackson, arm-in-arm with ten more Mau, also flashed onto the vessel's bridge.

Even caught off guard, Ot-Mul's forces were quick to react. With little time to actually count them, she estimated there were one hundred or more Craing combatants moving around the periphery of the bridge, as well as other soldiers now interspersed between the crewmembers sitting at various consoles and virtual holographic screens.

Energy weapons came alive and soon the large bridge was ablaze in a firefight. Three Mau were instantly killed before Orion could return fire. In the near distance, on a raised platform sat Ot-Mul and three other commanders. He, too, was gripping an energy weapon—prepared to join the fight.

But there was little for her to fear. Ot-Mul and his crew were no longer capable of doing much of anything. Orion was well aware that the despair and hopelessness she was now experiencing empathically from the Mau was not personally directed toward her or Jackson. But she was feeling it just the same—like nothing she'd ever experienced before—abject, total fear. She was afraid to move; afraid to look into the bleak, stricken, faces around her, as the remaining team of Mau slowly took up positions throughout the compartment.

Orion realized theirs was a truly devastating weapon, one there simply was no defense against. She watched as Ti slowly moved forward, in the direction of Ot-Mul. He, too, stood paralyzed—eyes wide with fear.

The Mau admiral, slowly and patiently, went for him. Her two arms rose up, almost gracefully. Her elongated face seemed mournful—her mouth a black abyss of everything dark and morose. Orion could almost feel Ot-Mul's fear and saw a wet stain spread across the front of his trousers as his bladder emptied. Unrelenting terror had thoroughly engulfed him.

Ti was now upon him—her fingers encircling his small, angular head. He did not resist ... could not resist.

As her own emotional suffering seemed magnified tenfold, Orion was forced to look away. Ot-Mul screamed—frightened beyond all comprehension. With tears in her eyes, she thought, just let it be over soon.

And then it was. Orion felt all fear around her dissipate, like a massive weight lifting from her shoulders. What remained was quiet stillness. The Craing crewmembers were dead. Every face contorted, grimacing—scared, wide-eyed, out of their minds.

Several Mau personnel assumed positions at various posts, including navigation. It was clear the Mau were claiming this ship as bounty.

Orion approached the Mau admiral and the small body lying at her feet. Well aware Captain Reynolds was watching the events taking place via her helmet cam, she knelt down and stared at Ot-Mul's paralyzed, dead, grimace.

★ ★ ★

Jason looked at the distorted face of what could only be described as that of pure evil. Ot-Mul was dead. He died perfectly. Appropriately. The war would end; probably, immediately. The hundreds, perhaps thousands, of Drac-Vin fleets—currently spread across all Allied space and beyond, would surrender ... would undoubtedly return home to the Craing worlds.

"The second battle droid is en route, Captain," Perkins said, now standing at Tactical.

And that's the irony of it all, Jason thought. The two remaining battle droids were unconcerned with Ot-Mul's sudden demise, oblivious to what death or defeat really meant. No, these two technological beasts would not stop until they had fulfilled their simple pre-programmed objective: Destroy *The Lilly* … and kill the captain of the ship.

"Captain, Admiral Reynolds sends his congratulations on defeating … and I'm quoting here, 'the little Craing bastard.' He also says the *Minian* is at least an hour, maybe two, away from reaching us. He said the *Minian* was embroiled in a battle with one of the battle droids. It suddenly moved off, but they've taken on damage to multiple ship systems, including their ability to phase-shift."

"Thank you, Seaman Gordon. What's our own propulsion status, XO?"

"*The Lilly*'s drives have been destroyed. Our phase-shift system is still down. We have no propulsion capabilities whatsoever, sir."

He turned to Ricket. "So … Where's your converted battle droid?"

"I've nicknamed the droid *Defender*. It was deployed to open space several minutes ago." Jason followed Ricket's gaze to the above display. Sure enough, a new live-feed segment was tracking the movements of Ricket's battle droid. He hadn't noticed it before, but with a larger turret head, this droid was somewhat different-looking from the other battle droids.

"Seaman Gordon … patch me through … ship-wide."

The young, red-haired communications tech looked back at Jason with concern.

"It's okay … go ahead and patch me through, Seaman." Jason collected his thoughts, let out a breath, and began to speak. "This is your captain speaking. Our ship … *The Lilly* … which, for many of us, has been our home-away-from-home for years—has fought her last battle. With shields and weapons ravaged … without propulsion or phase-shift capabilities … in all likelihood, she will be destroyed by the two approaching Drac-Vin battle droids. You, her crew, have served this ship

... and me, her captain, with honor and dignity. With all my heart, I thank you. Although we have won the war, the price paid for the same was this magnificent ship. All crewmen are to report to their immediate command personnel, and then proceed with abandon ship procedures. You will do so now, without exception. I wish you all my very best and bid you a fond farewell."

The silence on the bridge was crushing. All eyes were on the captain. Jason saluted and held his hand high to his head while he turned and met their eyes one by one. They saluted him, their captain, in return. "Go now ... that is an order."

Seaman Gordon wiped a tear from his cheek. "The *Perilous* is requesting—"

"Denied, Seaman. You know procedures ... all shuttles are to first assist with any abandoned crew personnel. Just patch me in to Lieutenant Grimes."

"Captain ... let us get you out of there," Grimes said on comms, sounding somewhat exasperated.

"Listen to me carefully, Grimes. In a few minutes, *The Lilly*'s crew will phase-shift into open space and need rescuing. They are your responsibility. Tell Billy that I specifically have no intention of committing suicide. We'll get out in time. Tell him and the others that. And Grimes, if anyone even attempts to rescue us, shoot them ... preferably set to stun only."

"Aye, Cap ... I promise," Grimes said.

"Seaman Gordon, direct Gunny Orion and Sergeant Jackson to remain with the Mau until they can be safely transported to an Allied vessel." Jason stood, and in a far less friendly tone said, "Out! Every one of you, off this ship now!"

The AI kept repeating the same ship-wide announcement: *Abandon ship ... Abandon ship ... Abandon ship ...*

He watched as the last of them—Ensign McBride and Perkins—hesitantly stood, nodded one final time at him, then scurried from the bridge.

Jason looked down and stared impatiently at the sole remaining crewmember. "Did you not understand the orders?"

Ricket returned the stare with the same intensity. "This ship, *The Lilly*, is as much a part of me ... as it is you, Captain. I could no more abandon this ship than you. There are still two battle droids out there that need to be destroyed. Let me, my friend, help you accomplish that."

"Just as long as you know what you're signing up for, Ricket. There is no walking away from this ... not this time."

"Then there is much to do before our demise ... it looks like *Defender* has engaged the first of the two battle droids."

CHAPTER 43

Jason's next order of business was to find the setting for his internal NanoCom and turn it off. It all started with an incoming hail from Billy—soon there were others: Mollie and Boomer, then Nan and Dira. He didn't accept their incoming communications. What was he going to say to them? His affairs were in order. In the event of his demise, they each would receive a personal letter—personalized letters he'd spent hours writing the previous evening. Surprisingly, his father had not attempted to communicate. He must understand the situation. Yes, of course he did.

Right now, he needed to dedicate what little time he and Ricket had remaining to at least attempt to destroy the two battle droids.

Ricket, standing at Tactical, gave Jason a rundown on what weaponry was still available to them: one plasma cannon, and one rail gun—although munitions, for the rail gun, were practically nil.

Jason accepted an incoming hail from Admiral Ti. Her face appeared on the above display. Perhaps it was only his situation, but she no longer looked quite so frightening to him. In her own Mau way, she was quite attractive.

"I see you have given the abandon ship order to your crew. I would like to assist you with the destruction of those three droids."

"Actually, one of them is ours. I thank you for your offer. Truly, I do. But I must decline."

"I do not understand, Captain. It is the least we … I can do."

"Admiral Ti, I've witnessed, first-hand, the destruction these battle droids are capable of inflicting. I suspect that once they have completed their objective—destroy *The Lilly*, as well as yours truly, and maybe attempt then to destroy the *Minian* … they will self-destruct. But if you fire on them, or if any other vessel does, they will engage you as an enemy and quite possibly destroy you. I cannot allow that. Cannot allow any more casualties. One way or another, the battle, the war, ends with me."

"I understand, Captain. I wish you well, then. You will be remembered, and honored, among our people. Goodbye." Her connection terminated. The logistics segment expanded out as Ti's new vessel, the *Assailant*, moved away. Within seconds, there were no other ships present in local space.

Jason kept a steady eye on the two enemy battle droids and Ricket's *Defender*. Over the past few minutes there was little direct confrontation. Not unlike a cat and mouse game, the three droids were moving about in space—darting one way then another—but not actually engaging each other.

"What the hell is going on?"

"Ot-Mul's droids are finding it difficult to maneuver around *Destroyer*, Captain. I had little time to integrate new technology, but one thing I could add was the droid's ability to phase-shift short distances. As you can see, it has the other two battle droids perplexed—they're not finding a way to approach *The Lilly*."

"Well, in the meantime, let's take advantage of that. We have one functional plasma cannon and one partially-working rail gun … let's give them something else to think about."

"*The Lilly* has no shields, Captain; those droids will return fire."

"Well, this waiting around is driving me crazy. Better to engage them with what we've got."

The Lilly's one remaining plasma cannon came alive, targeting the two battle droids. Even though both returned fire on *The Lilly*, Jason still knew it was the right course of action. *Destroyer* was moving in—attacking one of the battle droids. In a flurry of spinning reflective blades, the two combating battle droids fought with a combination of weapons fire from their turret heads, along with driving their mechanical arms and fists into each other. Unfortunately, they were so mutually engaged, the other battle droid was clearly making progress approaching *The Lilly*.

"What's that sound, Ricket?" Jason asked.

"The rail gun just came online. We have approximately thirty seconds of non-explosive projectiles available," Ricket said.

Jason watched as the approaching battle droid slowed, its own phase-shields beginning to heat up and turn red. "I think the rail gun's getting to it."

"The battle droid's shields just went down, Captain."

Ten more seconds and the rail gun expended all its munitions. The gun went quiet, but there was nothing left of the battle droid—it was completely destroyed. Jason smiled at Ricket and gave him a big thumbs up. "We might just make it out of this mess, after all."

But he'd spoken too soon. *Destroyer* was no longer faring well. Its reflective, razor-sharp blades were no longer spinning, and at least half were missing—pieces could be seen floating off in space. Ricket ceased firing the plasma cannon. The way the two droids were constantly turning, in such close proximity to each other, it was just as likely *Destroyer* would be hit by friendly fire and not the enemy battle droid.

"Any ideas?" Jason asked.

"Initiate the self-destruct process on *Destroyer* … it may produce a sufficient blast to take them both out."

"Do it … what do we have to lose?"

Ricket brought up his virtual notepad and quickly input something.

Defender was no longer fighting back. Instead, the battered droid was using its two claw-like hands to grab on to the other droid. The enemy battle droid seemed to understand what was going on, and its struggle intensified—becoming almost frantic in its attempt to escape.

"Ten more seconds, Captain, and *Destroyer's* power system will go critical and blow."

Five seconds later, *Destroyer,* missing both arms, was careening off into space by itself, the result of a substantial final kick from Ot-Mul's battle droid. In the distance, *Destroyer* imploded.

Ricket brought their remaining weapon back online. Plasma bolts hammered the droid's phase-shielding. Although it probably underwent damage in its fight with *Destroyer,* Jason couldn't see any. The battle droid was darting left, then right, then right again. Slowly, it was progressing forward, towards its single-minded, pre-programmed destination.

★ ★ ★

Admiral Reynolds stood with his hands on his hips as he yelled up to the chief of Engineering, three decks above him, standing on a catwalk. The admiral had opted to see what was happening first hand in bringing the *Minian's* propulsion system back online. Just minutes earlier, he'd been sitting on the bridge—waiting, having far too much time to think about the ensuing battle *The Lilly* was presently engaged in. Reports, coming in from *The Lilly's* crew earlier ordered to abandon ship, along with the ship's long-range sensors, were painting a dire picture. *The Lilly* was down for the count. Jason and Ricket had opted to stay behind. Of course they would. He'd have done the same. But that didn't mean he had to sit uselessly by and wait for the inevitable to happen. He was optimistic the *Minian* could destroy that battle droid.

"Chief, save me the technical bullshit ... what's the time-frame?"

The bald-headed Engineering chief leaned over the railing above. "Drives are still an hour out from going online. If I can expedite things within that time-frame, you'll be the first to know."

"You said that an hour ago, damn it!"

"Yeah ... well, that was before I knew the true extent of our damage. You're welcome to come up here and fix it yourself, Admiral. We need to extricate a section of scrap metal ... probably enemy fuselage, from an antimatter containment chamber. We screw this up and we'll all go *poof* ... so, please, let me get back to work."

The admiral didn't bother answering him. He was already strutting toward the *Minian*'s onboard Zip Farm. He hurried in the direction of the closest DeckPort, wondering if the *Minian*, too, might have been destroyed by that battle droid if the droid hadn't abruptly left the battle. The damage they'd withstood previously, from hundreds of Drac-Vin warships, was substantial—in all likelihood, the battle droid would have finished them off. As it was, not one of his fighters was in condition to phase-shift to *The Lilly*'s present coordinates. He considered sending a shuttle, or several shuttles, but he'd be sending them to their death. A shuttle was no match for a battle droid. He'd already deployed several cruisers—they'd reach *The Lilly* soon, within the hour, perhaps. Again, they'd be no match for the droid, and, most likely, even more lives would be lost attempting to engage it in battle.

The admiral entered the Zip Farm. Row after row of ten-foot-high by thirty-foot-long huge pieces of equipment occupied every inch of five separate compartments. He continued down one row, then up another. Black, heavy looking, and somewhat greasy to the touch, the Zip accelerators looked similar to early nineteenth-century locomotives. He'd been told their technology was developed on Alurian, a planet in the Corian Nez constellation system, one hundred-and-thirty light years from Earth. Caldurians uncovered this technology about ninety years ago and it changed everything. It was the reason why the Caldurians, for the most part, packed up and left this present reality for distant parts unknown, into the multiverse. With the *Minian*'s drive propulsion down, and the phase-shift system offline, the capabilities offered up by the Zip Farm could be their best opportunity for any kind of space travel.

The admiral found the tall Caldurian standing with two other crewmembers. They stood at a bank of mounted controls that took up an entire bulkhead. More Alurian technology was in here, also heavy and black—greasy-looking.

Granger looked up as the admiral approached. "It doesn't seem to be damaged, Admiral. Accelerators are all functioning fine."

"Excellent, then we can make use of—"

"Admiral, it's no different than what we did back at the Orange Corridor, months ago. But then we had some propulsion capability. Heading into the multiverse isn't your answer … you need to get the *Minian*'s drives back online."

"That's an hour of time *The Lilly* doesn't have," the admiral said. *An hour of time my son doesn't have to survive …*

CHAPTER 44

They had just reached the armory when *The Lilly* violently shifted beneath their feet. Both Jason and Ricket went down hard on the deck. Immediately, the alarm klaxon blared. Lights flickered and the AI's voice crackled to life: "Attention, there has been a hull breach ... Attention, there has been a hull breach."

"What's happening, AI?"

"Hull breach and enemy incursion on Deck 5. Environmental conditions have been compromised. Atmosphere is venting to space."

It was no surprise; the battle droid had breached the ship. "AI, I want constant video feeds of the battle droid's position continuously updated on my HUD."

"Yes, Captain Reynolds. The battle droid is currently ripping through inter-deck plating ... I believe it has locked on to your position."

Of course it has, Jason thought. *That thing's never going to stop tracking me. Me ...* The Lilly *and the* Minian *are in its cross-hairs. That won't ever change. Anyone else around me will be collateral damage. This technological assassin must be destroyed now.* But the truth was, he and Ricket were ill equipped to do that on their own. Almost tenderly, Jason placed an open palm on the closest bulkhead. Sadness and regret weighed heavy on his heart. Jason knew what had to be done. Ricket was watching him. Although the words remained unspoken, both knew what had to be done.

"Listen ... we need to slow it down. Whatever security

droids, maintenance Bots, anything … put them in its way."

"Yes, Captain Reynolds."

Ricket, already on his feet, disappeared into the armory as Jason scrambled after him. Ricket held out a multi-gun for him and took one off the rack for himself. Jason watched his HUD, now focused on Deck 5, as three hovering security droids fired on the battle droid. There was movement behind it, a flight deck maintenance droid holding what looked like a wrench.

"We need to get to Engineering before that battle droid gets in front of us."

Ricket filled a satchel with a selection of odds and ends, including spare multi-gun power packs, explosive ordnances, and two plasma pistols. Jason grabbed the strap of the satchel and headed out of the armory.

Ricket, close on Jason's heels, caught up to him at the DeckPort. "Captain, we'll want to enter Engineering on Deck 1 … I can directly access the reactor … misalign the collider beams."

They entered the DeckPort together, immediately exiting onto Deck 1. The noise emanating from the deck above them was incredible. It only highlighted what he was viewing on his HUD feed.

Engineering was accessible from all decks, since the massive drive system spanned the full height of the entire ship. Ricket and Jason entered the Engineering access hatch at a dead run. What Jason hadn't expected was the silence. *The Lilly's* dual drive system was always humming along, a constant drone that filled the large, expansive space. Right now, though, there was no sound … no hum.

"Ricket, should I be worried? I mean, other than the battle droid? I don't hear anything."

"That's to be expected, Captain. The drives are down. That's not a problem, in itself. The reactor may still be … for no better term … reactive." Ricket reached a narrow metal ladder and began to climb the rungs as fast as his little hands and feet could move. Jason followed, and asked, "Why not phase-shift where we want to go?"

"We don't want to be phase-shifting this close to the reactor."

Above him, Ricket scrambled onto a catwalk and sprinted to an inset, cubbyhole-like area. Easily ten feet high, and just as wide, the bulkhead before them was filled with transparent tubular containers. Each, depending on its placement, glowed like a neon sign: different hues of greens, blues, reds, and yellows.

"What is this?"

"These are the exposed ends of the collider tubes. I wasn't completely sure they were still activated. But they are."

"That's a good thing?"

"Most definitely, Captain. Now ... if we put enough of them out of phase, misdirect the collider beams ... the reactor will go critical. We'll want to be far away from here when that happens."

"How much time will we have?"

"I can only guess, Captain. Somewhere between five and fifteen minutes."

The sound of distant plasma fire abruptly ceased.

"You better get to it, then. Looks like we're going to have company soon."

Ricket moved closer to a group of tubes at the far right side of the bulkhead. "You stand over there, on the other side. We need to do this in unison. We need to manage the instability so it is at least somewhat synchronized."

"Okay, sure ... just tell me what to do."

Ricket pointed to a set of four small knobs beneath each tube that Jason hadn't noticed.

"These are the manual alignment adjusts ... used to get the tubes into rough alignment when the ship was first built, before the AI had made the necessary micro-adjustments."

"Can't we simply ask the AI to commence a self-destruct procedure or something?"

"No, Captain ... this is not a battle droid. No, the Caldurians did not include such a procedure for an entire ship. That would not coincide with their—"

"Whatever, Ricket! I don't care ... just tell me what to do!"

"Start turning them ... all of them along that side. We'll know when we've turned them enough."

Jason watched Ricket turn the knobs in no particular order and did the same on his side.

He saw that the battle droid had penetrated down into Deck 2, and was rapidly moving toward Engineering.

"We have to get out of here, Ricket."

"Not yet ... it's still not unstable enough."

Jason kept turning the knobs. He reached over his head for yet another set of knobs and heard something on the far side of the bulkhead. "I think the droid's here."

They both listened. It was a whirling, whining sound—and it was getting louder. "What you are hearing is the reactor complaining ... it's very unhappy ... we should leave the ship now, Captain."

"We do that and the battle droid will just follow us out. Track us, until it finds us and kills us. Nope, that thing gets destroyed along with *The Lilly*. We just need to keep it occupied for a few more minutes."

The AI was now repeating a new warning. "Alert, reactor containment is no longer stable ... Alert, reactor containment is no longer stable ..."

Jason was halfway back along the catwalk and running for the ladder when the battle droid crashed into Engineering above him.

He heard Ricket's voice over his comms, "The droid can disrupt the auxiliary power going to the reactor ... we need to get it out of Engineering!"

In a flash, Jason found himself and Ricket in the corridor outside Engineering, on Deck 1. "I thought you said not to phase-shift in here?"

Ricket didn't answer, quickly running down the corridor. Jason had taken three steps when the Deck 2 bulkhead tore open behind him. He turned, taking three plasma strikes directly to his visor; blackened scorch marks made visibility pretty much non-existent. Worse, his HUD was gone. There'd be no way to phase-shift now. Plasma fire was still coming, from in front and behind. Ricket was firing back at the battle droid. In his two tightly gripped fists, Jason physically pried open his helmet's visor—hell, if he couldn't see he was as good as dead anyway.

With the battle droid far closer now than Jason expected, he leveled his multi-gun and fired. He aimed for the small gun-turret head and hoped to disrupt its ability to fire back. It wasn't working. Jason felt his body racked with multiple white-hot plasma blasts. Pain enveloped his torso ... his chest. All it would take now was one shot to his head and it would all be over. He began weaving—darting unpredictably, from side to side. Another blast caught him in the side ... more pain ... excruciating pain. He didn't want to look down at his ravaged battle suit—afraid of what he'd see.

He continued to fire while progressing backward as quickly as his legs could take him. Where was Ricket's weapon fire? With a quick glance over his shoulder he had his answer. Ricket was gone. Had he been shot? Was he hiding behind a hatchway, somewhere along the corridor? The battle droid was gaining on him. Its mirror-like blades spun, and at times Jason could almost make out his own reflection.

Jason stumbled and nearly fell. He needed to get off this corridor, out of the field of fire. He continued to fire at the battle droid ... it was slowing, but still gaining.

A new noise eclipsed those coming from their weapons—the whirling-whining of the anti-matter reactor … Oh God … it was going to blow!

★ ★ ★

Dira and the others on board the *Perilous* stood at the starboard observation windows and watched *The Lilly*. The ship rescued twenty crewmembers and virtually every inch of the cabin was filled. Billy and Rizzo, outside the hull, had given up their seats so others could sit as they waited for the *Minian* to arrive. They kept giving assurances they had plenty of oxygen. Dira could see them suspended outside the *Perilous;* she'd almost be able to touch Billy, if it weren't for the bulkhead. He turned and waved, as though able to read her mind. Her eyes moved back to *The Lilly,* feeling a deep sadness within her at the ship's battered condition—her sleek black hull now pocked and cratered from weapon fire. *The Lilly* drifted lifelessly in space now and Dira wondered if she could, somehow, be brought back to her—

The explosion was immense. Spectacular. The flash was so brilliant that everything turned white, then blue, then, only the blackness of space remained. *The Lilly* was gone. Dira continued to stare at the spot where the ship had been only seconds earlier, and, standing there, she knew Jason was no longer alive. He was gone and she knew it without a single doubt.

Nan and the kids screamed. Someone was asking Grimes if she could read life signs … maybe Jason and Ricket had phase-shifted out in time. Maybe they were still alive. Bristol, sitting next to Grimes in the cockpit, violently shook his head, "No, no, no! Goddamnit! I would be able to detect them on sensors. Look at the fucking display … you see any new life-icons? No … nothing, nothing, nothing!"

Dira wasn't listening, not really. She didn't need to. She already knew he was gone … he wasn't there. Tears blurred her vision. As the same realization reached her heart she wondered if it would keep beating. Did she want it to? She turned her head and saw Nan holding her baby in her arms. Mollie and Boomer were melded into her … their arms encircling one another. They were all weeping.

CHAPTER 45

The *Minian* arrived within the hour. Admiral Reynolds was notified beforehand that *The Lilly* had been destroyed. Lieutenant Grimes told him that there were no indications that his son Jason, or Ricket, had made it out in time. Grimes, obviously emotional, conveyed her regrets; how she'd loved serving aboard *The Lilly* ... reporting to Captain Reynolds. She would miss him.

The admiral expected to see something ... perhaps a scattering of debris floating in space—something tangible. But there was nothing. For four days now, they'd gone through the motions—short- and long-range bio-sensor scans—multiple vessel searches conducted around the clock.

For the admiral, Jason's loss was immeasurably hard. Why now, when the war was finally over? Why now, when Jason had so much to live for?

The admiral was physically, mentally, and emotionally spent. But he wasn't given an opportunity to wallow in despair—far too much to do. Maybe that was a blessing. The *Minian*'s ready room was in a constant flurry of activity. No sooner would one crisis arise, be dealt with, than another would take its place. Currently, he was dealing with tens of thousands of Drac-Vin Craing and other species—alien crewmembers no longer having a home to return to. They were basically refugees. The admiral was finding most of the Allied worlds unreceptive toward their plight; not understanding why they couldn't, or wouldn't, just return home to Terplin, or Halimar, or some other Craing world. Some would ... others, for one reason or another, could not.

At the moment, Nan Reynolds was sitting across the table from him. She looked tired and, understandably, the usual fire in her eyes was gone. She was signing a stack of virtual memorandums and directives. As the still-acting president of the United States, she needed to return to Earth immediately.

She looked up from her work and offered him a weak smile. "You need to take a break. Get some rest before you fall over, Perry."

"I will, I promise."

"I have a favor to ask you."

"Anything," the admiral replied.

"I'm taking Mollie back with me today. But Boomer ... she says she needs to stay. Won't leave here ... not yet, anyway."

"That's understandable, Nan. She's been through a lot. I think staying here, at least for a while, will allow her to stay connected, somehow, with Jason."

"Then you'll let her stay?"

"Of course. In some ways it will make it easier for me, too."

With that, Nan stood, collected her virtual notebook, and came around the table. She gave the admiral a long hug. He felt raw emotion again pull his heartstrings. She stepped back and looked into his eyes. "What will you do now?"

"There's an old '49 F150 I started restoring ... I suppose it's time I finish it."

Nan smiled. "That sounds like a fine idea. Good for you." She waved bye and left the ready room.

The admiral didn't want to spend another second alone in the ready room. He had more goodbyes to say anyway. He left the captain's quarters and headed down the corridor toward Medical. He'd made this same walk on *The Lilly* a thousand times. Although the *Minian's* proportions were of a far greater scale, the two ships were really quite similar. He'd miss *The Lilly*; probably more than he could now realize. He'd also miss

Ricket. To him, the two were practically the same … inseparable … in his thoughts.

He arrived at Medical as Dira was preparing to leave. She was talking to two other medical techs, probably giving them some last-minute insights on working with the advanced Caldurian medical equipment. The technicians looked overwhelmed.

Dira turned toward the admiral as he approached.

"You heading out soon?" he asked.

"In a few. A part of me wants to stay. Actually, a big part."

"How you really holding up, Dira. You going to be okay?"

"I don't know. I miss him. It's funny … sometimes I think I can hear his voice in my head. Is that weird?"

"No, not at all. What will you do now?"

"With my father gone … I have responsibilities back on Jhardon. My home world is grieving the loss of their king."

"We'll miss you … I'll miss you."

"Thank you, Admiral. I hope we can keep in contact … would that be okay?"

"I insist on it," he said, as the two embraced in a final goodbye.

★ ★ ★

Boomer's tears were long since dry. What remained was a combination of resentment and anger. She'd just come from saying goodbye to her mother and Mollie, who were returning to Earth. Her mother had pleaded with her one more time to return home with them. Let her help her through this difficult time. But Boomer didn't want to be coddled. That was the very last thing she wanted. Now, as she walked the *Minian*'s corridors alone, she could think, could try to understand what had happened. *How long have I been walking? Twenty minutes, a half hour?* She stopped at an intersection of two identical-looking corridors. *Where the heck am I?* As similar as this ship seemed to *The Lilly*, it was also very, very different. At nearly a mile long, there were sections—complete decks— she was unfamiliar with. Some decks were closed off—no one allowed access to them. Her father reprimanded her once for exploring a closed deck that contained Caldurian laboratories and was some kind of bio-hazard area. A part of Boomer smiled. Exploring was the one thing she enjoyed doing more than anything else. Here on the *Minian* she'd have weeks, if not months, of exploring ahead of her. And there'd be no off-limits now.

"Are you lost?"

Boomer spun around to see the odd Caldurian man standing off to her right.

"Hello, Granger. No, I'm not lost. Not exactly. I just haven't been in this particular part of the ship before."

"I see." Granger continued to stare at Boomer, then gave her a warm smile. "You know, there are sections on this amazing vessel I think you'd be interested in seeing. I could show you—"

"I ... um ... prefer to be alone. But thank you anyway."

"I understand. There are areas that are unsafe for a little girl. I wouldn't want to see you get hurt. May I make some suggestions?"

She thought about that for a moment. She was kinda lost. A few suggestions couldn't hurt. "Okay, can you show me, after all?"

Granger smiled and looked upward, as if he were thinking. "Let me see ... You've already, of course, visited Medical, the bridge, the armory, and firing range ... probably the habitats—"

"What?"

"The armory, the firing range—"

"No! You said something about ... habitats?"

"Yes. Like on *The Lilly* ... but far larger; a much more comprehensive collection of habitats. There is a habitat that has Magnasium Cluk–Cluks you will love. And, of course, all the HABs you were familiar with on *The Lilly* are here—"

"Just take me … Now!"

CHAPTER 46

Four days, seven hours, and ten minutes earlier.

Jason's multi-gun died, its power pack completely drained. In the distance, on the looming battle droid's far side, Jason saw his pack lying on the deck. Somehow he'd dropped it. Fortunately, the droid was no longer firing back at him. Its turret head was blackened from countless plasma strikes, but the droid's ability to move seemed unaffected. It was now coming directly for him. Jason, limping, turned and ran as best he could down Deck 3's long corridor. *Where the hell is Ricket?* At this point, there was only one place he could possibly escape to—right there, on the left up ahead ... the Zoo.

Jason turned left at the entrance to the Zoo and saw it was completely trashed. Obviously, the battle droid had already been here, prior to finding them in Engineering. *Damn!* He'd stopped paying attention to the droid's whereabouts on his HUD when he was turning those damn knobs.

The Zoo was practically unrecognizable. The habitat portals—windows to other places, other worlds—were gone ... destroyed. Large sections of shredded bulkhead material were strewn around the deck—blocking his progression further into the Zoo.

Jason manhandled a large piece of metal out of his way, off to the side; then, he crawled under another section. Lighting fixtures above him hung precariously down from the ceiling, swinging back and forth like a pendulum.

"I'm here, Captain."

Jason followed the sound of Ricket's voice. Behind him,

he heard the battle droid entering the Zoo.

Ricket was standing at an access panel, located on the side of a habitat portal window that, it seemed, was unaffected. It was HAB 12. "It occurred to me, Captain, we did have one option. A way out of here without the battle droid following us."

"So, out of all the habitats … this is the only one? The only one still intact?"

Ricket, busy entering digits, looked relieved, hearing the familiar three consecutive beeps. "We must hurry, Captain. I fear *The Lilly* is on the verge of—"

The battle droid was crashing through the debris on the deck. Jason could see it quickly approaching, looking as if nothing could stop it.

Jason grabbed Ricket by the collar and pulled him into the portal of HAB 12.

The battle droid followed in their direction and abruptly stopped. It stood there, mere feet away from them, looming. Why was it just standing there? Did it not see them … was it confused? Jason tried to remember how long the portal window would remain open before automatically closing. Then he noticed Ricket still had a multi-gun hanging from a strap on his shoulder. *Should I move?* He had to chance it. Jason dove for Ricket's weapon, yanked it free from his shoulder, sending Ricket sprawling to the ground. Still in the air, he leveled the weapon on the battle droid and pulled the trigger.

The battle droid moved forward, pushing against continuous plasma strikes. One mechanical leg managed to step over into HAB 12. As it moved again, ready to completely cross over, the portal suddenly closed—slicing off the appendage within the blink of an eye. It stayed there propped up against the portal window … as if waiting to be reunited—to be made whole again. Now, through a distorted portal window, Jason watched as the one-legged battle droid lost its balance and toppled backwards to the deck.

Ricket got to his feet and joined Jason at his side. Ten seconds later, they saw a bright white, then blue, flash and the portal disappeared.

They stood together for some time. Neither spoke.

Startled, Jason heard the sound of metal scraping against metal, somewhere behind them. Well aware this was a dangerous place—he was fully prepared to see one or more Serapins ready to attack them from behind. What he wasn't prepared for was Jack, standing there in his green coveralls. Jack stepped down from the open doorway of an old Craing utility craft—the same one left abandoned months ago.

"Captain?"

"Um ... Jack. What the hell are you doing here?"

"I could ask you the same thing. But it was Bristol ... I caught him bringing his brother weapons, and one of those new-fangled SuitPac things."

Jason and Ricket exchanged glances.

"Where's Stalls?" Jason asked, suddenly aware this place was even more dangerous than he first thought.

Jack slowly turned, stared off into the distance, and pointed. "He's up there ... somewhere on that cliff, that little rock outcropping. You see it?"

Jason knew exactly where Jack was pointing. There were few, if any, locations as safe as that one. Twice he'd camped there.

"He surprised me ... thought I'd be left here to die. But twice, he's dropped off cooked meat and water. I'd be dead if it wasn't for him."

"He's a psychopathic killer. Why he brings you food, keeps you alive ... I have no idea. But I guarantee it is for his own needs, not yours. Maybe it's to show he's a changed man ... not the same ruthless killer we've all come to know. I'm sure he thinks the day will eventually come when we'd let him out of here."

Ricket looked around, then back up at Jason. "We could

be here a long time, perhaps indefinitely. I do not believe we can survive both the Serapins, and the pirate, Captain Stalls."

"I'm with you on that, Ricket. How 'bout you let me borrow that battle suit of yours? The one I'm wearing is useless. I'm going to pay a little visit to our pirate friend on the cliff."

★ ★ ★

Jason left the multi-gun with Ricket, telling them to stay put until he returned. He used the battle suit's phase-shift capabilities to get to the base of the towering, five-hundred-foot-high cliff. Halfway up the rocky surface he saw the flat outcropping. He also saw another life-icon on his HUD. If Stalls was wearing his battle suit, Jason knew that he, too, appeared on Stalls' HUD.

He observed Stalls' specific location and decided to phase-shift to the other side of the little plateau area. He set the co-ordinates, phase-shifted, and appeared near the edge, closer than he planned to be. He looked behind him and saw nothing but sky and several hundred feet of vertical rock surface leading far down to the ground below.

In front of him, a line of trees obstructed his view to the rest of the plateau. Doing his best to stay quiet, he crouched low and winced, still sore where the battle droid's plasma fire penetrated his battle suit. His internal nanites would be working overtime for a while yet. He stopped and took cover within the tree line. Up ahead, he saw the distinct outline of an RCM. The tent-like structure sat in the middle of the overhang. Stalls' life-icon didn't correspond to the location of the RCM ... Good, Stalls wasn't home.

Jason moved out of the trees and slowly approached the RCM—using it as cover as he moved into the open. There were only so many places to go. Peering around the corner of the RCM, he saw a campfire and some kind of animal cooking on a spit.

Jason knew exactly where Stalls would be, the only other place he could be. He double-checked his coordinates and phase-shifted there.

The sound of water gently cascading into the natural pond brought back fond memories of when he and Dira swam together here. Swam … other things, too.

Stalls, in the water, floated on his back, his head positioned beneath the waterfall. It looked relaxing. Jason figured there were worse places to be stranded. The pirate was naked and he was singing.

Stalls' multi-gun and a pile of clothes lay on a nearby rock. On top of them rested a small metallic box, about the size of a pack of cigarettes. Jason casually walked over to the clothes and picked up the SuitPac device. He found a nice rock to use as a seat and waited.

Five minutes later, Captain Stalls floated out from the cascading water and stood up in the pool. His eyes locked on to Jason.

"That looked quite relaxing, Captain Stalls."

He looked to the pile of clothes. "You can't. Without that … I'm dead."

"That's not a very positive attitude, Stalls. I've learned to never underestimate your resourcefulness. With that said, you still have much to account for. You're a shit, Stalls; luckily, I've decided to let you live. With that said, I'll let you keep the multi-gun … but I'll be taking the SuitPac, and these too." Jason leaned over, picked up Stalls' clothes, and, smiling, phase-shifted away.

★ ★ ★

Boomer ran into the *Minain*'s Zoo and abruptly came to a stop. This wasn't like *The Lilly*'s Zoo at all. She was standing at a wide, circular entrance, where four separate corridors fanned out before her. Each one, she could already see, had dozens and dozens of habitat windows. It was magnificent … it was huge!

Granger was back at her side. He returned her smile. "I thought you'd like this."

"It's amazing. But I need to find the same habitats that were on *The Lilly*. Take me to them, please!"

"I'm sorry, Boomer. But they're interspersed all over … you'll just have to look for them."

Starting with the corridor at her far left, she ran. As she moved past the habitat windows, her head spinning left and right, she saw amazing, crazy-looking creatures. A dinosaur in one, a walking fish in another. She stopped and took three quick steps backward. It was HAB 4! Alice, her drog, was in here … somewhere. She continued on, slower now, conscious she could easily pass by other *Lilly* habitats. She saw the water habitat, where the Drapple swam. She ran on and on. One window after another, she passed in front of some familiar habitats. Familiar, but not exactly the same: The portals, too, were in slightly different locations—close, but not quite the same.

She walked fast now—a perspiration sheen on her forehead—her hair damp. She just finished the second corridor, and was entering the third, when she stopped and screamed out loud.

Granger came running up, his face full of worry. "What! What is it, Boomer?" She was wide-eyed—her arm outstretched and finger pointing. She screamed again.

Granger looked into the portal window, into the habitat. Dusk was falling on a desert scene: A campfire blazed next to an old, beat-up spacecraft, and three individuals were laughing, looking no worse for wear. "That's my dad … Oh my god … that's my dad!"

EPILOGUE

Jason retrieved two bottles of beer from the cooler. On his way down to the yard he heard the same cursing he'd been listening to for the last hour. *Why in hell does he put himself through this?* He descended the steps down to the gate, opened it, and let it slam shut behind him.

As he entered the scrapyard, Jason stepped on something sharp. *Shit! I should have put on my shoes.* He found the old '49 pickup where it always sat. The hood was up and more cursing erupted from beneath it. Jason placed the cold bottle on the fender and peered down at the little engine block, and the back of his father's head.

"You're blocking my light!"

"Sorry … hey, why don't you take a break?"

"In a minute … I think I've almost got it."

Jason wasn't sure what his father *almost got* under the hood, but he knew his father, in his own way, was happy. He was away from the necessity of making life and death decisions; the crushing stress of too many people wanting too many things from him.

Jason plopped himself down on the rickety lawn chair and took a pull from his beer. The warm Santa Ana wind was kicking up and he used his shirtsleeve to wipe his forehead. Two months had elapsed since his release, by Boomer, from HAB 12 … actually, now HAB 331, within the *Minian's* Zoo. Nothing was the same now. Maybe that was for the better. Billy and Orion were out there somewhere, catching zombies for the government. They'd started their own little business, had asked Jason to join them. But that life had no appeal for him, not in the least. More than half the population was gone. But the country, the world, was on the mend. And on the positive side, people around the globe had stopped fighting each other—Jason wondered how long that would last. He wondered if the planet had really returned back to some nostalgic period in time where helping each other actually trumped taking advantage of one another. Was there ever such a time?

Nan was still the president and not just loved by the people, but beloved. It had turned out that a woman president, at least this one, was a very good thing. Eventually the *peovils* would be dealt with … from what he'd heard from Billy, they were making good progress around the world.

Ricket was still on the *Minian* and, along with Granger and Bristol, getting the ship fully operational again. Jason's thoughts moved to his friend Traveler, and he smiled. Over the last few months, the number of rhino-warriors had grown exponentially. The habitat they'd been living in had not been large enough to support their now independent society. What had surprised Jason the most was that Traveler and the others wanted to live on Earth. The last Jason heard was a significant section of North Korea had been appropriated for them. With a late influx of *peovils* into that geographic area, much of that section of the world was unpopulated … at least by humans.

His father extricated himself from the old Ford. He found the beer and brought it to his lips. He faced Jason and leaned against the truck's front grill. "I over-tightened a sparkplug. I can't get it the hell out off there."

Jason laughed. "Maybe I can loosen it. That, or we'll get one of the droids … Teardrop's around here someplace."

His father continued to stare at him. "What are you going to do with yourself?"

"I'm doing it … absolutely nothing."

"You're going to drive me crazy."

"I'm going to drive *you* crazy?" Jason answered with a smirk.

But Jason knew he was driving his father crazy, and everyone else, too. Nan repeatedly told him to find something to do with his life. If he was adamant he wasn't going back into space, then he needed to do something ... *hell, maybe I'll get a job.*

"You know, Dira's been leaving me messages. Says you've been avoiding her ... won't talk to her."

"Dad, that's none of your concern. But, if you have to know, I've decided there's no sense in pursuing that relationship. Think about it ... she's certainly got more important things going on in her life than me ... like overseeing an entire planet. So, just drop it, Dad ... that ship's already sailed. Got it?" Jason scooted his chair closer to a stack of wheel rims—he sat back and stretched out his long legs. "I'm fine right here."

The admiral was no longer looking at his son. Off in the distance, where an old Cadillac sat next to a battered school bus, two figures were approaching. "Looks like we've got company."

"Well, they can just turn around and head back the way they came," Jason said, taking a swig of beer. Shuttles had been coming and going—phase-shifting in and out from the underground base all day. He'd head down there tomorrow; see what the hubbub was all about. He glanced in the direction of the path again. He now recognized them. It was Ricket on the left and Dira on the right. She was now close enough for him to see that she was smiling. He wondered why she had on a spacer's jumpsuit.

They stopped five feet from Jason's chair.

"Good afternoon, Captain," Ricket said.

"You don't have to call me that any more, Ricket. Jason will work just fine. And good afternoon to you, too."

"Don't I get a hello, Jason?"

"How are you, Dira? I'm actually more than a little surprised to see you. Why would the Queen of Jhardon be standing in my scrapyard, wearing a spacer's jumpsuit?"

"That's a fair question," she replied, pulling up another rickety lawn chair next to his. She took his half-empty bottle and drained it in one swig. "The thing is ... I'm not the queen of anything. With the help of my good friend Ricket here, and the delivery of one, I'm sure, very expensive Medi-Pod ... my mother, the real queen, has made a full recovery."

Jason continued to stare at her. He saw that his father and Ricket were enjoying the show. Before Jason could think of something clever to say, Dira was out of her chair and sitting in his lap. Her arms went around his neck and she kissed him long and hard.

When she finally let him catch a breath, he let himself smile a little. "I'm not so sure this chair can support two of us."

"That's okay ... I'm used to taking chances. And I'm not going anywhere."

The End

Thank you for reading Call To Battle. *You have reached the end of the* Scrapyard Ship *series!*

Brain cells are already at work conjuring up new adventures for one, perhaps two, new spinoff series. Hope you join me when that happens—together, we'll uncover how amazing the Minian *truly is ... remember, much of that vessel is still unexplored. I've come to think of the* Scrapyard Ship *cast of characters as real living beings. Personally, I'm still curious what's in store for Mollie and Boomer. Will Traveler, Billy, Rizzo, Dira, and Captain Jason Reynolds reunite to face new villains? Perhaps there's trouble brewing ... somewhere within the multiverse. Hmm.*

If you enjoyed **Call to Battle**, *please leave a review on Amazon.com — it really, really helps!*

To be notified of the next spinoff series of books, send an email to: markwaynemcginnis@gmail.com, *Subject Line:* **Scrappy Spinoff**. *I'd love to hear from you! Thank you, again, for joining me on these SciFi romps into space and beyond.*

ACKNOWLEDGMENTS

I am grateful for the ongoing support I receive for the *Scrapyard Ship* series books, as well as for the other books I've written. This book, number nine, came about through the assistance and combined contributions of others. First, I'd like to thank my mother, Lura Genz, for her tireless work as my first-phase creative editor and a staunch cheerleader of my writing. I'd like to thank Mia Manns for her phenomenal line and developmental editing … she is an incredible resource. And Eren Arik produced another magnificent cover design. I think it's my favorite so far. I'd also like to thank those in my writer's group who have brought fresh ideas and perspectives to my creativity, elevating my writing as a whole. Others who provided fantastic support include Lura and James Fischer, Sue Parr, and Chris Derrick.

OTHER BOOKS BY MWM

Scrapyard Ship

(Scrapyard Ship series, Book 1)

HAB 12

(Scrapyard Ship series, Book 2)

Space Vengeance

(Scrapyard Ship series, Book 3)

Realms of Time

(Scrapyard Ship series, Book 4)

Craing Dominion

(Scrapyard Ship series, Book 5)

The Great Space

(Scrapyard Ship series, Book 6)

Call To Battle

(Scrapyard Ship series, Book 7)

Mad Powers

(Tapped In series, Book 1)

Lone Star Renegades

(Lone Star Renegades Series, Book 1)

11560080R00155

Printed in Great Britain
by Amazon.co.uk, Ltd.,
Marston Gate.